US bestselling author J. D. Tyler is best known for her dark, sexy, paranormal series Alpha Pack, and the Firefighters of Station Five series under her pseudonym Jo Davis. PRIMAL LAW, the first book in her Alpha Pack series, is the winner of the National Reader's Choice Award in Paranormal. She's also been a multiple finalist in the Colorado Romance Writers Award of Excellence, a finalist for the Booksellers' Best Award, has captured the HOLT Medallion Award of Merit, and has been a two-time nominee for the Australian Romance Readers Award in Romantic Suspense.

When she isn't writing, J. D.'s idea of a good time certainly isn't cleaning house (sniff), bungee jumping (not in this lifetime, or the next), or camping (her idea of 'roughing it' is a slow bellboy). She enjoys reading, being pampered like the diva she is, and spending time with her awesome family. J. D. lives in Texas, USA, with her two children. Visit her website at www.JDTyler.com and follow her on Twitter @JDTylerAuthor

Praise for J. D. Tyler:

'Readers will fall head over heels for the Alpha Pack!' *New York Times* bestselling author Angela Knight

'Try Tyler's sizzling new supernatural series featuring the Alpha Pack – a specialised team of wolf shifters with Psy powers. Tyler has set up an intriguing premise for her series, which promises plenty of action, treachery and scorchingly hot sex' *Romantic Times*

'A thrilling, passionate paranormal romance that you will not soon forget. Filled with action, hunky shifters, a feisty heroine, witty banter, danger, passion, romance and love, this is a book I hated to see end . . . J. D. Tyler is definitely a "must-read" author' *Romance Junkies*

'In a genre where the paranormal is intense, J. D. Tyler may just be a force to be reckoned with. Th̶ ̶ ̶ ̶ ̶ ̶ ̶eted from start to finish' *Night (̶*

By J. D. Tyler

Alpha Pack Series
Primal Law
Savage Awakening
Black Moon
Hunter's Heart

Writing as Jo Davis

Sugarland Blue Series
Sworn to Protect
Hot Pursuit

The Firefighters of Station Five Series
Trial by Fire
Under Fire
Hidden Fire
Line of Fire
Ride the Fire

SHADO Agency Series
I Spy A Wicked Sin
I Spy A Naughty Game
I Spy A Dark Obsession

When Alex Was Bad

HUNTER'S HEART
J. D. TYLER

headline
ETERNAL

Published by arrangement with NAL Signet,
a division of Penguin Group (USA) Inc.

First published in Great Britain in 2013
by HEADLINE ETERNAL
An imprint of HEADLINE PUBLISHING GROUP

1

Cataloguing in Publication Data is available from the British Library

ISBN 978 1 4722 0092 1

Offset in Palatino by Avon DataSet Ltd, Bidford-on-Avon, Warwickshire

Printed and bound by CPI Group (UK) Ltd, Croydon, CR0 4YY

Headline's policy is to use papers that are natural, renewable and
recyclable products and made from wood grown in sustainable forests.
The logging and manufacturing processes are expected to conform to the
environmental regulations of the country of origin.

HEADLINE PUBLISHING GROUP
An Hachette UK Company
338 Euston Road
London NW1 3BH

www.eternalromancebooks.co.uk
www.headline.co.uk
www.hachette.co.uk

To Kierin "KK" Stevens, my biggest fan and softball catcher phenomenon. Good luck as you begin college, not that you'll need it. You're going to set the world on its ear and achieve all of your dreams, and you'll do it your way. You're an awesome, special young lady and I'm proud to know you.

Ryon's story is for you.

ACKNOWLEDGMENTS

As always, special, thanks to:

My wonderful family for always being there to support and encourage me. I love you all.

The Foxes and my best friend, Debra Stevens, for saving my sanity with impromptu lunches and refreshing spiked beverages, and always being there when I need a shoulder to cry on.

My friend Mary Anne Rocha for making sure I take a "gamble" on life and unleash my inner wild child from time to time.

My agent, Roberta Brown, for always being my cheerleader and my guide.

My editor, Tracy Bernstein, for endless support, patience, and words of wisdom.

All of the crew at New American Library, including the other editors and copy editors, art department, marketing team, and publicists. You guys are awesome!

And the readers, for your enthusiasm for the Alpha Pack that ensures they live on. You rock!

HUNTER'S HEART

One

"The guy bringing up the rear is always the one who gets eaten, you know."

Ryon Hunter made a face at Aric Savage's back as their team of shifters, the Alpha Pack, crept stealthily in human form down the garbage-strewn alley. Or half of them, anyway.

The other half were elsewhere in the Big Apple, quickly and quietly searching the night for a gang of rogue vampires reported to be on the hunt, killing humans by draining them and leaving their corpses to be found by puzzled and alarmed citizens. The Pack's commander, Nick Westfall, had given them a simple mandate: find the bastards and neutralize every last damned one of them. Otherwise the public would have questions, ones that had answers the Pack and the very few authorities in the know didn't want them getting hold of.

Vampires in New York City. Sounded like an apocalypse movie.

If people only knew of the very real paranormal world that lurked in the shadows, there would be mass panic. The Alpha Pack's job was to make sure that never happened. They hunted the most dangerous creatures in the world, taking them out before humans had a clue they were there. The less dangerous ones were brought in for possible rehabilitation, and integration into their world.

Peering into the gloom, Ryon forced himself to concentrate. Spirits beckoned to him from every corner, their ghostly forms fading in and out as they entreated him to listen to pleas he couldn't hear. Didn't *want* to hear. As the Pack's Channeler/Telepath, this was his gift—or rather, his curse.

As a Telepath, Ryon was capable of pushing his direct thoughts into other people's heads. He could also catch a reply from one of his teammates if they pushed back hard enough, even though none of the rest of them shared his gift. But his oh so wonderful abilities didn't stop there. Being a Channeler meant that Ryon could also communicate with the dead, if he really tried. Which he rarely wanted to do, but the ghosts just wouldn't leave him alone. Lost souls were drawn to him like metal shavings to a magnet, and New York City held so many of them it was like wading through pea soup.

Even worse, the ghosts seriously pissed off his wolf, who snapped and snarled inside him every time one got too close. Which was constantly.

Nobody, not even his Pack brothers, knew how very close to the breaking point the spirits had driven him.

A slight scuffing sound came from behind him, like a shoe on concrete, and Ryon whirled. His enhanced eyesight scanned the darkness, but all was still. Quiet. So quiet that it took him a couple of seconds to figure out why that bothered him.

The spirits had vanished.

"Shit," he breathed, spinning around to catch up with his group. "Guys—"

The alley exploded in a flurry of dark figures, rushing them from all sides. He just had time to see Aric and Hammer engage in battle with four rogue vampires when a fifth tackled him from the side, slamming him into the wall of a building.

Grunting in pain, he shoved at the vamp, grimacing at the stench of fetid breath wafting over his face. The rogue had him pinned and bared his fangs, going for Ryon's jugular. Twisting, Ryon managed to get enough leverage to put his back to the wall and shove the thing off him. The vamp stumbled backward and Ryon grabbed for the silver knife strapped to his thigh, cursing himself for not already having it in his hand.

He took the snarling vamp to the ground, and in one swift movement, thrust the blade under the breastbone, burying it deep into the monster's black heart. The vamp's squeal joined the others as Aric and Hammer took out their opponents. But they weren't out of the woods.

Another wave of the rogues emerged from the shadows, intent on destroying their adversaries and feasting on their blood. Before Ryon could stand up, two vamps leapt on him, slamming him to the dirty concrete. He'd fought greater numbers than this before and won, but they had him off-balance. They got him facedown, one sitting on his legs, twisting an arm behind him and taking the knife, while the other grabbed a fistful of his hair and pulled his head back to expose this throat.

"Get off me, you fucker!" His wolf, enraged, demanded release as he bucked. Tried in vain to throw them off. Knowing he could fight them much better on four legs, with his own set of sharp teeth, he gathered his concentration for the shift.

"Uh-uh," the one sitting on his legs sang. "We can't let the puppy come out to play."

How do they know—

A hard punch landed in his side. Hot, agonizing fire spread through his torso, seized his lungs. His cry came out as a hoarse wheeze as he realized the vamp had stabbed him with his own silver knife, buried it to the hilt between his ribs. He renewed his struggle to throw them off, but it was no use.

"Hold still, pup," the other crooned in his ear. "This will be over soon."

Then the creature's fangs sank deep into Ryon's throat, silencing his shout. The agony was indescribable, drowning out even the burn in his ribs. The sickening slurp of the thing feeding at his neck made him want to vomit, but he couldn't move. Could do nothing as his sight began to dim, his brain spinning with dizziness.

The one who'd been feeding raised his head, and

spoke with reverent wonder. "It's true! Shifter blood is like the purest cocaine! So good . . ."

"Let me try," the other insisted.

"No! This kill is mine!"

Their argument saved him. That, and his Pack brothers rushing to his rescue after taking care of the other rogues. Distantly, Ryon heard the sounds of a fierce but brief fight as the vampires turned to meet the new threat. Then sudden silence, broken by harsh breathing. Boots, jogging toward him. Cursing.

"Motherfucking hell," Aric snapped. "Help me turn him over. Careful."

Hands lifted him, and soon he was on his back. He tried to make out their faces, to say he was all right. But warm blood gurgled in his torn throat instead. Fuck, he couldn't breathe!

"Don't try to talk," Hammer instructed him. "You're gonna be all right, my man."

Aric examined Ryon's side, muttering. "Stabbed him with his own goddamned knife. We've got to leave that in there for now, or he'll bleed out."

"But he can't shift unless we remove it. If he can shift, maybe he can heal faster."

Aric's voice floated above him. "Ryon? Can you hear me?"

He nodded, once.

"Good. If we take out the knife, can you shift?"

He nodded again, or thought he did. Concentrating, he attempted to call his wolf, but it howled in pain. Retreated deep inside him, strength draining.

"Ryon? Hang on, man . . ."

His Pack brothers' curses, their insistent pleas, melted far away. Into nothingness.

Daria Bradford tossed back her single shot of whiskey, relishing the warmth that slid down her throat to her stomach. The nights grew cool in the Shoshone National Forest in the early fall, so the small indulgence was welcome.

Sitting by the fire, she picked up a bottle of water and rinsed her shot glass. Then she dried it before returning the glass and plastic travel flask to her backpack. The nightly ritual comforted her, made her feel more at home, so far from civilization. It was a tradition she and her father had shared before he retired from the life's work he'd loved so much. The work that she carried on.

Her father had taught her all he knew about studying wolves. As a young girl, she had accompanied him on many a trip. After high school graduation, unlike many of her peers, Daria had known exactly what she wanted to do with the rest of her life—she would follow in her father's footsteps. And so she had, becoming a wildlife biologist who specialized in the field of studying what, to her, were the most beautiful and elusive creatures on the planet.

Her father had been part of the conservationist group in the 1980s that was instrumental in saving wolves in the Shoshone from the brink of extinction. Watching them thrive once again was one of the two great joys in his life, along with doting on his daughter. But eventually his arthritis prevented him from scaling the mountains and valleys he loved so much, so he now lived vicariously through her tales. She made sure to bring him plenty to hear over their cozy nights by the fire, their whiskeys in hand.

Smiling to herself, she thought of all she had to tell him when she went to visit in a few weeks. The wolf packs she'd checked on so far were doing very well, the pups growing. By the dancing light of the fire, she retrieved her spiral notebook and logged her notes on each of the local pack members for the day. Then she put it away and crawled into the tent, zipping it shut against any nighttime visitors that the flames didn't dissuade.

Exhaustion crept into her bones and muscles, but it was the nice sort earned from an honest day's work. She crawled into the sleeping bag and before long, sleep cocooned her and she drifted off, content.

That's when the nightmare invaded.

She was standing in a dark place. A dirty corridor. City noises came from nearby—traffic, people talking. Then came the shouting. She moved closer to the noises, and realized it sounded like fighting. As she crept forward, she saw dark shapes. Pale, humanlike figures dressed in rags, snarling, yellowed fangs slashing in the gloom.

They were attacking a group of men, and for a few moments, it appeared the evil ones would win. How she knew the defenders were the good guys, she couldn't say. She only knew she was invisible to them as they battled, as the men gained the upper hand at last.

But one of their number went down under two of the dark ones. There was a flash of silver, his choked cry ending terribly. Suddenly. One of the attackers yanked back his head and ripped into the man's throat with those awful yellowed fangs.

Stumbling forward, Daria shouted at them to stop, but nobody heard. Her breath froze in her lungs as the man's companions came to his rescue, dispatching the remaining creatures. That's what they were—creatures—but she couldn't put a name to them. Thoughts of the ugly ones vanished as she walked close, looked down and studied the man whom his friends were trying so hard to save.

He was, without a doubt, the most beautiful man she'd ever seen. He was lying on his back, arms and legs limp. Moonlight fell into clear, crystal blue eyes and glinted off his shaggy blond hair. His nose was straight, and he had grooves around his mouth and full lips that hinted at a man who smiled frequently.

But at the moment, he was struggling to breathe. A splash of red marred the torn flesh at this throat, and there was more of the crimson lifeblood flowing from around the hilt of the knife buried in his side. Worry for the man and a deep, sudden sadness overwhelmed her. She tried again to speak, but could not make a sound.

Then his gaze found hers, widened. Just for a moment, the world narrowed to the two of them. Raising his arm, he reached for her with bloodied fingers. She wanted to hold his hand, bring him what solace she could.

Then she was sucked backward, falling out of the dream as she cried out in protest.

No!

"No!" Daria's shout rang in the tent as she bolted upright.

Hand on her chest, she sucked in several deep breaths. Gradually, her racing heart calmed, but the horror of the nightmare remained. Because she knew better than anyone that it was no dream. The scene had been a vision.

Only her father knew of the "gifts" bestowed upon her, supposedly by a Native American ancestor. Everyone else would think her crazy, so the two of them guarded her secret with great care.

All of her life, she'd been plagued with visions of scenes that were either imminent or had just occurred. Most of them were useless, nothing more than innocuous flashes. In the more serious, detailed ones, she typically didn't have a clue who the person in the scene was, and couldn't do anything to help. Well, not directly. Her other gift—astral projection, the ability to send her physical body into a dreamlike state and visit another place in a spirit form—was also useless if she didn't know who to help, or where they were.

Squirming on her sleeping bag, she worried over the handsome blond man in her vision. Who was he? What were those horrible things that had attacked him and his friends?

Most important, was he going to survive?

She didn't know why he mattered so much. Why the need to find him and make certain he was alive was like ants crawling over her skin. Maybe, with this one, she could find out. Because, unlike all the others, for one brief instant, Daria and the man had connected. Even now, as the rest of the vision seemed distant, a thin tendril remained, trailing from her consciousness to his. She felt it, but would need to project astrally to access it. However, she couldn't do that until she'd recovered some. The strength of this vision had left her drained.

Settling down again, she tossed until daylight broke, sleep elusive. Rather than being rested, she was tired and rattled. She'd been so afraid she'd fall asleep and wake up to find the thread connecting her to the sexy stranger had vanished. But it was still there, waiting.

Centering herself, she sat with her legs crossed and closed her eyes, arms loose in her lap. Focusing inward, she let the sounds of the waking forest carry her away. The telltale tingle danced over her skin, the signal that her body was going into its trancelike state. Slowly, her consciousness separated from her body, leaving it behind. Looking back, she saw herself sitting peacefully in the tent and, satisfied, set out to follow the thread.

At first the journey was easy. Not confined to flesh, she soared over the trees, basking in the sunlight and the beauty of the day. Onward she traveled, the connection leading her to a curious break in the forest, a place where the trees had been cleared. In the center of the clearing sat a large building boasting several wings. The thread led to one of those wings in particular.

In seconds, she stood in what appeared to be a hallway. Before her was a door, and beyond it, she knew she'd find the man she sought. Going forward, she simply walked through it, intent on reaching the still form on the bed—

A loud shriek snapped Daria painfully back into her body. The sound echoed through the mountains, causing her pulse to stutter in her chest. "What the hell?"

As the sound died away, she tried to figure out what in God's name it had been. The creature's angry, baritone cry reminded her of something prehistoric out of an old *Godzilla* movie. Unbelievable, but accurate. As the call died, chills pimpled her skin. Whatever it was, it could be miles away.

That idea was enough to get her moving. She felt too much like a sitting duck here, and she couldn't try the projection again for a while anyway. Quickly, she broke camp, packing her tent and supplies, and then making sure the fire was completely out. Then she headed down the trail on the way to her next site.

Thoughts of the blond man were never far from her mind as she hiked. She much preferred to think of him rather than the terrible dream, or the disturbing bellow from some strange animal. Could a grizzly bear make a sound like that, if it was in dire pain? She didn't think so. But out here, what could be large enough to make that noise and be heard for miles?

Don't think of it. Think of him.

She put the mystery animal from her thoughts and lost herself in enjoying the day. She tackled a couple of steep switchbacks, and by noon, tired and sweating, finally stopped to rest. Dragging off her pack, she rolled her shoulders with relief and bent to reach inside for her water.

A familiar stench hit her nose and she straightened slowly. Blood and rotting flesh. Standing stock-still, she turned only her head, scanning the area for signs of the remains that must be nearby. Up ahead, she spotted some broken branches off to the side of the trail. Beyond that, perhaps thirty yards into the foliage, there was something lying on the ground. Studying the lump, she thought she saw blue jean material, maybe a boot.

"Aw, shit."

Quickly, she grabbed her handheld radio from the backpack. If it was a body, she'd have to call the rangers' station and report it, then wait for them to arrive. She needed to check in with them anyway, let them know she was all right. Carefully, she ventured off the trail and picked her way to the lump on the ground. As she got closer, her fears were realized.

"God in heaven," she whispered.

Once, the body had been a human, but whether it was a man or woman, she couldn't say. The corpse had been literally torn to pieces. She spotted part of a leg, an arm. The torso was mostly gone, eaten. Huge teeth had ripped massive chunks of flesh from its victim, the marks so big she couldn't fathom what creature had made them. There was no head to be seen.

Stumbling a few steps away, Daria fell to her knees and vomited. Her stomach turned inside out, though, thankfully, there wasn't much to purge due to her lack of breakfast. As the heaves subsided, one thought screamed into her brain.

What if the killer is still here?

Swiping at her mouth, she pushed up and slung her backpack to the ground, radio in hand. Then she dove for the water hooked to the side and rinsed her mouth several times. Took a long drink. She had to call this in, but did she dare wait around for the thing to come back for seconds?

Raising the radio to her face, she was about to depress the button when a low growl made every hair stand on end. Turning slightly to the right, she blinked, not sure about what she was seeing. As it stalked forward, head lowered, she sucked in a breath.

The creature was a snow white wolf. It wasn't very large—female if she had her guess. The she-wolf made another threatening rumble and continued to advance. All sorts of useless knowledge came to mind, such as the fact that there had never been a documented case of a wolf attacking a person.

Tell that to this one.

Daria depressed the button on her radio, intending to speak to the rangers, but she was too late. At that moment, the wolf launched itself forward. With a cry, Daria abandoned her belongings, spun around, and ran for all she was worth. And knew she'd done exactly the wrong thing. Her dad would rake her over the coals for making such a rookie move.

Legs pumping, she veered off the trail, searching frantically for a good tree to shimmy up. But there were none with the branches low enough. Snarling, the wolf snapped at her boots. She pushed on, faster.

As she topped a rise, the terrain suddenly fell away and she skidded to a stop, right at the edge of a deep ravine. "Fuck!"

She whirled to find the she-wolf right *there*. Panting, baring her teeth. Teeth that were nowhere near big enough to have caused the destruction of the dead hiker, but that hardly mattered right now. Looking around, she scanned the ground for a rock, anything. She didn't want to throw her radio and risk damaging it, but it might make a good club.

She and the wolf locked gazes in a standoff. Daria was struck by the intelligence there, the lack of madness. What the hell was going on? Then a crash sounded from the forest. And another. The sound of heavy steps. More hikers? Maybe help was here.

The moment of distraction cost her. The wolf gathered itself, leapt, and knocked her backward. Daria staggered, tried to regain her balance.

And stepped into thin air. She fell, screaming, and then her back connected with the rocky ground, knocking the breath from her lungs. She tumbled, ass over elbows, rocks gouging and scraping, tearing her clothes. The slide went on forever it seemed.

Until she came to an extremely abrupt stop that made her bite her tongue. Warm blood flooded her mouth. She tried to move, but couldn't. She was lying mostly on her back, her body wedged in a crevice formed by some boulders. Her left arm stuck out at a weird angle, bloody bone protruding through the skin. Trying to move, to get some sort of leverage, only caused waves of agony to pound her battered body.

Her radio? She moved her neck, attempted to see. There was nothing but rock all around, and her broken body was firmly trapped. The radio was gone, the cell phone in her pocket crushed . . . and nobody knew Daria's exact location. In the Shoshone, it could take days for her to be found. Months.

Or her bones might still rest here decades from now.

She thought of her father, and his devastation when he learned his only child was dead. Lost to the very forest they had both loved so much. It would kill him.

Though it was too soon to attempt another projection without draining the last of her strength, she had no choice. She thought of reaching out to her father, but he was too far away to make a successful connection. But there was someone who was much closer. Ignoring the horrendous pain of her injuries, she closed her eyes. Found her center. It took much longer than usual.

Eventually, she felt the familiar tingle. The buzzing sensation that meant she was leaving her earthly form and traveling over time and distance. Determined, she once again followed the thread to the one she knew in her gut would understand her message. There was no time to lose.

She flew over the trees, soaring. Eventually, she reached the place she'd found him before, the big building in the forest. A curious place that appeared to be some sort of compound with another big building next to it—a hangar, going by the jet parked next to it—and yet a third building under construction, not far from the main one.

In moments she found herself in the hallway. This time, a woman with long, curly brunette hair emerged, carrying a clipboard. She wore a lab coat, and Daria realized she was a doctor. The woman was taking care of the sexy stranger. The doctor passed by, not having seen Daria at all.

Daria drifted into the room, her attention immediately focused on the tall figure in the bed. Knowing time was short, she moved forward, to his side.

Tentatively, she reached out and gently touched the face of the handsome blond man. Watched as he opened his gorgeous, crystal blue eyes—eyes that widened as he saw her astral form hovering by his bed. He might not hear her, or understand. But she had to try.

"Please, help me."

Two

Holy shit, his entire body hurt like hell.

Caught between exhaustion and the inability to sleep, Ryon tried hard not to squirm in his hospital bed. Nothing was more miserable than being injured, overtired, and insomniac, and every small movement he made caused waves of pain to throb in every muscle and limb.

Beside his bed, Dr. Mackenzie Grant, or "Mac" as most of the guys called her, was checking his chart and making thoughtful humming noises to herself. Whether her opinion on his progress was good or bad, he couldn't tell. Uncomfortable, he tried to move up on the pillows a bit and was rewarded with a sharp stab of agony in his side.

"Here, let me help you," Mac said, moving quickly.

Cutting the doc his most pleading look, he cleared his sore throat as best he could. "Pain meds," he rasped.

That fucking vamp had really done a number on his windpipe. "Can't sleep."

She gazed at him in sympathy, touching his arm. "I know, sweetie. But you've got another hour before your next dose, so hang in there, okay?" He nodded. "Do you think you can shift yet? That would help speed the healing process."

Concentrating, he called to his wolf. But the creature whined and curled into a firm ball inside him, hurting and still more than a little freaked out by the vampire attack. Carefully, he shook his head. "The silver, from the knife . . ."

"It was inside you too long," she finished with a sigh. "Getting you well will take some time, but thankfully you've got plenty of that. Try to rest and I'll send Noah in an hour to give you more medicine for the pain. Try to rest, okay?"

"Sure." As if that would happen.

Disappointed, he watched her leave the room and resigned himself to a long day of excruciating boredom, not to mention aches and pains. He couldn't concentrate to read and didn't feel like watching TV. How he was going to keep from losing his damned mind, he didn't have a clue.

He'd just closed his eyes when a sense of someone—or rather something—approaching flooded his awareness. A spirit? Or a flesh-and-blood person? He only knew he felt a tug that was familiar somehow, and it took him a moment to think why.

This was the same tug he'd experienced last night,

in the aftermath of the attack. Lying there in the dirty alley, bleeding out, he'd seen the most beautiful ghost hovering over him. As such, he shouldn't have been able to tell the color of her eyes, but they were a warm brown that soothed him. Promised him refuge. Her hair was long and shiny, the deepest black, her cheekbones high and almost sharp, her nose thin. Full, sensual lips just made for kissing.

Through his agony he'd noted her features in an instant, and now he mulled over the fact that he'd never had a spirit appear to him quite so intact, so detailed. Almost as though she were real, not a ghost. Impossible. Right?

Opening his eyes, he sucked in a sharp breath. It seemed he'd get another chance to find out, because the woman in question was standing beside his bed looking down at him anxiously. Her form was translucent, flickering as though her energy was waning.

"Please, help me."

"Jesus!" Reacting, he jerked upright and then hissed in pain. "What the hell?"

Ghosts shouldn't be able to speak and make themselves understood so clearly. But this one wasn't having any problem in that area.

"Help me," she entreated again. "I'm hurt and there isn't much time."

He blinked at her. "How do you think I can help you? You're dead, sweetheart," he said, his tone firm but gentle. Most of the spirits couldn't accept their demise.

"No, I'm alive! I was working a few miles from here and I was pushed into a ravine." She began to appear more desperate. "If you don't find me, I'll die out here. You have to believe me."

A chill snaked down his spine. Maybe she was telling the truth. "Okay, honey. Tell me where you are and I'll come to you." He hoped.

"North. Past the second ridge." She began to fade.

"Wait! That's a lot of miles to cover. Can you be more specific?"

Her reply was broken, the sound going mute at intervals. "The rangers . . . checkpoint . . . camp."

"You were camping? What was that about the rangers?"

"Hurts," she whispered. "Hurry."

And then she was gone.

"Fuck!"

Ryon stared for a few seconds at the spot where she'd been, wondering if she'd reappear. But the very real urgency in her plea got him moving. Despite the pain it caused, he scooted to the side of the bed, removing the sticky heart-monitor pads and ripping out his IV line. The back of his hand bled, and he licked the wound, sealing it, then pushed to his feet.

Sucking in a sharp breath, he braced a hand on the bedside table and held his injured side with the other. Ten minutes ago he wouldn't have been able to get out of bed. But that was before an intriguing spirit had appeared at his side to beg for help—and his wolf had come roaring to life inside him. Now his constant companion was anxious, insisting they race to help this unknown woman.

Ryon struggled to control the shift. Apparently, hiding and licking his wounds like a big baby was no longer on the wolf's agenda. The creature was practically clawing him apart from the inside out in his hurry to be gone. He had something much more important to focus on now, and he wasn't going to let anything keep him from finding the gorgeous vision.

Ryon had to alert his team. Pushing out the door, he stumbled into the corridor of the infirmary and ran straight into Noah. The blond nurse grabbed and steadied him, fussing.

"What the heck are you doing out of bed? If you need something, use the call button!"

"No time," he said hoarsely. "Gotta find Nick. We've got a problem."

Scowling, the younger man steered Ryon back into the room. "Sit your butt down in here while I get hold of him, or you're going to be the one with the problem when I sedate your stubborn self."

Ryon complied, but he didn't have to like it. Until he let his wolf out, he wasn't going to have the strength to walk across the compound, much less run through the mountains searching for an injured hiker. He listened impatiently while Noah used the room's phone and made the call to Nick. As he did, it occurred to Ryon that he wasn't thinking straight—he could've simply used his ability as a Telepath to reach Nick himself, pushing his thoughts into his commander's head. If that wasn't proof that he had no business leaping from bed to run through the Shoshone, nothing was.

But that wasn't going to stop him.

Noah replaced the receiver and turned, grabbing the discarded wires from the heart monitor. "He's on his way. Scoot back and I'll fix this."

"No. I'm not staying here."

"Ryon—"

"I said no!"

"Fine! Stubborn furballs, all of you." The nurse stomped out, leaving the door open behind him.

Ryon felt bad for snapping, but anxiety was riding him hard. He needed to be gone, like five minutes ago. Dammit, he'd apologize later.

Nick walked in a couple of minutes after Noah left, his expression concerned. The Pack's commander was a big SOB who put off a *don't fuck with me* vibe that was best heeded. Oh, Nick was a good guy, but more than a little intimidating.

The commander pushed a hand through his dark hair, his eyes piercing Ryon's. "I knew a big change was coming for you. I just didn't expect it to arrive so soon."

The hair on the back of Ryon's neck stood up. In addition to being a rare white wolf—born, not made—the commander was a PreCog, which meant he could sometimes see events before they happened. Or get a sense of something important on the horizon. As much as Ryon hated his own *gift*, he wouldn't trade with Nick for anything. Some people might think being able to see the future would be cool, but Ryon thought it would totally suck to know the bad stuff.

"What did you see?" he asked in curiosity. And with a bit of dread as well.

"A woman," Nick said simply, with a bit of reluctance. "And the fact that she's going to shake up your world pretty thoroughly."

Oh, crap. "How so?"

"You'll just have to find out for yourself. But for that to happen, we'll have to get going." The man cocked his head. "Did she appear to you?"

Evasive bastard. "Yes, and she's hurt. She didn't say her name, but she told me she was pushed into a ravine past the second ridge, to the north."

"Pushed? By whom?"

"I don't know. She tried to say something about the rangers and a checkpoint, but the message was garbled at the end."

"Okay. I'll go by my office on the way out and give the ranger station a call while you grab a few of the guys." He eyed Ryon. "That is, if you're healed enough to go."

"I will be after I shift," he insisted. "My wolf is going nuts and if I stay behind, it won't be pretty."

Nick paused, considering. "All right. I trust you to know your limits."

"I'll meet you at the hangar with others. And thanks, Nick."

"You're welcome. I'll speak to Melina, Mac, and Noah

on the way out, tell them what's going on and get them to accompany us in a second vehicle."

"We're bringing her here?" he asked in surprise. "What about the humans' Search and Rescue team? Sounds like she'll need a regular hospital."

A mysterious smile played about Nick's lips. "I have a feeling that's not going to work out so well."

"What—" Much to his annoyance, his boss left without explaining. "Damn."

Ryon stood, shrugging off the annoying hospital gown. Next went his briefs, tossed to join the gown. Naked and trembling from that small exertion, he focused on reaching out to his wolf in preparation for the shift, a process that wasn't typically as fluid and easy for him as it was for some of the other guys. Now, however, his wolf surged to the surface and completely took over, his anxiety to get to the injured woman almost a physical need.

Muscle and bone popped, morphed. His body rearranged itself, fur sprouting from his skin, muzzle lengthening, tail growing, hands and feet becoming paws. All of this in less than five seconds.

Immediately he felt stronger. Not fully healed, but he would last until the raven-haired beauty was found and brought back safely. The pull to do just that got him moving.

Steady on four legs, he bolted from the room and down the infirmary's corridor. Ryon ran straight to the recreation room where many of his friends could be found loitering away their downtime on any given day, and he wasn't surprised to find that today was no different.

Hammer and Aric were there, playing a video game on the Wii, and Micah Chase and Kalen Black were watching a rerun of *Ghost Hunters*. The foursome stopped what they were doing, giving him their full attention as he skidded to a stop and shifted back.

"Damn, my eyes!" Aric moaned as the others laughed. "I guess you're feeling better, huh? At least put on some pants."

They all knew the redheaded wolf was teasing—the Pack had been together long enough that they didn't care about nudity before or after their shifts. But Ryon didn't have the time or patience to play along.

"I need you guys," he said, holding on to the sofa for support. In human form he wasn't as well as he'd like, but it couldn't be helped at the moment. "We've got an injured hiker out there, and we're mobilizing."

Hammer, the team's gentle giant and Nick's right-hand man, rubbed his bald head, perplexed. "That's not our job. What about Search and Rescue?"

"The woman appeared to me in astral form and begged for my help," he explained impatiently, unable to hide his anxiety. He chose to leave out Nick's interesting response to that very question Ryon had asked. "Getting S and R involved will take time she doesn't have. There's no way a bunch of humans will be able to find her before we do, and she's going to die if we don't hurry."

Aric stood. "In that case, I'm in."

The other three echoed him, and Ryon looked to Micah. The brown wolf/Dreamwalker had been rescued along with Aric, weeks ago, by the Pack and Rowan, Micah's sister, an LAPD cop who turned out to be Aric's mate. Micah had fared much worse in the lab facility where he and Aric had been held, and had endured heinous experiments for months at the hands of the now-deceased Dr. Gene Bowman. Micah was horribly scarred inside and out. But with drugs and therapy he was making progress, it seemed.

"You ready to test the waters?" Ryon asked him. He was fairly sure Nick wouldn't object to their Pack brother stretching his long-unused muscles while assisting on a simple rescue. If so, he'd take the heat later.

Micah nodded eagerly, pushing a long strand of brown hair from his face. "You bet. If I have to stay behind again, I'll lose what's left of my mind."

"That's settled, then. We're meeting Nick at the hangar with the medical team. Anybody know where Jax is?" Jaxon Law was their unofficial Pack leader, right after Nick.

"I'll find him and Rowan. We'll see you there." Aric jogged off.

"I'll get dressed and be there in a few."

Ryon shifted again and took off in the direction of his personal quarters. Everyone had his own apartment at the compound and Ryon's was situated at the end of one of the wings that housed the Pack and the rest of the staff. At his door, he shifted to human form again and cursed the necessity. His wolf was much stronger and faster in many aspects. He could follow a scent trail and locate someone in a way that was impossible as a man. But they would need vehicles and emergency equipment. No help for that.

Anxious, he punched his code into the security pad and let himself into his quarters. As quickly as possible, given his own injuries, he dressed in a T-shirt, jeans, and hiking boots, and then braced his hands on the dresser. Mirrors didn't lie, and this one was telling him to go straight back to bed and stay there for another week.

Unfortunately, on top of looking like shit, he felt even worse. As he headed out again, the stab of pain in his side reminded him that he'd missed the promised dose of pain meds. But it wasn't the pain that concerned him—he'd been through plenty of scrapes and survived. It was the possibility that his body might fail him before he found the woman.

He didn't doubt that if something happened to him, the Pack would find her. But every instinct in his body screamed that it was vitally important that he be with them. He couldn't fail.

Half-limping, he jogged into the hangar to see Nick and the others waiting. The group of men, plus the medical team, was swallowed by the cavernous space that held a number of vehicles, including SUVs, three Hueys, and a private jet. Several pairs of eyes turned in his direction, and a couple of his buddies exchanged dubious looks.

Aric shook his head. "You need to sit this one out, bro."

"I agree," Jax said, crossing his arms over his chest.

"Forget it." Slowing to a walk, he joined his team. "The woman reached out to *me* for help, nobody else. That makes it sort of personal."

Jax persisted. "We'll find her and bring her here. You've done enough—"

"We're wasting time," he snapped. "Can we just get on with the plan?"

Anger flashed in Jax's gaze and for a couple of heartbeats, Ryon thought they were about to get into it. Nick didn't intervene, simply watched and waited. Even Aric, the smartass, went silent. But then his friend relented, albeit reluctantly. "Fine. But if you pass out, I'm not carrying your stubborn ass back to the vehicles."

"Like nobody's had to carry *you* before," he shot back. Jax had no comeback, and the decency to appear contrite.

The tension gradually dissipated as Nick brought them up to speed. "I contacted the rangers' station and learned some interesting things. First, the woman we're looking for is probably Daria Bradford. She's a wildlife biologist studying the wolf population in the Shoshone—the real kind."

Daria. What a pretty name. Ryon's insides fluttered, but he hid his reaction.

Micah snorted. "Wolves? How's that for irony?"

"They're also not too concerned about her just yet. Miss Bradford checked in with the rangers this morning as scheduled, and gave them the coordinates for her next campsite. She's not due to call in for another few hours."

"So how did you explain the inquiry?" Ryon asked.

"I told them I'd heard a call over the radio on my office from someone in distress. Of course, they were baffled that they didn't hear anything, but they were too distracted by another development to focus too much on the discrepancy."

"What's going on?"

"A couple of campers have gone missing, a man and his wife from Nebraska who are, or were, here on vacation." Nick's expression was grim. "They arrived eight days ago, according to a daughter who spoke with them by cell phone before they settled in. The couple didn't check in with the rangers when they got here, though. They were only supposed to camp for four nights, and then head home, calling their daughter when they left. They never made that call and by the morning of the sixth day, she started to panic."

"So, Search and Rescue is already out there, looking for them," Ryon mused. "This could complicate our effort to find the biologist."

Nick shrugged. "Maybe, maybe not. We'll stay out of their way, but it won't hurt for us to keep an eye out for the missing couple while we're looking for Miss Bradford. We'll definitely have to be cautious about shifting with extra people combing the forest. Don't let out your wolf, or panther," he said, nodding to Kalen, "unless absolutely necessary."

"Are we taking a Huey?" Aric asked, gesturing to the big helicopter.

"Yes," Nick confirmed. "If we find the woman, we'll

need to get her back here as fast as possible because she's gravely injured."

Aric frowned. "Why not just let the humans take her in? Ryon said it would take the rescue team too long to mobilize, but considering that they're already out there, wouldn't that make more sense?"

Ryon opened his mouth to protest, but Nick beat him to the punch. "Are you questioning my orders?"

The redhead blinked. "No, sir. Just asking."

"Good. Trust me when I say it has to happen this way."

"Yes, sir," he drawled. "You're the PreCog."

"Smart of you to remember. You'll pilot, take Micah and the medical team with you. There's a sufficient place to land about a mile from where Miss Bradford last made camp. The medical team will hike with us. You and Micah stay with the copter unless you hear different."

Aric didn't look pleased to be left out of the search, but he didn't argue. Maybe he figured he'd pushed Nick enough. "Will do."

The commander handed Aric the coordinates, then addressed the group. "Ryon, Jax, Kalen, A.J., Rowan, Hammer, and I will take the two new Range Rovers. We'll park as close as we can to the landing site and hike to her last camp, then go from there. Any questions?"

After so many years together, they knew the drill. Even the two relative newbies, Kalen, their Sorcerer/ panther shifter, and A.J. Stone, a human who'd once been a police officer and was a damned fine sniper, pulled their weight as though they'd been with the Pack forever. They all moved like the proverbial well-oiled machine.

They loaded into the vehicles, Ryon behind the wheel of one of the Rovers. He watched as the blades of the Huey started to whirl, and the roof of the hangar began to slowly slide open to allow it to take off. When it lifted from the ground, the noise was deafening. The sight never failed to awe him. Aric could pilot almost anything with an engine and, being a Telekinetic, plenty of objects that didn't to boot.

After the copter cleared the building and swept away, the roof began to close. Ryon took the lead, driving out of the hangar and onto the private road leading from the compound. They'd have a couple of security gates to pass through, their property being restricted to outsiders, and then they'd take one of the main roads normally used only by park officials. Beside him, Nick punched the campsite's coordinates into the GPS.

The drive took almost half an hour. Too long. Inside him, his wolf paced anxiously, straining to get on with the hunt for the woman. Daria. With difficulty, he shut off the questions churning in his mind because the answers didn't matter right now.

"I wish Zan and Phoenix had been able to come along," Jax said from the back.

Ryon glanced at him in the rearview mirror. "Me, too. It sucks that they're out of commission."

"Yeah. But hopefully they'll be good as new when they get back from their vacations."

Zander Cole was a black wolf, the team's Healer, and also Jax's best friend. Zan was sorely missed as a friend, but more than that, his skills were often crucial in the field when they incurred severe injuries. But Zan had been badly hurt himself a few weeks ago, when the Unseelie king Malik had tried to destroy them all. Kalen had unleashed the full fury of his Sorcerer's power, killing Malik, but Zan sustained a head injury in the blast that had left him deaf and suffering from terrible headaches as a result.

After that horrible nightmare, Nick had granted them all well-earned vacation time and they'd spent the past few weeks rotating out so they weren't all absent at once. Soon, Zan and Phoenix would return and all would get back to normal—whatever *normal* meant to them.

Using the rangers' service road, Ryon managed to get them all the way to the flat clearing where the Huey rested. Once they'd parked a safe distance from the copter, they unloaded the backs of the Rovers and divided among themselves the packs that contained rescue equipment such as harnesses, ropes, pulleys, and a carrying basket for the injured party. There was a bunch of other stuff they might not need, but it was best to be prepared.

He saw Mac, Melina, and Noah jump from the copter and shoulder their backpacks filled with first-aid supplies. The trio joined them and waited for Nick's instructions.

"We'll stay together until we reach Miss Bradford's

last camp. Then we'll fan out and do a sweep in the direction of her next site. She told Ryon she was pushed into a ravine, which means she went off the trail at some point. Stay sharp. You all know what signs to look for." He paused. "And one other thing—be alert for whoever, or whatever, attacked the victim. We don't want any more nasty surprises. Christ knows we've had enough of those," he muttered, gesturing for them to move out.

Ryon couldn't agree more. All of his senses were wide open as they walked, scanning the area for anything that didn't belong. Especially the damned ghosts, who never left him alone and yet were strangely absent today. Could be that no one had died in this area in the past few years, if ever, but that typically didn't make a difference. Spirits were drawn to him and would travel from far and wide to try to communicate with him.

He should be glad they were making themselves scarce, but he wasn't. There was a weird vibe in the air. A disturbance in the atmosphere that he couldn't pinpoint. It was a tangible feeling, not simply an intuition that something was wrong. He and Nick were in the lead, so he halted in his tracks and turned to the others. They stopped and waited in question.

"Does anyone else feel that?"

After a few seconds of silence, Micah said, "I do."

Nick glanced between them sharply. "Feel what?"

How to explain? "It's like a vibration in the air. A sound wave or something, only with no sound."

Jax frowned. "That makes no sense."

"This is going to sound bizarre, but . . ." Micah shifted, looking uncomfortable. Then he pointed to the scarred side of his face. "My skin is prickling, almost like I have ants crawling on me. But just on this area of my face, nowhere else."

They stared at him, and Ryon's unease intensified. He couldn't imagine what the hell that could mean, but it probably wasn't going to be good.

Nick looked to Ryon. "Do you sense an actual presence? Are your spirits telling you anything?"

He gave a humorless laugh. "What spirits? I think they all got the hell out of here and I don't blame them. As far as a presence, there's something making the disturbance. I just don't know if it's a living thing, or if there's another explanation."

"All right. Let's keep going."

They started out again. Nick didn't have to remind them to stay sharp. Considering the weird vibe, plus the injured biologist and missing campers, it was clear that something bad was going on in their forest.

And the thought came unbidden that Malik was the last creature to stalk it.

No *way* could that Unseelie asshole have risen from the dead. Because that's what he was—a deep-fried crispy critter sent to hell, thanks to Kalen. Any alternative was unthinkable.

Reaching the first campsite took longer than Ryon would have liked. At least his head had cleared some on the way and he was able to focus as they walked into the deserted area. He looked around, disappointed.

"There's not much to see," he observed, digging the toe of his boot into the cold, black ashes left from the fire. "She was here, and then she left."

"In a hurry, though. She left this behind." Micah held up a travel-sized bottle of whiskey that was three-quarters full.

Jax smoothed his dark goatee thoughtfully. "You know you're booking out when you don't notice you've left the booze behind, or you do and don't bother to go back for it."

Ryon walked over and took the bottle from Micah. "I wonder if something scared her and she took off from here. Maybe she was running from whoever pushed her into the ravine."

"Nah," Jax said. "I think she was nervous at first, cleared out in a hurry. If she ran from here she would've left everything, not just the bottle."

"True." Holding the bottle up to his nose, Ryon sniffed. A faint tinge of sweetness that didn't belong to the liquor inside teased his senses, and he unscrewed the lid. The full bouquet of the whiskey was pleasant, though that wasn't what hit him the hardest.

She had touched the glass. It carried her rich and earthy scent. How he knew it was hers when he had never scented her before was an easy one to answer.

His wolf was going fucking berserk.

"You've got her scent?" Nick asked.

"Yeah."

"Let me get a whiff."

Nick took the bottle and sniffed it. Then inhaled

again, giving Ryon a bemused look. "I don't smell anything but whiskey. Wonder why you picked it up but I
can't."

"Got no clue." He had a feeling Nick did, though.
Damned if he was asking in front of his Pack brothers.

Nick waved a hand at the trail ahead. "We'll keep
going and spread out some, but no farther than shouting distance. If you pick up her scent again, let us
know."

Quickly, Ryon took the bottle back, screwed the lid
on again, and stuffed it into his pack. She'd want a nip,
later. Especially after she recovered enough to recount
what had scared her. Almost killed her.

He and Nick walked the center of the trail while the
others split off to the left and right of them, searching
deeper into the woods. Now and then, Ryon caught the
barest hint of her essence in the air, or on some brush.
No sign of her, however, or where she might have
veered off the path.

Until Micah called out from the left of the trail and
stepped from a copse of trees, waving an arm. "Hey!
Over here!"

Guys, Micah has something to the left of the trail, Ryon
pushed into their heads. It was easier and more effi-
cient than yelling.

He and Nick struck out through the trees, hurrying,
the third group behind them. Micah disappeared
briefly and he worried they would lose him, but it
wasn't long before he and Nick spotted Micah, Hammer, Mac, and Noah in an area where the trees thinned

a bit. Micah was agitated, glancing their way, and then down at a lump on the ground. Hammer was outwardly calm, his expression unreadable.

The first fact Ryon became aware of was the stench. The putrid odor of death clogged his nostrils and threatened to send up the meager contents of his stomach. As he and Nick approached, he was damned grateful that his breakfast had consisted of little more than dry toast and some juice. Apparently, Mac, who was Kalen's pregnant mate, wasn't so lucky.

"Excuse me," she croaked. "I'm going to be sick."

Ryon felt sorry for her. The doc was a pure professional, but pregnant women sometimes couldn't handle certain sights and smells very well. Hell, he'd almost been sick and he didn't even have an excuse. Ryon almost went after her, but Kalen showed up and intercepted his pea green mate, leading her away from the gruesome scene.

"Fuck me." Noah breathed. "As a nurse I've seen plenty of dead people, but nothing like this."

Ryon nodded. "Me, neither. Christ."

"Can't tell if it was a man or a woman," Jax observed. He coughed, holding a hand over his face. Not that it would help.

Rowan, Aric's mate, had been quiet throughout the search, until now. "Woman," she said, pointing. "Look how small the shoes are, and the laces are pink."

Noah arched a brow. "That doesn't mean anything. *I* have pink shoelaces."

Ryon shot him a grin. "So it's like *that*, is it? Shoulda

figured." Noah winked at him and several of the guys laughed. The exchange dispelled some of the depressing atmosphere, but Nick wasn't amused.

"Focus, idiots. We've got a murder here and two more possible victims we need to find."

Sobering, Ryon crouched near the body and studied it. God, it was torn to pieces. Hardly recognizable as human, just shredded clothing here and there, clumped with bloody flesh and muscle, writhing with maggots. A sliver of garment that used to be white caught his eye, however. Reaching for a stick on the ground, he used it to lift the white strip of cloth from the clump.

"It's part of a bra," he said, then dropped the stick in disgust. "Rowan's right."

"There's her backpack," Micach observed. Everyone turned to look at it. "But it's strange that it's not torn up and there's no blood on it."

Ryon stared at it, chilled. "It might not belong to the this victim." He gestured to the mangled body.

"A companion?" Nick wondered aloud. "Or the woman who came to you for help?"

Just then, Ryon's eardrums were nearly shattered by a high-pitched wailing noise. "Shit!"

Bracing a hand on the ground, he searched for the source of the shrieking. He wasn't surprised to note that none of the others heard the racket. Nor was he shocked to see the spirit of the female victim sitting beside her own body, covered in blood, rocking as she wailed out her terror.

"Ryon?" Nick barked. "What is it?"

"The woman," he said hoarsely, pointing to the ghost they couldn't see. "She's there, screaming. She's rocking, too, staring at the blood all over her."

"Christ."

Ryon tried getting her attention, reaching out a hand. "Ma'am? Hello? Can you tell us your name? What happened to you?"

The wailing stopped briefly as she blinked at him. He hated that vacant stare. The mind that no longer was at home, working like it should. She couldn't make sense of him.

And just like that, she vanished.

"She's gone," he told them. He heard someone say "thank fuck" and silently agreed. "She didn't tell me anything."

Nick blew out a breath. "Okay. We've either got a crime scene or a grizzly bear mauling, but it's going to take experts to tell which one. I've got to radio Sheriff Deveraux, get the county folks on the way. Then we've got to find Miss Bradford before we run out of time."

At the reminder of the missing biologist, Ryon stood. Sniffed the air. At first it was hard to smell anything but the awful odor from the body, and he began to doubt he'd be able to pick up her trail again. But then it was there. Her sweet scent, beckoning him on.

"Daria was here," he told them. "I'm positive. Her scent is all over the backpack. I think it's hers."

They waited as he made a circuit of the area. Frustration grew as the scent faded in and out, weaker in his human form. His wolf snarled again, demanding to be unleashed. His companion could track her much faster, and he was getting hard to control.

He turned to Nick. "I need to let my wolf out. Tracking is too dicey in this form."

"And if the humans see you?"

"You can say I'm your pet. A wolf-dog hybrid. Please, we don't have much time to debate about it."

Nick hesitated, but gave in. "Fine. Put your clothes in your pack, and someone will carry it."

He heaved a sigh of relief. "Thanks."

Undressing quickly, he shoved his clothes into the pack and immediately dropped to all fours. The shift happened in a blink, leaving him disoriented for a second. Never had it been so fast, and he knew the woman was the reason. Vaguely, he heard one of the guys exclaim over the speed of his shift, but he lost the comment amid the overwhelming scent of the female his wolf sought.

There was nothing now but her. The need to find and protect the woman. She wanted him, had come to him. No one else. He had to find her, to know why.

Forgetting about the body, he honed in on Daria's scent and bolted in the opposite direction of the trail, farther into the forest. She had discovered the body, and had run. He understood that something had frightened her into taking off, causing her to move in the wrong direction. Something more than just finding a corpse.

The tangible prickle was still in the air. Stronger now than before. He ran, the pain of his own injuries a dis-

tant memory, of no importance. Not when he was on
the precipice of losing something monumental, something he couldn't name. And if she didn't survive—

No. That could not happen. He wouldn't allow it.

He ran so fast, he almost tumbled headlong over the
edge of the ravine she had told him about. Skidding to
a halt, he scrambled back from the edge and then
peered over. Stared into the gorge and wondered how
far she had fallen. Where could she be?

Pacing the lip, he put his nose to the ground and
searched. Up and down, again and again. Until finally, he
found where she'd gone over. He felt her then, her life
fading. Heartbeat slowing. How was this connection possible?

Sitting on his haunches, he let out a long, lonely howl.
Then he plunged over the side and hit the rocky slope,
sliding, aware of shouts from above. He almost lost his
footing once or twice, but managed to control his de-
scent. He was nearly to the bottom when he saw her.

Daria was lying wedged in a tight crevice, her arm
sticking out at an impossible angle. Her clothing was
torn and bloody. Scratches marred her arms and what
he could see of her face. Long raven hair covered much
of her features, billowing slightly in the wind. She
didn't stir as he rushed over. Didn't move at all as he
nosed her good hand, licked her face. Whining, he huddled as close to her as he could, his wolf taking charge
of the man for the first time in his memory. In a heartbeat, in the wake of her suffering, he was lost to the
beast within.

Daria. Hurt.

The wolf heard the calls from above, and tensed, growling softly. A menacing warning to those who approached. They would not get near her. He would not allow it. She suffered, and he along with her.

"You found her!" a dark-haired man said, moving closer. "Good work. Let me—"

Baring his fangs, he moved to place his body between the man and his female. Crouched, ready to spring, and rumbled a warning deep in his chest. *Hurt. Mine.*

"Shit. Ryon, it's me, Nick." Holding out a hand, the man edged closer. "Ryon, get hold of your wolf."

Mine! He snarled at the man called Nick and the others who crept up behind him, wide-eyed.

"We know, buddy. But she's hurt and needs medical attention, remember? We can't help her if your wolf won't let us near her."

"Christ, has he gone feral?" someone asked.

"No," Nick said quietly, eyes never leaving the wolf's. "He's protecting his mate."

"His *what*?" A pause. "Oh, fuck."

"That's one way of putting it."

Mate? Mate. Mine!

Nick raised his voice, speaking urgently. "Ryon Hunter, do you hear me? Make your wolf stand down now or she's going to die. Your mate will *die*. Do you understand?"

Your mate will die.

Ryon struggled to gain control over his wolf, but

forcing him into submission wasn't easy. The beast was so enraged by his female's suffering it was damned near impossible. But gradually, he exerted his will over the snarling beast and won the battle.

Mate. Nick had said . . . the woman was his mate? She would die?

Sitting back, he let the shift flow and in seconds found himself in human form, blinking at the others. "Nick? What the hell is going on?"

"Later. Right now we've got to make sure she survives. I'm going to be honest and tell you there's only one way to do that."

"Which is?" He had a feeling he knew what his commander was going to say. His serious expression said it all before he even spoke.

"If you want Daria to live, you'll have to bite her."

With those simple words, Ryon's life was changed forever.

Three

If you want Daria to live, you'll have to bite her.

Ryon stared at Nick, heart thudding in his chest. "You mean claim her."

"Yes. Give her some of your blood first, then the bite. If she's going to survive, you have to hurry."

There was no time to sit around debating how this one act was going to completely alter his life, and the beautiful young woman's as well. No time to fear how much she'd resent him for playing God, not a second to lose agonizing that she'd hate him forever.

There was no choice, really. Because no way in hell was he going to let his mate die.

Working carefully, he helped Nick and Jax extract Daria from the crevice and move her to level ground, on her back. She was too still, her tanned face gray, lips turning blue. The biologist was clinging to her life thread with every ounce of strength she possessed, and her core of inner strength gave him hope.

He wasted no time in shifting one finger into a claw, using it to slice open his wrist while Nick pried open her mouth. Blood welled and he placed his wrist to her lips, squeezing to hurry the flow. The crimson liquid dribbled between her lips, a macabre sight and yet a lifesaving measure. If only her body would accept the offering. Embrace it. Heal.

"Come on, honey," he encouraged. "Drink this."

For several long moments, nothing happened. Ryon stroked her throat, encouraging her to swallow, to no avail. Despair began to weigh heavily on his heart, much greater than the sadness of not being able to save a stranger. His wolf howled inside him, forlorn.

Ryon and his wolf had scented their mate. If Daria died, so would they.

"Daria, please," he whispered. "Work with me. Live."

She twitched, her head moving slightly to the side. Then she coughed and swallowed. He let out a sigh of relief as she repeated the action, licking her lips to get the life-giving blood that had spilled there. Her eyes remained closed, but he felt it. A spark flared within her, a tiny light of hope that reached out to him tentatively, seeking an anchor. Meeting the light halfway, he pulled it into himself, holding on tight.

A hand landed on his shoulder. Nick's voice was urgent. "Bite her now, Ryon. Bind her to you, or she won't survive."

"Where? She's hurt all over." Desperate, he scanned for a good spot.

"Anywhere. Her wrist will do for now."

He'd been alone for so long, had never dreamed he'd find a mate. A wave of disappointment washed over him that it must happen here, like this, in front of his Pack brothers, as he fought for her life. Then he shoved down the self-pity. There would be time for intimacy later. He should be grateful fate had sent her into his world.

Gently, he lifted her good arm and brought her wrist to his lips. His fangs lengthened and his wolf growled in anticipation. Reining in his aggression and possessiveness wasn't easy, but he managed to sink his canines into the tender flesh without ripping or clamping down too hard.

Instantly, his tongue was flooded with ambrosia. He had a mere five seconds or so to marvel at the rush that quickened his pulse before his world detonated into a brilliant solar blast that almost knocked him backward. The thin light that had been threaded between them when she accepted his blood was anemic compared to this. A thick golden bond arced from his body to hers, crackling with electricity and then detonating like a supernova. His fangs slipped from her wrist and he felt himself fall backward, into a strong embrace.

"Gotcha," Jax said in his ear. "You okay?"

Was he? He blinked into the cloudless sky, taking stock. Nothing hurt. In fact, he'd never felt better in his life. Even the pain left over from the vampire attack seemed pushed so far into the background as to be almost nonexistent. All that remained was the fiery glow that spun between him and Daria.

"Yeah. I think so." With Jax's help, he sat up and studied the woman anxiously. "She looks better, doesn't she?"

"Her color has improved." Nick patted his shoulder. "You've given her a chance she didn't have before. Now get dressed before Jesse sees you naked and thinks something really kinky is going on."

"Would serve him right, the grouchy bastard." In spite of the seriousness of Daria's situation, he smiled a little. Sheriff Jesse Deveraux knew their main secret and had kept it well, even if he didn't much like it. Bastard or not, it was good to have a human ally in law enforcement.

Ryon almost felt sorry for the sheriff. Whatever was going on in the Shoshone, the man was going to have his hands full real quick.

Nudging Ryon aside, the medical team—minus Mac, who was forbidden by Kalen from descending the steep hill—went to work hooking up the biologist to an IV and a heart monitor. Melina and Noah straightened her broken arm as well, causing the woman to moan in agony even in her unconscious state, and making Ryon's wolf very unhappy again. But he kept a leash on the beast.

Once the arm was in a sling, Daria was declared fit for transport. Carefully, with Nick's and Jax's assistance, they transferred their patient to the basket, strapped her in, secured the basket to the pulley and ropes, and began to guide it up the incline. It was a long, tedious process that had them all sweating by the time they reached the top, and everyone was relieved to start the journey back to the Huey.

Ryon remained glued to her side as his friends carried the basket toward the trail. Her color did appear better. She was far from healed, but she would be. He couldn't wait to get to know this woman who had reached out to him, and in doing so, had set them on a path that would alter their destinies.

Would she be shy and kind? Or brash and loud? She worked alone, at one with the nature around her. She loved wolves. That had to be a positive sign, right? And she apparently treated herself to a bit of the hair of the dog once in a while—no pun intended. The recollection of the little bottle of whiskey made him smile. Getting to know her might be fun.

And maybe he wouldn't feel so alone anymore.

When they reached the clearing where they'd found the mutilated body, Ryon wasn't surprised to see the entire area crawling with park rangers, the county cops, the medical examiner's people, a crime scene unit, and Deveraux himself, standing tall among the ordered chaos, a thunderous expression on his rugged face.

"Westfall!" He strode toward Nick, a man on a mission. "Why is it that every single time things go to shit in my county, you and your band of misfits are smack in the middle of it?"

"Good to see you, too, Jesse. Hey, are you putting on weight? Don't worry. You carry it well."

"Don't fuck with me, friend. Not today." He jabbed a thumb in the general direction of the remains. "What do you know about this?"

"Not a damned thing, nor do I want to," Nick replied drily. "That's why I called you. I think you've either got a rogue grizzly, or a serial killer. Neither of which are my problem."

The sheriff's gaze went to Daria. "Yet this injured biologist *is* your problem? How does she fit in with the killing?"

"I don't think she does, except I'm speculating she found the body and something scared her into running. We're going to find out, though."

"Then I'll need to question her," Deveraux persisted. "You taking her to the hospital?"

"No, to the compound." Nick pinned the other man with a steely glare. "I need you to keep her whereabouts quiet."

"Goddamn." He blew out a breath. "As much as you fuck me up the ass, I ought to start keeping lube handy."

Nick fell silent for a few seconds, a faraway look in his eyes. Ryon recognized it, having witnessed it before, and no doubt so had the Pack members present. Their commander had "seen" an event, something vital to their future.

Whatever the vision was, Nick shook it off. "Come to the compound when you're free. I'll explain as much as I can."

"What, you're actually going to let me enter the exalted inner sanctum? Tell me what the holy hell you guys do up there?" The sheriff shook his head. "Miracles never cease."

"I know I can trust you," Nick said simply. "And for the record, I was wrong—your body over there isn't just your problem, nor is it the last one. I have a feeling we're going to have to work together on this case. Just buzz the security box at the gate and someone will let you inside."

"Fine. I'll see you later." The sheriff stalked off, barking orders to anyone within earshot. Everyone jumped like rabbits to do his bidding.

Nick waved on his team. "Let's get her out of here."

As they walked to the Huey, Ryon mulled over Nick's intriguing statement to the sheriff. Something big and scary was in the shadows, waiting.

And he suddenly knew with absolute certainty that it wasn't just his and Daria's lives that were about to be changed forever.

For an endless stretch of time, there was nothing but blackness. Pain.

Then there were voices. Snarling. A dog? What was a dog doing here? Then hands, lifting her body. Agony.

More discussion. The snarling ceased, and there were soothing words. One of the voices sounded familiar. He was important, but she couldn't recall why.

Then, something incredibly sweet trickled into her mouth. The taste was amazing, but her throat refused to work and she feared choking. Gradually, that changed. Something began to happen. Synapses fired, creating tiny explosions in every cell, making them come alive. At last the muscles in her throat cooperated and she drank the essence, greedy for more and more. When the wonderful liquid was taken away, she felt the loss like a physical blow.

The letdown didn't last. Her arm was lifted and a warm pair of lips settled against her flesh. Lips? Before she could think on it further, sharp twin points pierced her skin, and a silent cry lodged in her chest. She couldn't scream, and even if she could make a sound, it wouldn't be from agony.

The greatest pleasure she'd ever known shot through her veins. Spread liquid heat to every part of her and detonated into a million shards of white-hot crystal, then solidified into a golden cord. She should've been frightened, but she wasn't. The cord bound her firmly to the stranger. Her stranger, and yet it seemed she knew him somehow. She struggled to capture the memory, but it escaped.

The sharp points withdrew and she felt bereft, but not as badly as before. She could handle it now because she sensed him hovering close. Watching over and protecting her. How could she know this? But she did. Secure in the knowledge that all would be well, she drifted. Fell into a deep abyss.

When she surfaced again, it was to the sensation of floating, and an occasional rocking motion. The movement made her nauseated, but she was too weak even to throw up. Just as bad was the deafening noise threatening to split her aching head in two. It dawned on her that she was being transported, and the rapid *whump-whump* sound told her she was in a helicopter.

Flying. Another reason to be sick, if she had the energy. She was an earth-loving girl. If she'd been meant to fly, she would have been born with feathers. Her distress must've been apparent somehow, because a man's gentle hand stroked her hair, caressed her face. She wondered whether he was speaking to her, too, though there was no way to tell over the racket from the aircraft.

Despite the noise, her sickness, and fear, darkness pulled her into the depths again. She surfaced once more, when the helicopter landed, and there was a flurry of activity as she was rushed into some sort of building. A hospital? Her brief glimpse of it gave the impression that it wasn't like any hospital she'd ever seen. The area outside seemed rural, lots of trees. No parking lot filled with cars, no activity.

Strange. But all of that was swept away when, inside, she was rolled into a small, sterile room and a pretty woman—doctor?—with long, curly brunette hair smiled down at her.

"Miss Bradford? Just relax. We're going to take care of you, and you'll feel better soon. I promise." She patted Daria's arm. "Do you understand?"

She nodded. Or thought she did. Then the good drugs must've kicked in, and she knew nothing else for a very long while.

*   *   *

The Huey landed and Ryon jumped out, watching helplessly as the medical team whisked Daria out of the transport. He jogged after them as they rushed the gurney through the double doors, down the hallway to the infirmary, and into one of the trauma rooms. There, however, he was blocked by Noah, who placed one palm on Ryon's chest.

"Sorry, man. You have to stay out here," he said firmly, not without sympathy. "Better yet, head back to the waiting area."

"But—"

"No buts. We'll let you know how she's doing soon."

The nurse wasn't going to be budged. Worse, Ryon was holding the man up from doing his job. With a sigh, he gave in. "All right. But let me know the second you can tell me how she's doing."

"You bet. Don't worry, okay?" With an encouraging smile, the nurse disappeared.

"Dammit!" Raking a hand through his hair, he made his way back to the waiting room. Frustrated, he paced like a caged animal for several minutes, until Aric showed up, Rowan with him.

"You've gotta settle down or you're gonna give yourself a stroke," the red wolf observed. "Sit."

"I can't. She's back there, suffering, and there's not a goddamned thing I can do about it!"

Rowan stepped in front of him, clasped his shoulders, and tried to soothe him. "Daria isn't feeling any pain right now. She's in good hands, and she's going to get better fast, thanks to your bonding."

"She's not hurting *now*, but she will be when she wakes up," he rasped. "And I'll have to tell her what I did to save her life."

"One step at a time. You don't have to get into that right away."

"Yes, I do. If I let it slide, even just until she's better, it'll be the same as lying. What if she hates me for it?" The possibility had him breaking out into a cold sweat. His wolf would go insane, taking the man right along with him.

Taking his hand, Rowan pulled him over to sit in a chair and took a seat beside him. "She might be scared or upset, at first. Don't let that eat at you. There's nothing you could've done differently under the circumstances except allow her to die, and then you would have been next. Once she understands that, everything will be fine."

"I hope you're right." If she rejected him, the consequences he'd suffer didn't bear thinking about further.

A couple of hours passed. His Pack brothers came and went, checking on him and asking for word about his mate. At the moment he was alone. Tired from his constant pacing, he slumped into a chair again and stared out the window, contemplating this turn of events.

Why did he care so much about Daria? On both a primal and intellectual level, he knew what she was to him. Unlike Jax and Aric when they'd met their mates, right from the start there had been no question in his mind, or his wolf's, that Daria was his mate. His wolf's reaction, the beast's attraction to her, was like a blow upside the head with a tire iron. His beast wanted to claim her, mark her with his scent. And much more. But the *man* cared more than one would for a stranger. It both excited him and scared the shit out of him.

Odd that he'd met her twice already—just not in person. On both occasions she'd reached out to him across miles. Had she somehow sensed their bond, causing her to act?

"Ryon?"

Pushing to his feet, he saw Melina Mallory coming toward him. The doctor's short cap of dark hair was growing out, almost touching her collar, and framed her elfin face in a flattering way. It softened her features, made her more approachable. The rare warm smile hovering on her lips boded well, and he just about fell over in relief before she could speak. In typical fashion, the no-nonsense doc got right to the point.

"Daria is lucky to be alive. She sustained a broken arm, a broken rib, various cuts and bruises, and serious internal bleeding, which is what almost killed her. That said, she's doing well."

He gave a humorless laugh. "Doesn't sound so good to me."

"I'll be honest. If it hadn't been for the mating bite, her story would've ended in that ravine. But you reached her in time, did what had to be done, and that's what matters. She has no serious head injury and her other wounds are healing faster than I've ever seen on a human," she mused.

"Really?"

"Yes. It's quite extraordinary." Melina gazed at Ryon thoughtfully. "I've seen shifters heal rapidly plenty of times. It's just part of your abilities. However, this is the first time we've been able to observe the same healing property at work in a newly mated human. I would love to know whether the bite is only capable of mending one's fated mate, or if it would work on any human."

"Well, it's not like we can go around chomping down on random injured humans in order to find out." A thought struck him. "When our SEAL team was attacked in Afghanistan six years ago by those rogue wolf shifters, we were human. Those of us who survived healed fast, and became shifters. Our Psy gifts were enhanced by the change, too. But none of those ugly bastards were our mates."

"Good point. So it would seem that one doesn't have to be a shifter's mate to benefit from the bite." She paused. "Maybe a human just has to possess a Psy ability."

Ryon considered this, and nodded. "That could be the connection. Maybe that's why we survived the attack when so many others didn't."

"Or it could be simply a thing between mates. Anyway, it's certainly a theory worth more study."

"This is all fascinating, but—"

"I know, you want to see Daria. Impatient, aren't you?" She graced him with a full-fledged smile. "Noah's putting her into a room now, second one on the left. He'll come and get you when he's done."

"Thanks, Melina," he said with feeling. "For every-thing."

"Don't thank me. You're the one who's got your work cut out for you these next few weeks and months, getting her settled in. Helping her accept a whole new reality. I don't envy you that task."

Giving his hand a quick squeeze, she turned and walked briskly away. In less than five minutes, Noah was there.

"You can see her now." With a sympathetic smile, the nurse left.

Somehow, walking into her room was the hardest thing he'd ever done. For a long moment he stood inside the door and studied the slender, battered woman on the bed.

She was lying on her back, lashes like black lace on her high cheekbones. Her arms were on top of the covers, the right one in a cast and sling resting on her stomach, and he noted the scratches on the left arm weren't quite as angry and raw in appearance as they should be. Her color was much improved, and he noticed for the first time that her skin was a rich bronze, whether from being outdoors a lot or from her heritage, he could only guess. Maybe a bit of both.

As he moved closer and took a seat beside the bed, he was relieved to see that her breathing was deep and even. She seemed to be at peace.

He worried about how long that would last.

For several long moments, he contemplated Melina's parting words, that she didn't envy him the task

ahead. Daria might forgive him, but getting there probably would not be a joyride.

Despite his relief at seeing her already healing, the
first hint of trepidation seeped through like black
sludge.

Daria had to forgive him. Had to. The alternative
was unthinkable.

I shouldn't be alive.

That was Daria's initial thought as she blinked into
the sunlight filtering through the crack in the blinds in
the sterile room. Yes, she was completely positive she
had been dying out in that isolated stretch of wilderness, lying broken at the bottom of a ravine.

How am I here? How?

Gradually, bits and pieces returned. Rescuers had
found her. *He* had been among them, the one she
sought. Talking to her, encouraging her to live. What
was his name?

Her thoughts were sluggish, but she finally recalled
she didn't know it. As more of the fog lifted, she realized
that her vision of him being attacked hadn't revealed that
piece of information. Nor had they exchanged names
when she'd come to him astrally and begged for help.
Then a slight rustle sounded from her right and she
turned her head to see the man in the flesh, dozing in a
chair beside the bed.

She sucked in a sharp, involuntary breath, ignoring
the pain it caused. However beautiful he was in her
vision was *nothing* compared to the real thing. Even

with his long, lean frame sprawled in the uncomfortable-looking chair, shadows under his eyes, and snoring a little as he slept like the dead, he was stunning male perfection.

He wore faded jeans and a short-sleeved button-up shirt that wasn't tucked in. The buttons were open half-way down his torso, as though he'd thrown on the shirt and couldn't be bothered to finish with the task. Though she couldn't see his feet, she guessed he must be wearing tennis shoes.

Taking in her surroundings, she noted that this room was much like the one she'd visited him in—when? She had no idea how long she'd been here. There was no clock on the bedside table or on the wall. There wasn't much of anything except a pitcher of water, a plastic cup, the chair, her bed, and a rolling food tray that held a vase of pretty flowers.

She blinked at them, and suddenly remembered her dad. Were they from him? If so, where was he? Maybe he'd gone for some food.

The blond man stirred in the chair and opened his eyes, revealing the crystal blue that she remembered. Stretching his back, he sat up, and in spite of his obvious fatigue, he smiled at her. His teeth were straight and white, and the effect on his already breathtaking looks made her heart skip a beat.

"Hi there." The rich timbre of his voice was smooth, sexy. Like the rest of him.

"Hello." Her own voice was raspy, as though she hadn't used it in months. "Where am I?"

"A . . . private facility." Before she could question him about that, he scooted closer and laid a big hand on her arm. Or rather, over the sling and cast covering her arm. "How are you feeling?"

She paused, taking stock of her body. "Sore. Hurts a little." Then she frowned. "Seems like I should be in more pain, though. Good drugs, maybe."

Those gorgeous blue eyes grew solemn. "Something like that. Do you remember your name and what you were doing in the Shoshone?"

"I'm Daria Bradford, and I'm a wildlife biologist specializing in the study of wolves." She swallowed, the dryness in her throat making her hoarse. Immediately he caught on and poured her a cup of water, sticking a straw in it. Then he held the straw to her lips.

"Just a few sips. Don't want you to get sick."

The water was heaven. More so was the solicitous attention from this kind stranger. "Thank you." She sat back and he placed the cup on the table.

"You're welcome." He paused. "Do you recall how long you'd been in the area before you fell into the ravine?"

She nodded, the slight movement making her neck twinge. "Almost two weeks. And I didn't fall, I was pushed. I told you that before."

A blond brow arched attractively, disappearing under the fringe of bangs that fell into his eyes. "When you astrally projected yourself into my hospital room. You have a gift."

There was no accusation in his tone. No stunned disbelief, no censure or disgust. Just honest interest. Why wasn't he shocked? "Yes."

"All right. Why did you go off the trail? Why did you run from the scene of the body you found, and who pushed you into the ravine?"

"Back up. I can't believe you're taking it so well that I have a Psy gift."

He laughed softly. "Trust me, nobody around here will bat an eyelash at that."

"What do you mean?"

"All in good time."

"What's your name?"

"Ryon Hunter," he said softly. "At your command."

He was gazing at her as though she held the answers he'd sought all his life. It made her feel warm and fuzzy all over. Weird. And sort of nice.

"It's good to meet you." It came out sounding shy, though she wasn't typically a shy person at all. This man got to her, and she didn't understand why.

"You mean good to meet me *again*."

"That's true." More questions hovered on his lips, she could tell. But he simply waited. "How long have I been here?"

"Since yesterday. You were out all night."

"Okay. To answer you, I broke camp yesterday morning and left in sort of a hurry because I heard something that frightened me. A screeching sound."

"Screeching? Like a bird or something?"

She shook her head. "No. Have you seen any of the old *Godzilla* movies? That awful sound he makes when he's trashing Tokyo? That kind of noise, exactly. It echoed through the mountains." This information earned her the dubious look that the revelation of her Psy gift had not.

"It sounded like Godzilla?"

"It did," she said stiffly. "Every living thing in the forest went still and silent. My job entails working in nature, being alone and isolated for weeks at a time as I study the wolf packs and check their progress. I don't scare easily, and I wouldn't exaggerate something like that."

He held up a hand. "Sorry. I didn't mean to imply you would. I just can't come up with anything that would make a noise like that."

"Whatever it is, the creature isn't any type that belongs in this area, I can assure you."

After a moment, he nodded. "And then?"

"I hurried out of there, but as the morning went on I managed to convince myself it was nothing. Until I found the body." The memory threatened to make her ill. "I can't remember what got my attention first, the sight of clothing on the ground, or the smell. I went over to investigate, see if the person was alive, and the body was mutilated. I've never seen anything so gruesome. Ever."

"Me, neither," he agreed grimly. "We discovered the corpse just before we found you, and we're pretty sure it was a woman, from parts of her clothing."

She shuddered. "I didn't look that closely. I got sick and then fetched my radio, started to call the rangers. That's when the wolf showed up."

At that, Ryon tensed. "What did it look like?"

"That's one of the strange things—it was snow white. Very rare in the wild for an albino of any species to survive."

"White? Was it a male?" he asked, his expression serious.

"Female, sort of small. But she appeared large enough when she bared her teeth at me and started chasing me away from the scene of the body. I ran, and came to the edge of the ravine. When I turned to face her, she lunged and pushed me over the edge."

He looked stunned. "Jesus. Maybe the woman was her kill and she didn't want you near it?"

"Could be, but I have my doubts. Have you ever seen a wolf do that to a human?"

"Not a *real* one," he muttered.

"What?"

"Nothing. Anyway, we'll know more soon, when the medical examiner finishes with the body." He fell silent for a moment, studying her. "I saw you a couple of nights ago, when I was attacked by some . . . subjects my team and I were chasing."

"I'd wondered if you knew I was there, or remembered," she said quietly. "I'm not sure what drew me to you, to be honest. I fell asleep that night and had a vision of you in the alley with your friends, fighting some humanlike creatures that looked like vampires. Crazy, I know."

A faint smile curved his lips, but he said nothing. The smile wasn't mocking, and his eyes were devoid of humor.

"I have real-time visions sometimes when I sleep. I'm projected into the scene whether I want to be there or not."

"Wouldn't that be Dreamwalking, in that case?"

"No. Dreamwalking requires the person, or both parties if there's more than one, to be dreaming, and the scene isn't necessarily real, or happening at all. It's often a fantasy that disappears when the person wakes. It didn't actually happen, but the memory can be shared if there's more than one Dreamwalker involved. A meeting of the minds, if you will, rather than reality."

"I see. So you really *were* there, in the alley with me."

"Yes. Even in my sleep, I projected a form of myself to the actual scene that was taking place."

"Okay." So simple, his acceptance.

"Just *okay*? Where is your attitude, the sarcasm? What did you mean when you said nobody around here would be surprised by my gift?"

"Because nobody will." He sighed and braced his elbows on his knees. "You asked me where you are. Right now you're a guest of the Institute of Parapsychology, housed in a secret location in the Shoshone National Forest."

"The Institute of Parapsychology," she repeated, turning over the term in her mind. Gradually, it dawned on her. "The study of the paranormal."

"Yes. As well as the effects of that world on all of us who live here at the compound."

She digested this. "And just who are you?"

"My team is called Alpha Pack. We each have different Psy abilities and we get called all over the world to handle paranormal predators like the rogue vampires you witnessed us battling."

"They really were vampires?" she whispered.

His voice was gentle, almost apologetic. "Those fangs weren't fake, honey. Neither was the silver knife that one bastard buried in my side."

"Why silver? Wait— How are you even out of your hospital bed two days after being stabbed and having your throat ripped out?" She sat upright, heart beating wildly in her chest. "I saw it! And now there's nothing but some pink scars on your neck!"

"You're right, you did see me torn and stabbed. But I heal fast. All of my kind does."

"What kind is that?" She was almost afraid to know.

"The type that doesn't react well to silver, so that much of the legends is true." He gave her a sad smile. "You might as well know . . . we're wolf shifters, Daria."

Ben Cantrell fell to his knees in the undergrowth, sick and exhausted.

What had happened? Where had he been this time?

His confused mind finally registered the blood. His hands were coated in the vile stuff. His arms, chest, some splattered on his legs. Reaching up, he felt his face, and recoiled in horror. Blood, on his mouth.

"Oh, no. *No*."

Not again. Please, not again.

But to his lawyer's mind, the evidence was irrefutable. He laughed at that, a mad, hysterical sound. Because he'd never work as an attorney again. Would never be human. His life had been stolen from him and he would never get it back.

Unless he found the ones who could help. He'd set out searching for them, but now struggled to recall who he was supposed to find. But he'd remember. He would. And they *would* help him.

They had to. Or soon, Benjamin Cantrell would be lost forever.

Four

Ryon's guts clenched as he studied Daria's reaction. The woman paled under her tan, her lips parting in shock. Then she dropped her gaze to the sheets. "I can't buy that."

"I know it's a lot to take in, but it's true. I wouldn't lie to you."

She looked up. "I believe you *think* you're telling the truth, but—"

"You can perform astral projection," he pointed out. "You know about Psy gifts, and you saw the vampires with your own eyes."

"There have been documented case studies of people who have psychic abilities and can do or see all sorts of things they shouldn't be able to," she said. "Some can predict the future, read an object to see the past, move items with their minds, find missing people. You name it. But you're asking me to believe you can change forms? I'm sorry, Ryon. You're delusional."

"I expected you to react like that," he said, trying to hide his disappointment. "I can't blame you. But I *can* prove it."

"You can change into a wolf, here and now." Her tone was flat.

"Yes."

She flicked her good hand at him. "Okay, so do it."

"I don't think so. Not yet."

Some of the hardness left her expression, and her tone became kind. "Have you sought help for this fantasy? There are some really good doctors who can treat that sort of thing."

He stood. "I don't need a doctor. Not for being delusional, anyway. I'm going to let you rest because you have a lot to take in, and this is enough for the time being."

"Will you be back?"

She sounded hopeful, and that eased some of his anxiety—and his wolf's. But not all. The beast paced inside him, not happy at being doubted. It was much too close to rejection.

"Yeah." Leaning over, he kissed her cheek, then straightened. "I'll be back soon, no worries. Sleep."

"All right, I'll try." She didn't look convinced, though.

Giving her a reassuring smile, he turned and walked out while he still had the strength to leave. He'd pushed far enough, and her scientist's mind needed precious time to absorb the truth of his words. She wasn't ready to see him change into his wolf, but she would be. As a biologist, and his mate, though she didn't know that part yet, she wouldn't be able to help her curiosity. She would continue to be drawn to him.

He hoped.

Leaving the infirmary, he headed for Nick's office. The door was cracked when he got there, and he heard his commander inside, talking. Guessing the door wouldn't be open if the boss didn't want to be disturbed, he knocked lightly and waited.

"Come in."

Pushing inside, he saw Nick sitting behind his desk, Sheriff Deveraux reclining in a chair across from him. Deveraux was about Nick's age, and Ryon supposed women would find him good-looking in a rugged, outdoorsy way. Ryon stuck his hand out to the visitor.

"Sheriff," he said politely. "I've seen you a couple of times, but we've never been introduced. I'm Ryon Hunter."

The other man grasped it briefly, his gaze sharp but not unkind. "You're part of the Alpha Pack that Nick has been telling me about?"

Ryon looked at his boss, who gave a slight nod. The sheriff had been unwittingly pulled into the Sluaghs' attack on a local family several weeks ago, and rudely made aware that the paranormal really existed. Since then, the commander had obviously been easing the lawman into their world, and so it was okay to talk freely in front of him.

"Yes, I am. I don't mean to interrupt, but I just came from visiting Daria, and I thought Nick would like to hear what she said about yesterday's events. You too, Sheriff, since you're here."

They listened intently as he described the great screeching noise Daria heard, and how it frightened her into breaking camp. If they'd expected Ryon to tell them that the culprit who chased her from the scene of the body and pushed her over the ledge was a Sluagh, or some previously unheard-of creature, they were wrong.

"It was a white wolf?" Nick repeated, going still. "She's certain?"

Ryon rolled his eyes. "Of course she's sure. She's got a broken arm, not brain damage. On top of that, she says the wolf is female."

The commander's face paled, and he stared at the top of his desk. "I haven't had any visions at all about any of this, just a sense of wrongness. Danger. I'm not sure what any of it means, and I'm hesitant to guess."

"But you *do* have one," Deveraux pressed.

Nick sighed. "I don't think the wolf is responsible for the killing, but we won't know for sure until Kira and Melina finish testing that DNA sample of the victim they liberated from the crime scene."

"I'll pretend I didn't hear that." The sheriff scowled.

"No offense, Jesse, but I have a hunch your medical examiner is going to come up with some very strange findings on that body and isn't going to know what to make of them. Which is for the best. But my lab people will know what the results indicate, or at least have a good head start."

"You might be right, but I don't like it," the man muttered. "You'll keep me in the loop."

"You bet."

Mollified somewhat, the sheriff stood to leave. "Nothing to do for now but wait and see. Search and Rescue is still looking for the couple that vanished—or the husband at least. I'm betting the mutilated woman is the wife."

"You're probably right."

Deveraux shook hands with both of them again, and then saw himself out. Ryon waited until the lawman was gone before he spoke.

"You sure we can trust him?"

"Absolutely," Nick said. His mouth curved into a wry smile. "He's so old-school, all this paranormal stuff is about to burst a blood vessel in his brain, but he's a good man. He's on our side, for all the bitching he does."

"Good to know."

"How's Daria?"

"Unsettled," he admitted. "Just because she has a Psy gift that she acknowledges doesn't mean she's ready to accept that we're shifters or that other creatures exist. She wanted me to change and prove I'm a wolf, but I could tell she wasn't really ready for that. I don't want her to push me away."

"She's had enough to deal with," Nick agreed. "You did the right thing giving her some time."

"Thanks."

"But don't take too long to tell her the rest. It's a delicate balance between giving her time to adjust and coming across as though you were hiding the truth."

"Yeah, I know." Hanging his head, he studied his shoes. He was so damned tired, his body still healing, and yet he hadn't been able to rest for worrying about her.

"You're about to fall over. Go crash for a while, or you're not going to be any good to the team or your mate."

"I think I'll do that."

He'd try, anyway. Back in his quarters, he tossed on the bed and fantasized about a striking, raven-haired woman who might not want a thing to do with him. He thought only of kissing those plump lips, caressing toned, soft, honey brown skin. His lids grew heavy and yearnings followed him into his dreams where she tormented him endlessly, leading him to the edge, so in danger of falling. Only to pull back and leave him hurt, confused.

God, her lips were soft. His tongue slipped inside and he explored her mouth, groaning at her sweet taste. His fingers dipped into the swell between her breasts and stroked the creamy mounds. Sought lower, skimming down her flat stomach . . . until she caught his hand.

"Ryon."

"Baby, please. I need you."

"I can't." She shook her head.

"Why not?" Pulling back, he studied her expression. He saw fear, confusion. Not the ideal emotions to inspire in his mate.

"This is too soon," she said softly. *"I don't know how I feel about this. About whether there's an us."*

His wolf howled inside and a bubble of panic lodged in his throat. *"Of course there is. Don't you feel something growing between us?"* he asked hoarsely. *"I already care about you, Daria."*

She shook her head. *"I cared about someone else not too long ago, and he broke my heart. I thought what he and I had was real, but it wasn't. How can I trust again?"*

"Let me show you." He was begging shamelessly, and he couldn't help himself. *"Let me prove how good it can be with the right man."*

"I don't think I can. I'm sorry." She gave him the saddest smile.

Then turned and walked away.

"Daria, no! Don't leave me!"

Ryon bolted upright in bed, heart hammering in his chest. Not a vision—that wasn't his gift. Just a dream turned nightmare, he realized. A horrible, stupid nightmare with no basis in reality. God, he wanted her so much.

As proof, his unsatisfied cock was hard and aching, pointing at the ceiling. He needed relief or he was going to die of blue balls. Unzipping his jeans, he pushed them down far enough to free his tackle, and cupped a hand, squeezing the tight orbs. It felt so good he did it again, manipulating the sac and teasing the perineum. One finger trailed down to his hole, giving it a naughty rimming and stimulating his arousal to near pain.

Taking himself in hand, he gripped the hot, hard flesh and began to stroke. Up and down, hissing in pleasure at the little shocks of sensation that skittered from his nerve endings to heat his groin. The feeling was awesome, but it was nothing compared to what happened when he imagined Daria crouched between his thighs, jet-black hair spilling over his lap as she sucked him down her throat.

"Oh, shit."

That tripped his trigger, and his hips bucked as he worked his rod with abandon and just let himself go. In seconds that familiar buzz started at the base of his spine, signaling orgasm. His release exploded like a shot from a gun, creamy white ropes of cum squirting to land on his stomach and chest. On and on he spurted until his balls had emptied and he was jerking with aftershocks, wishing it hadn't ended so fast.

"Damn," he rasped. "Time for a shower."

Now that the high had ended, he felt empty. Sort of lost. With a sigh, he rose and padded to the bathroom, turning on the water to let it get hot. As he stepped into the steamy spray, he groaned and tried to shut the nightmare out of his mind.

But now that it was stuck in his brain, he couldn't dislodge it.

Getting to know Daria, much less winning her over, might be his biggest challenge yet.

On the second day of her stay, Daria awoke feeling much better. So much, in fact, she was suspicious of exactly why she wasn't hurting beyond a twinge or two. And why in the hell the scratches on her body weren't more than pink, healing lines that looked a few weeks old instead of two days.

She stared at one of the marks on her left arm in growing dread. What kind of medicine speeded healing like that? Nothing she'd ever heard of.

It was then that she noticed two faint puncture marks inside her wrist.

Again, the memory of voices, the men shouting as they worked to save her life, flooded in. This time came the recollection of a slight, pinching pain on her wrist. Had she imagined that? If so, why were there marks on her skin?

Restless, she glanced at the chair beside the bed, wondering where Ryon had gone. Her new protector had been by her side off and on since his team had brought her in, and at first she was relieved whenever he would duck out. Then the stretches of time he was gone seemed interminably long, when she was awake to realize it. Now, she had to admit to herself that she missed him.

They had talked a little, though he avoided the subject of the Pack's specific missions and the paranormal world they fought in. Instead, he made small talk about Wyoming, his friends in particular, their strengths and idiosyncrasies. They were an odd group, but close as brothers, and his love for them shone with every word. As if her thoughts had conjured him, Ryon stepped through the door carrying a plastic grocery sack and approached with a tentative smile on his sexy face. "How are you feeling?"

Her heart lightened just to see him, though she kept her enthusiasm in check. "Almost human again."

He looked away, his expression sheepish, and she wondered what on earth was wrong with him. But then the odd moment passed and he brightened again.

"Well enough to get out of here and have a bite to eat in the cafeteria with me? The food there is awesome."

"They're springing me so soon?" she asked in surprise.

"If you promise to take it easy for the next few days. Nick took the liberty of having one of the guests' quarters made ready for you, if you'll do us the honor of staying while you recuperate."

"That's nice of him." It was. She also found it faintly disturbing, being taken in just like that by a compound of men she didn't know and who didn't know her, but she knew her nerves were on edge. Anyone's would be after what she'd been through.

"Great," he said, taking her words as acceptance. He looked vastly relieved, more than he should at the news that a stranger was staying. "I put your clothes and camping gear in your room already. I hope you don't mind."

"Of course not. Thank you." She gestured to the sack. "What's in there?"

"Oh, these are some of your clothes. Didn't think you'd want to leave here with your butt hanging out of that gown. Not that I'd mind."

His statement and the impertinent grin made her laugh. "You must be a handful."

"I can be. Want to find out?"

He was so cute, she couldn't possibly take offense. "Not before you feed me. I was promised a meal, right?"

"You bet." Handing her the sack, he backed away. "I'll get a wheelchair while you get dressed."

"A wheelchair? I don't think I'll need one of those."

"Trust me, you do. After what you went through it's a miracle you're breathing."

"And why *am* I breathing?" she asked pointedly, gesturing to the pink scars on her arm. "Why am I practically healed?"

"All in good time. Baby steps, huh?"

Frustrated, she watched him walk out and shut the door behind him. Clearly, he was reluctant to get into many more details with her, but given the way she'd reacted to his delusion of being a wolf shifter, she wasn't really surprised.

But *was* it a fantasy on his part? She should be dead, not getting ready to leave, even in a wheelchair. Her bizarre recovery aside, she'd soon get the straight story on Ryon. She was sure his teammates would clue her in that he was suffering from some sort of mental illness and they humored him. That was the only explanation, and it made her sad.

Getting dressed took her longer than she had imagined, and she was just slipping on the borrowed tennis shoes Ryon had brought when he walked through the door pushing the wheelchair. But he wasn't alone.

"Daria, I'd like you to meet my commander, Nick Westfall."

Ryon's boss was an imposing man with short, feathery dark hair with the slightest bit of silver at the temples, and steely blue eyes. He carried himself with his back straight, his projected demeanor warning *don't mess with me* even though he had yet to open his mouth. When he did speak, however, his tone was kind.

"Miss Bradford."

"Daria, please."

He nodded. "I'm Nick. I try to keep my team in line, and sometimes I actually succeed. We're glad to have you here, even though it's not under the best of circumstances."

"Thank you. I appreciate your taking me in like this. I could go to a hotel if it would be less trouble—"

"Not at all. It's our pleasure, and we wouldn't hear of turning out a fellow nature lover after what you've been through." His lips turned up a bit. "You might want to hide out here anyway, at least until the media frenzy dies down."

She stared at him. "I don't think I like the sound of that."

"We have some reporters lurking outside the first gate, and they've asked to talk to the biologist who found the body in the woods. If you want to speak with them, I'll set up a place for you to meet."

Shuddering, she rubbed her arms. "And if I don't?"

"I'll make them go away."

Simple as that. She had no doubt he would follow through, and with pleasure. "I don't want to relive what I found for the media. Let the authorities talk to them."

The commander's expression reflected approval. "I think that's a wise decision. You will have to talk to Sheriff Deveraux, though. Ryon told him your story, but he wants a statement from you directly."

"I guess that's to be expected, but I don't want to talk to anyone else."

"Then you won't. Now, I'll leave you in Ryon's capable hands." He winked, turned and left.

"Nick is an interesting man," she said to Ryon.

"He's the best superior I've ever had." His voice told her of his real affection for the man. "He'd do anything for any of us."

"He strikes me as that kind of boss and friend."

"Yeah." He paused. "Are you hungry?"

"Starving." Her stomach rumbled again.

He helped her into the chair, holding on carefully when she swayed. Perhaps she did need the thing after all, since she wasn't nearly as steady on her feet as she'd thought she would be. He didn't say *I told you so*, just got her situated and rolled her out by an adorable blond male nurse who waved at them as they went past.

"That's Noah," Ryon told her. "He's a fixture around here."

"Yes, I met him. He came in to check on me from time to time. Very sweet guy. Does he live at the compound, too?"

"All the staff does."

That was so weird to her. "Why?"

"My team is required to live on base. We get dispatched at a moment's notice so it would waste valuable time if we had to wait on everyone to get here from town. Living on-site, we can train, plan maneuvers, discuss ongoing cases, and generally be ready for whatever comes our way. We get time off, though. We relax when we aren't busy."

"Sort of like the military."

"Exactly."

"What about the doctors and other staff? Surely they could live in town."

"They could, but we're kind of isolated. It makes more sense to live here rather than driving to and from town."

"Very logical, but why do I sense there's more to it than that?"

"There is. All of the traffic coming in and out of our compound would attract too much attention. We definitely don't want that."

"Because of what you do here," she said, unable to mask the doubt in her voice. "You're out saving the world from paranormal predators like vampires and such."

"I know you don't believe me yet, but you will. It's true."

They would see about that. Her broken arm was still in a sling—even some sort of new super-healing ability couldn't fix that overnight—and she examined again the healing pink scratches on her arm. And the two mysterious puncture marks on her wrist. Unbidden, something Ryon had told her before popped into her head.

But I heal fast. All of my kind does.

Staring at the punctures, a question came to her that she wasn't ready to deal with. She wasn't ready to know the answer, and so she shut it down. For the moment, anyway. Instead, she busied herself taking in the compound's interior as her companion rolled her along.

The décor was nothing like she would've expected of a place where a military-style team was housed. Instead of being stark and white with serviceable industrial-tiled floors that had no personality, the walls were painted a soft sandy beige, and the hallway was carpeted in a short, smooth weave that allowed the chair to make easy progress. There were nice fixtures on the walls, giving off plenty of light instead of drab fluorescent ones overhead. The place was homey. She was impressed, and that only increased when they arrived at the cafeteria.

The area was really a large dining room. It was filled with several tables that allowed the occupants to sit in groups and chat, which many were presently doing. Food was served in the middle of each table, family-style, and they ate off real dishes and used actual utensils instead of paper plates and plastic forks.

A wide door beyond the dining area gave her a glimpse of the big kitchen beyond, where a number of cooks were busy going about their tasks. The wonderful aroma brought her attention back to the food, which consisted of hamburgers with all the fixings, and fries.

Ryon rolled her to an empty spot, making sure she could reach the table. "How's this?"

"Fine, thanks." She noted that some people were watching them with interest, Daria in particular, and she smiled at some of them. Nerves tried to get the best of her, but she pushed them down.

"You okay?" he asked in concern, taking a seat across from her.

"Yes. I'm just not used to being around so many people."

"I can imagine, being out in the woods so much. Do you miss the interaction, or are you one of those who only comes back to the real world when you have to?"

She looked at him in surprise. "That's a perceptive question. I don't think anyone has ever asked me that." Reaching for a bun, she thought about it. "I do miss being around other people, talking, laughing, and sharing stuff. I love my job, but it's so isolating that I sometimes miss doing something as fun and simple as meeting the girls for drinks or going to a movie."

"Stuff other people take for granted. I totally get that."

He did, and she found it was nice. "Do you miss having a regular job?"

He smiled. "Honey, I wouldn't even know what that means. I'm happy here, doing what I do."

Warmth slid over her, her entire body reacting to his calling her *honey*. Even when her ex-fiancé had used endearments, she hadn't felt as though she wanted to wrap herself in the man and never emerge. It was a good feeling, and scary.

They piled goodies on their burgers and munched for a while, and she took the opportunity to study him, trying not to appear as though she was doing it. He was so handsome, with those crystal blue eyes. And she had a thing for blonds, always had, maybe in part because she found her own black hair so plain and boring. She found herself wanting to bury her fingers in those sunlight tresses and do delicious things to his mouth.

She almost choked on a bite of burger.

"You okay?"

"Fine," she said, coughing. In the next instant, she was very glad she'd swallowed that bite of food.

From her seat she had a good view of the entrance, and when she turned her head slightly to the right, something, or some*one*, strolled in that she'd never forget.

"What the hell?" she whispered, burger plopping to her plate, forgotten.

Just inside the entrance to the dining room stood a tall, breathtakingly beautiful male creature. An other-worldly being, not a man. He stood six feet tall, maybe a little more, and was slender, jeans slung low on his hips. He had a gorgeous face with high cheekbones and large, golden eyes like an eagle's that almost glowed.

But his most stunning features were his waist-length jewel blue hair that cascaded like ribbons in water, and the magnificent feathery wings of the same color that had brushed the top of the doorframe when he'd stepped through. The wildlife biologist danced in glee at this find. The woman stared, not sure whether to greet him or run and hide.

"Incredible." She couldn't take her eyes off him.

"Isn't he?" Ryon's voice was wry, tinged with humor. "Sariel tends to suck up most of the air when he's in the room."

The male made his way toward them, having noticed Daria. His wide smile was warm as he stopped beside their table.

"Hello there! You must be Miss Bradford, our guest."

He bowed slightly. "I'm Sariel, or Blue if you prefer. For obvious reasons."

Her mouth worked, speech having died between her brain and her mouth.

Ryon interceded with a chuckle. "She's going to need some time to get used to us, buddy. Just call her Daria. Daria, this is our resident Seelie prince."

"Removed from my throne," he said smoothly. "Titles don't mean much here, unless you're the commander."

"What's a Seelie?" she managed at last.

Blue explained patiently. "A member of the Fae realm, a world that exists parallel to this one. The portal to the Fae realm is located in a country you call Ireland. The Fae consist of two groups—the Seelie and the Unseelie. Members of my Court consider us to be the *good guys*, if you will. Though we all know not every world is made of entirely good or bad people."

A shadow passed over his face as he related that last bit, and she wondered at it. "What are the Unseelie, then? The *bad guys*?"

"Essentially. They devote their existence to pleasing themselves, no matter who they hurt. Their minions are the Sluagh, Seelie who've given themselves to evil, and have fallen."

She took this in. "And you're a prince."

"Yes, formerly from the Seelie Court. Old news, and a long story." He waved a hand at a vacant chair. "May I join you both?"

"Sit," Ryon said. "Eat. You're way too skinny. Haven't you been following the diet Melina put you on?"

Blue, as Daria was starting to think of him, wrinkled his nose at the hamburger patties as though they were the most revolting things he'd ever seen. "I seriously doubt those should be on anyone's diet."

"You just need to gain weight, man. Doesn't matter how at this point."

Blue glared at his friend. "Thank you for so helpfully pointing that out." He reached for a bun and piled it with vegetables, leaving out the meat altogether and ignoring the fries.

Thankfully, Ryon didn't comment on his choice. She could see that Blue was rather sensitive about the subject of his eating habits. She wondered if food was so different in the Seelie Court that he couldn't find things here to satisfy his palate. Then she ground to a mental halt at the direction of her thoughts.

She was pondering the eating habits of a Fae prince. As though that were perfectly normal.

We're wolf shifters, Daria.

She had believed Ryon to be mentally ill. And the proof that he wasn't was sitting here, politely chatting away with the man who'd appointed himself her friend and protector.

Ryon had been telling the absolute truth about his world and the creatures in it.

And *her* world had just been irrevocably turned on its head.

Five

R yon witnessed the exact moment Daria *knew* the truth.

He saw it in her brown eyes, on her stunned face. She was shaken, but didn't do anything dramatic like dissolve into hysterics, and for that he breathed a sigh of relief. That didn't mean they were out of the woods on her acceptance of things, but it was a start.

To her credit she held it together, focusing her attention on Blue, who preened under the attention. The prince regaled her with tales of his brothers, his adventures with them, and the good times they had. Well, before he'd been thrown out of the realm when Elders in the Seelie Court found out that Blue was a bastard. A product of the Unseelie king Malik's forcible taking of the Seelie queen, Blue's mother.

"I'm so sorry," Daria said, her pretty face empathetic.

Blue smiled, though Ryon knew it was a front. "I'll see my brothers and Mother again one day. In the meantime, I have Kalen. He and I recently found out that we're half brothers."

"Who's Kalen?"

Ryon pointed to the man, who was sitting at a nearby table, eating and talking with Aric and Aric's mate, Rowan.

"Wow, physically you guys are total opposites," Daria observed. "He's completely Goth, and you're like sunlight and sky."

Ryon had gotten so used to Kalen, he didn't notice anymore how different the man was from the others. But it was true. With his layered, black rock-star hair falling to his shoulders, the black jeans and T-shirt with his new black leather duster over it, and the matching kohl-rimmed green eyes and nail polish, the guy definitely made people look twice.

Blue smiled. "Sunlight and sky? That might be the nicest thing anyone's ever said to me."

She shrugged. "Well, it's true."

Ryon knew she had definitely earned a friend in their Fae prince.

"So," she went on, "how are you and Kalen half brothers?"

"It's complicated, but I'll try and simplify. We had different mothers, but like me, Kalen's father was also Malik, the fortunately now-deceased Unseelie."

"Kalen fried his ass in a big battle we had with Malik and his forces not long ago," Ryon supplied helpfully.

"Did Kalen live in the Seelie Court, too?"

"No. If he had, we would've met long ago. He was raised in the human world, led to believe he was human with magical powers. His grandmother didn't want him to learn the truth of his ancestry, in order to keep him safe from Malik and his minions." Blue sent his half brother a look filled with sympathy. "When she died, the man Kalen believed to be his father threw him out of the house, leaving him to survive on the streets. He was fourteen."

"Rotten bastard," Daria hissed. "What happened then?"

"He survived for years, until the Alpha Pack found him in a nearby cemetery, raising a corpse to speak to it while investigating the man's murder."

"Hold up—Kalen raised a corpse? Out of the ground, and spoke to it?" Her eyes were wide. "As in 'Hellooo, Mr. Corpse, let's have a chat and tell me who killed you?'"

"Not so simple as that. It's not easy to raise the dead, you know."

Daria blinked at him. "Guess not."

"So Kalen was taken into the Pack. He was just finding his place here when he met Mac and started to fall in love with her, and then Malik came along and tried to steal him away from all of us to use his Sorcerer's power."

"So, he's a Sorcerer and can raise the dead. What else?" She said it sarcastically, as if there couldn't be anything else.

"He's also a black panther. That's all."

"Sure." She rested her elbows on the table and looked around the room. "So Kalen is married to the doctor, Mackenzie Grant."

"Mated, not married. Much stronger bond than some piece of paper," he said. "But yes, and they're expecting their first child."

"I sort of got that from the baby bump she's carrying around. Any other *mated* pairs here, as you call them?"

"Aric and Rowan. Aric has been with the Pack since the beginning, like a lot of the men, but Rowan recently joined the team. She's a former police officer from some vile place called Los Angeles." Daria snickered. Blue pointed to the redheaded wolf and his brunette mate. Then he gestured to a goateed man and a small blond woman.

"Then there's Jax and Kira. Jax is an original member, a silver wolf and RetroCog, meaning he can touch an object and see important events surrounding it. Kira is one of our lab assistants who specializes in DNA and gene strand stuff. Don't ask me more about that, it's confusing. She's also working to build a sanctuary for displaced paranormal beings, and I'm helping her," he said proudly. "That's my job here."

"I think you'll be wonderful at it."

He beamed at the praise, his feathers rustling. "I hope so. Kira is a dear friend of mine and I would hate to let her down."

"I doubt that will happen."

"We have several creatures depending on us, and I'm sure more will come."

That seemed to unsettle her, but she said nothing about it. Blue pointed out some of the other guys, but it was apparently too many people for her to take in. She just nodded politely and chatted with the prince, finishing her burger. When they were done eating, Blue rose.

"It's been a pleasure talking with you, Daria. I'm sure we'll get to know each other much better." He slid a sly smile at Ryon.

Ryon wondered if the prince had the ability to sense their bond, but he couldn't very well ask. He knew that Daria would likely start to feel it, too, if she hadn't already. He'd have to explain soon, as Nick advised, or she might think there was something wrong with herself. He was afraid she would be upset, too.

Blue left to join Kalen. Ryon wiped his hands and laid aside his napkin. "Would you like to see the compound?"

Her eyes held his for a moment, something sparking between them. "I'd love to."

His heart did a little happy dance, but he forced himself to stay cool. This was not a woman to be pushed, and yet he'd had no choice but to change her entire life without her input. He hoped she would forgive him.

Taking the handles of her chair, he guided it into the hallway and turned the corner. "How about the recreation room first? If you're by yourself and can't find who you need, there's always someone relaxing in there."

"Sounds good." She gestured to the place in general. "It's very homey. Not what one would expect."

"The women rallied when we first opened the place and demanded new paint, carpet, the works. They said if they had to live here, they weren't going to live in a drab white box."

"Nick approved that? He doesn't seem the type."

"Nick wouldn't have cared, but he wasn't our commander back then. Our boss was Terry Noble. He was killed in an ambush several months ago, along with some of our team."

"I'm sorry to hear that," she said honestly.

"Our job is dangerous, and death is always a high risk. But we all miss him, Ari, and Jonas. Those are the other guys we lost." He paused. "We thought Micah and Phoenix had been killed along with them, but it turns out that they were being held in a lab facility run by Malik, where his doctors were performing experiments on humans and shifters, trying to perfect a super-soldier."

"That's horrible! I'm glad you were able to get back two of your guys, though. Maybe the others are still out there somewhere?" she asked hopefully.

God love her. "It would be a miracle. All of Malik's labs have been destroyed, as far as we know, and none of the other Pack members were found."

"You never know."

"True. But on a happier note, this is the rec room." Pushing her inside, he came around to stand where they could see each other. "We have all sorts of games in here. Ping-Pong, board games, and the Wii. We're thinking about buying another TV and game system because there's always someone hogging the one we do have."

"Neat room, lots of comfy furniture. I can see why everyone likes to hang out here."

"Just beyond those doors is a field with a picnic area where we play football, baseball, grill out, and whatever other excuse we can think of to get outside."

"With scenery as beautiful as that outside your door, I can see why." She gazed outside thoughtfully. "How can you have a compound in the middle of the Shoshone when it's government land?"

"Because the government sanctions our being here. Those in power who need to know, do."

"I see."

They left the rec room and he took her to the gym. Micah was shooting hoops. Jax was there, apparently working off lunch, lying on his back on a bench, lifting weights. A small, furry brown creature was perched on his chest, curled up dozing with a look of pure bliss on its teddy-bear face. Ryon glanced at Daria, who was frowning at the creature.

"What is that?"

He pushed her closer, chuckling. But not too close. "That's Chup-Chup. He's sort of like a gremlin, or something. Nobody's really sure."

"One of the rescued critters Blue was telling me about?"

"Among others."

"Hey, guys," Jax called as they approached. He heaved a couple more bench presses, then sat the bar in the holder and wiped at the sweat on his brow with his hand. "Move slow and easy. You know how Chup is about strangers."

"*You* ought to know," Ryon said, ribbing him. "Took you and the furball long enough to make peace."

"Don't remind me. There are body parts that still hurt at the memories." Laughing, Jax stroked the beast's small head. "He likes me well enough now, though."

"I think the steak treats probably helped change his attitude."

"Hey, he has a fondness for women. I had to fight dirty."

Daria leaned forward. "Can I hold him?"

Jax considered Chup warily. "I don't know. Depends on him."

Just then, the creature sat up, stretched and yawned. Ryon privately thought the thing was cute as hell, but he wasn't about to touch it. He'd seen the little shit almost take off Jax's hand once, and that had been enough to convince him that his calling did not lie in taming animals.

Jax sat up carefully, cradling Chup against his stomach as he let the creature become aware of Daria. It leaned forward, sniffing curiously, eyes wide. Then it started straining against Jax's hold, wanting to get to her. Jax allowed it to crawl into her lap, watching it carefully for any sign of aggression and to make sure it didn't hurt her broken arm. So did Ryon, but all the creature did was to begin making his contented little *chup-chup* noises.

It cuddled against her, whirring like a small motorboat as she scratched its ears with her good hand, both of them clearly in heaven. "I've never seen anything like this," she said in awe. "This is just amazing."

Jax nodded. "He's come a long way. He rarely bites anymore, only if someone startles him, and we're damned careful not to do that."

"I'll bet. Do you know where he came from?"

"Originally? No idea. We found him on an op a couple of years ago when we were dispatched to eliminate some rogue demons. Chup had been in their cave, but we're not sure why he was with them."

Of course, her mind caught on one word, and she stilled. "Demons?"

Jax cringed. "Uh, yeah. Anyhoo, he's happy these days, thanks to Kira working with him."

"He sure seems to be."

She was really taken with the creature, and Ryon enjoyed watching her so much he hated to leave. Eventually, Chup scrambled from her embrace and reached for Jax in a clear plea to be taken back.

"Spoiled rotten little menace," Jax grumbled. But he scooped up the beast, his actions belying his words.

"Thank you for letting me hold him."

"Hey, don't thank me. The brat makes his own decisions." With a wink, he went back to his workout.

Ryon escorted her from the room, taking her outside. She was quiet as they enjoyed a turn around the grounds, and he could tell she was still thinking about the gremlin.

"It's a real shame the world can't find out creatures like Chup exist," she said, almost sadly. "But I understand why that would be a disaster."

"It *is* a shame, isn't it? We can enjoy them here, though. In the end, that's the safest thing for them and the general population."

"Don't you worry about Chup or the others getting loose?"

"Some. We take precautions, though. Chup has earned full run of the building, and Blue has improved in being integrated, but some are still in cells in Block R—that's rehabilitation. We're replacing Block R with the sanctuary Kira and Blue are starting."

"Blue was in a cell at one time?" She was horrified by this news.

"For a while, until Kira joined us. When we brought him here, he was traumatized and uncommunicative. He was severely depressed and tried to harm himself, and we didn't know what else to do with him. It took Kira to make us see that he needed compassion, not chains."

"She sounds like a special woman."

"She is. Kira has totally changed our ideas on dealing with paranormal beings. Not all of them are bad, any more than all humans are bad. Some are just confused and hurt."

Daria thought about this. "In a way, she does what I

do—study different life-forms around her and tries to make sure they're thriving."

"That's a good comparison, yes."

When her questions tapered off and her head started to nod, he knew she was getting tired. "You need to rest after your ordeal. Why don't I show you to your quarters and you can sleep for a while?"

"That sounds good. I guess I'm not as healed as I thought."

"A couple of days and you'll feel like a million dollars."

At her door, he punched in the security code Nick had texted to him while they were walking, and then told it to her. "I'll write it down so you can keep it with you. Once you learn the number, it's quicker and easier than using a key."

"Okay."

He rolled her inside and found the rooms were sort of bare, devoid of the homey touches that cheered these functional spaces. "Sorry it's kind of plain. This room has never been occupied, that I know of."

She gave him a droll look. "I'm used to camping outside, with bears, wolves, big cats, and any number of snakes and insects that love to inhabit my sleeping bag. I'll deal."

"Good point." In her bedroom he gave her a hand up out of the wheelchair, and then sat her on the bed. "Do you need me for anything else?"

"I'm fine for now, thank you."

Damn. He was hoping she'd say yes. *Give her time, Ryon.*

Leaving her temporarily, he went and found a note-pad and pen on the bar that separated the kitchen from the living room. Quickly, he wrote all the information he thought she'd need and carried it back into the bed-room. She was lying curled on her side, drowsing, when he got there.

"I wrote down my cell phone number, the number to my quarters down the hallway on the right, and the code to your door. If you need anyone else here, there's a list of extensions in the nightstand drawer."

"Thanks. I don't have a cell phone anymore, though, to call you with."

"Use the one there," he said, pointing to the cordless by the bed. "We'll run into town tomorrow and get you a replacement."

"Okay." He hesitated to leave, and she gazed at him for a long moment, lids heavy. "I really like you, Ryon."

His lips turned up. "I like you more than a little bit, myself."

"Why do I feel this pull toward you?" she asked sleepily.

"Why do any man and woman feel chemistry?" His tone was light, but his gut clenched. He knew she wasn't just talking about simple man-woman attrac-tion, and her next words proved it.

"What I'm feeling is more than that, though I'm plenty attracted." She paused, her brown eyes liquid with heat. "It's like there's some sort of golden thread connecting us. Does that make sense?"

"It does, yes." Reaching out tentatively, he brushed a strand of black hair from her face, ready to withdraw it if she protested. When she didn't, instead turning her face into his touch, his wolf practically whined in pleasure, and the man celebrated this small progress.

He'd have to come clean, soon. He couldn't put it off much longer.

For now, he'd leave her with something that she'd hopefully think about, in a good way, after he was gone. Kneeling by the side of the bed, he brought his face close to hers. Looked into her eyes, questioning silently, again giving her time to call a halt to the kiss he was about to plant on those plump lips.

Invitation was clearly etched on her pretty face, and he closed the small gap between them, bringing their lips together. Lightly at first, then with more pressure, fusing their mouths. His cock went rock-hard in his jeans, pushing insistently against its confines and demanding to be let out to play. She wasn't ready for more, however, so he reined in the impulse to crawl onto the bed with her.

They explored each other, tasting, tongues dueling. She was sweet, ambrosia on his tongue, the flavor unique to his mate. He figured his flavor was the same for her, and wanted to ask, but he didn't dare. Not yet. This was a good start, his mate welcoming his kiss, and he was thankful for that.

Finally, he pulled back, and saw the dazed expression on her face. She felt desire for him, the *want* plain to see, even if he hadn't picked it up from their bond. She desired him, but was uncertain. Confused.

He hated that confusion and the circumstances that had made it necessary. They should have met, fallen in love first. Then become Bondmates later, when they were both ready. But life didn't always happen according to a neat little plan, and the wolf shifter's makeup didn't allow a lot of time for courting when he met his mate. Ryon's mating certainly hadn't gone the way he'd always envisioned it.

"I'm going to let you rest, okay?" he asked softly.

"Will you be back later?"

His heart lightened. "I will. I'll check on you in a while and we'll have a talk."

"I'm looking forward to that. I suspect I have a few more surprises in store."

God, she had no idea. Giving her another kiss, he headed out, his emotions a weird mix of trepidation and joy.

He had a beautiful, smart, kind mate. Any man, or wolf, would be proud to have her at his side.

Now, if she didn't hate him for what he'd done, his life would be perfect.

Daria's senses reeled long after Ryon walked out the door.

"Holy shit, that man can kiss," she whispered to herself, staring at the ceiling. Her body was a sensitized mass of nerves, all straining for the man who'd left her alone when she hadn't wanted him to go.

His closeness, his warmth and clean manly scent, called to her as no other man's had, ever. The attraction was a tangible thing between them, waiting to be explored and unleashed. She had no doubt that they would end up in bed, sooner rather than later. They both wanted it, and she couldn't think of a reason why two consenting adults should deny the pull. He wanted her as much as she wanted him. She felt it.

That gave her pause. *Felt* it? Yes, she had. And not just in the "normal" way that people meant when they said they experienced attraction for someone. It was almost as if she could touch his attraction for her, the need and want in him, as though she had some sort of hotline to his feelings and emotions. How was that possible?

Raising her good arm, she examined her wrist again. The punctures were barely visible now, and the rest of the scratches were all but gone. Just in the few short hours since she'd last looked. One inescapable conclusion kept coming back to her, and it made her pulse flutter in anxiety.

Ryon, or someone, had bitten her. They were wolf shifters and as such, had special healing abilities. Daria should have died. At some point after that, she had been bitten. And now she was almost ready to go hiking, she was so well healed. Had one of them bitten her in order to save her life?

Okay. Assuming that was true, why would Ryon be so reluctant to share that with her even when she'd asked about the marks? Saving someone's life was a great thing, and so what if they used a bit of an advantage nature gave them to do it? There had to be more to the story. That would explain why he didn't want to discuss it.

She had a suspicion she wasn't going to like the explanation, or else he wouldn't be working so hard to avoid it.

Giving in to the lingering tiredness, she dozed for an hour or so. When she came awake, she sat up, restless. Her arm was itching around the spot of the bite mark, and she felt like she was about to jump out of her skin. A walk might help, so she decided to act.

First, she did away with the annoying sling, tossing it to the nightstand. She held her casted arm this way and that, and experienced no pain. Padding to the bathroom, she took care of business and then took a bath, which was a long process since she had to be careful of her cast. Just that small routine made her feel better. Next she dug in her backpack for her brush and a scrunchie to make a ponytail. Items in hand, she returned to the bathroom mirror, brushed out the long tresses and pulled all of it back, securing it with the stretchy band.

Scrutinizing her face, she wondered what Ryon saw when he looked at her. When she studied herself, she always saw a no-frills woman who never wore makeup of any kind. But then, makeup never looked right with her bronzed skin tone, even if she didn't spend most of her year in the wilderness where there was no one to appreciate it or care. She supposed her face was nice enough, with high cheekbones, thin, arched brows, and thick black lashes framing her brown eyes.

Nice, but plain. Nothing to account for the intense desire that had been rolling off Ryon like steam from a boiling pan of water. Not that she was about to complain.

In the bedroom, she retrieved the piece of paper Ryon had written the important numbers on, and pushed it into the pocket of her jeans. She walked out of the quarters into the hallway, firmly closing the door behind her, and glanced around.

Setting off in the direction of Ryon's room, she came to the door that corresponded to the number he'd written on the paper. The man owed her a talk and he was going to follow through.

After knocking, she waited for any sign of life beyond. She was just getting ready to knock again when the door swung open. Ryon stood there bare-chested, and she couldn't help that her eyes immediately fell upon the broad expanse of taut skin. He was toned a golden hue, a fair-haired man with the complexion of someone who was outside frequently. His pecs were dusted with just the right amount of hair, enough to tickle and fun to play with, but not too furry.

"Hey there," he said, eyeing her curiously. "I was going to check on you soon. Everything okay?"

"That's what I'm here to find out." She wasn't going to be swayed by his hunky self standing half-naked in the doorway.

His expression became serious. "You deserve the

truth. Why don't you come in and we'll talk about—"
A buzzing noise interrupted what he was about to say.
With a grimace, he pulled an iPhone from this front
jeans pocket and looked at the display. "Nick. I have to
take this."

Turning, he went back into his quarters as he answered and waved her to follow. From his end of the
conversation, she could tell that hers with Ryon would
have to wait.

"Hey, boss." Pause. "Now?" Pause. "All right, I'll
tell her." He ended the call.

"What is it?"

"Nick wants you and me in the conference room for
a meeting with the team." He made a face. "It has
something to do with the body in the woods."

She shrugged. "I don't know what more I can con-
tribute, but I'll sit in and listen."

"Let me just put on a shirt." Quickly, he disappeared
into his bedroom.

"Don't bother on my account," she muttered.

He called out. "What?"

"Nothing!" Damn, wolf shifters must have supernatural hearing, too.

He emerged wearing a dark T-shirt that read NEVER
ENGAGE IN A BATTLE OF WITS WITH AN UNARMED PER-
SON. She snorted and he glanced down at it. Then he
snickered. "Oh, well. Guess it'll do."

They walked out together, and he kept his pace
slower so she could keep up. Her energy wasn't 100
percent, though her pain was pretty much in the past.

"You're doing great without the wheelchair," he observed.

"I just needed that extra bit of time to get back on my feet, but now I'm fine."

"We'll get Melina to x-ray that arm again. She might be able to take the cast off."

She gaped at him. "After a couple of days? Are you nuts?"

"Nope. You'll see."

He didn't offer more, and it frustrated her to no end. She tried to put it out of her mind as they came to the conference room. Inside, the Pack guys were assembled, some sitting around the huge oval table, some standing or leaning against the walls. All of them appeared interested in what Nick, at the head of the table, had to share with them.

"I've had some news from the sheriff," he said by way of calling them to order. When the room stilled, he went on. "This afternoon the body of the second hiker was found about two miles from the woman. They're almost positive it's her husband, from the clothing and some of the belongings that were scattered. Deveraux slipped us a sample of the man's tissue, for comparison against the woman. Of course, our lab is looking for shit the humans would never dream of."

A few grim chuckles followed that statement.

"And have they got anything from the woman?" Micah asked.

"Yeah." Nick rubbed the back of his neck, as though he was searching for the exact right words for what he had to tell them. "There was no wolf DNA present in the saliva on the lady's tissue, either natural wolf or shifter. Even if the white wolf was capable of shifting into half-human form, our lab doesn't feel there's any way she could've done that sort of damage. The teeth marks aren't consistent with the length or curvature of our fangs."

"What *are* they consistent with?" Aric crossed his arms over his chest.

"This is the fun part. The marks in the tissue and the way the victims' bones were crushed match an animal with the massive skull of say, a tiger, and the teeth of an alligator. The skin was punctured, two jagged rows of long teeth evidenced there, just like a roadmap of the creature's mouth."

"Jesus," Ryon breathed. "What the fuck?"

Grabbing a remote control for the projector, Nick turned on the device to shine an image on the wide screen. "*What the fuck?* about sums it up. This is a computerized composite image of our mystery creature based on the lab's findings."

"How the hell did they come up with something like that?" Jax blurted. "That thing is impossible."

"Nothing is impossible, as we all know firsthand. The victim's tissue was slathered with the DNA of the attacker, and it turns out that the DNA contained shifter gene strands of a tiger, a bear, a wolf, a huge lizard— and a human." This caused some exclamations of shock. "I created this picture with the lab's help, as a beast that contains similar characteristics of their findings, using the strongest traits of each shifter, and merged with a human. It won't be exact, but we're dealing with something like this guy."

Daria stared at the rendition. The beast had to be at least eight feet tall, with a thick skull shaped like a tiger's and a maw similar to a gator's, but with the mouth much shorter. It stood erect on two hind legs, thighs thick as tree trunks. Its chest was like a barrel, arms strong, hands and feet sort of webbed, with sharp claws on the end. The hide was tough and scaly-looking.

The creature was the ugliest fictional monster Daria had ever seen. Only it wasn't a costume for some alien movie. It was fact.

Everyone looked their fill for a few moments, the mood somber. Finally, Ryon spoke. "I hate to say this, but there's only one way I can think of as to how this monster came into existence."

"Unfortunately, you're on the right track. When we liberated Malik's and Bowman's test subjects from the last lab, one of them obviously escaped." Nick heaved a weary breath, but met his men's gazes steadily.

"And now we have some poor bastard who was turned into a mutant killing machine wreaking havoc on the general population."

"Jesus Christ," someone moaned.

Nick gave a grim laugh. "I have a bad feeling we're going to need more help than that."

Daria had a bad feeling he was right.

Six

Jax was pissed. Ryon watched his friend, knew he was taking the news badly. As they all were.

Jax yanked at his goatee in anger. "I don't see how it's possible we lost one. We were careful!"

"You can't take this personally," Ryon told him. "It's not your fault, or anyone's. Remember, the building exploded and some of us were injured. In the chaos, one of the test subjects ran. It's a pretty believable and understandable outcome."

Kalen pushed from the wall where he'd been leaning. "I just remembered something. Right before the building blew, Bowman was excited, talking about a test subject that was almost a perfect example of the super-soldier they were trying to create. He apparently had more tweaking to do, but in his twisted mind he was nearly there. What if that's the one who escaped?"

"It's a good theory," Nick said. "No one on our list

of survivors has anywhere close to the horrible genetic mutation that our subject has acquired. So, it has to be one that got past us, perhaps Bowman's pet. Do you recall what Bowman said about the subject?"

Kalen nodded. "Yeah. He said something like 'Bring the wolf to OR-4. I want to try to splice his DNA with human subject 356 again. I'm on the verge of a break-through.'"

"That could be important. Every bit of information helps."

"You know," Micah said thoughtfully. "if this crea-ture is in fact one of the poor bastards like me who got experimented on, that might explain why I felt him at the first victim's murder scene."

Ryon nodded. "That's right. I felt a vibration, but for you it was like ants crawling on your skin."

"A lot of tests were done on our skin," Micah said. "Might be why I get a prickling sensation when he's close."

"So what's the plan?" Ryon asked.

Nick clicked the remote and brought up a map of the Shoshone. "The forest is too vast to search the entire region at once. I think we should split into teams and look in the areas in the grid close to where the bodies were found. See if we can find where the creature is holed up."

"And if we do find it?" Aric snorted. "Should we ask it nicely to come with us? Man, I'm no pussy, but that thing? That's seriously messed up."

"I'm with Aric," Hammer put in. The big, quiet man

usually just listened and used his muscle whenever and wherever needed, and he had plenty of that. But even he appeared worried. "We've got no idea yet what that thing can do."

Their commander shared their concerns, but his directions stood. "Unfortunately, this is one of those cases where we won't know until we dive in. I wish there was another way, but there isn't."

"When do we leave?" Jax asked.

"First light." His smile was grim. "When it's up and ready for breakfast."

More grumbling ensued. Micah shifted in his seat. "A question. Since the white wolf has been ruled out as the killer, why did it push Daria into the ravine?"

Nick was silent a moment. Whatever his thoughts were, he wasn't happy about them. "I don't know. But I'm going to find out."

Interesting choice of words. *I'm going to find out*. Not *We'll find out*. But Nick always played his cards close to the vest. Getting a secret out of him was like sneaking a gold bar out of Fort Knox.

"Everyone can go, except Ryon and Daria."

The others filed out, shooting them looks of sympathy. As good a boss as Nick might be, nobody liked to be the one singled out for a meeting when he took on that tone. Once everyone was gone, Nick moved closer to him and Daria, taking a seat at the table across from them. Most of Nick's attention was for his mate, and Ryon was puzzled. But not for long.

"Daria, I spoke with your father today."

That gave her a visible jolt. Her eyes widened. "Dad? How did you get in touch with him? Why?"

"Actually, he got in touch with me. The news story about the killings here went national and your name was mentioned as the wildlife biologist who stumbled onto one of the bodies and became injured."

She rubbed her temples. "Oh, no. I didn't think he would hear the story all the way in Missouri."

"Yeah. He's apparently been going nuts calling the Sheriff's Department for the past two days trying to find out where you were. Of course, that information was being kept secret and Jesse has been so swamped that he missed receiving your dad's messages until this morning."

"What did he tell Dad?"

"Just that you were fine, staying with friends while you recovered from your so-called scrapes and bruises," he said wryly. They all knew the danger had been much more than that. "He promised your dad you would call."

"Damn. I'd hoped to get through this without him finding out." She frowned.

"Any particular reason?"

She leaned back, looking annoyed. "He's a worry-wart. Dad and I are close, and he'd be in my hip pocket if he could, keeping his baby safe."

Nick's sudden smile was wistful. "Dads are like that. You should cut him some slack."

Ryon wondered at his tone, the expression, but the moment passed.

"Well, thank you for telling me. I would've called him in another day or two anyway, though I wasn't going to mention my, um, adventure."

"You should know that he's been trying to reach you since before he knew you'd been hurt. Not only does he want to make sure his daughter's all right, he has some news from home and needs you to call right away."

Daria looked alarmed. "Is he okay? Did he say what's wrong?"

"Your dad is fine," Nick assured her. "No, it's something else. He wanted you to hear it from him."

"He told you what it is?"

"Yes. But I think you should talk to your dad."

Nick, what's going on? Ryon asked through his telepathic link.

Daria will tell you when she's ready. Just be there for your mate.

So I'm here for moral support?

Basically.

That doesn't help me much.

You'll understand soon.

Jesus! Half the damned time, that's all the man had to say. He would either speak in riddles or not give any information at all. It made Ryon want to hit something.

Nick rose, signaling the conclusion of their brief meeting. Ryon frowned at his boss, but the man wasn't giving anything away. After issuing a reminder to Ryon that the team was leaving early in the morning, he headed out.

Ryon took Daria's good hand as they walked into

the hallway, and she looked at him in surprise. Pleasure also blossomed on her face.

"It's been forever since someone held my hand."

"That's a shame," he said with a grin. "Because if ever there was a pretty hand made for holding, this one is it." He brought said hand to his lips and kissed the back of it. He loved her sweet scent, sort of like orange and ginger. He'd smelled a candle like that once in some fancy bath store. He liked it, a lot.

"What a sweet thing to say."

Only her worry seeping through their bond regarding the impending talk with her dad put a blight on his mood. Just a temporary one, though, because in the wake of that came a tentative caress against their bond. A brush of contentment and well-being that couldn't be faked. He doubted she knew she was doing it, reaching out to him as a mate, and that both scared and elated him.

The last thing he wanted was for her to feel trapped.

"Would you like to come to my room to make your call?" he asked, trying to keep the boyish hope from his voice. "I'd like to make you dinner instead of going to the cafeteria."

She brightened. "You can cook?"

"I'm a pretty damned good cook, if I do say so," he said proudly. "My mom made sure I knew how when I was growing up, and I found it to be very therapeutic."

"That's cool," she replied with enthusiasm. "I can't cook to save my life, except for the prepackaged stuff I have to keep with me when I'm staying in the field, performing my studies."

"MREs. God, I remember those days from the SEALs."

"Meals ready to eat, the bane of my existence." She smiled. "We have something in common."

"Oh, yes." He grimaced. "I had to endure those for far too long. Every single one I choked down made me long for my mother's kitchen."

"You're lucky. My dad is a fair cook, but not a ton better than me. We ate out a lot."

"Nothing wrong with that, but it's good to enjoy a home-cooked meal once in a while. I'm going to spoil you."

"Well, Mr. Hunter, I'm going to let you." She sounded light, happy. It was a good look on her, too.

"Great! What's your favorite food?"

"Um, anything someone else cooks?" She snickered. "We already established I'm grateful for whatever isn't freeze-dried."

"Seriously, there must be some hard limits. Stuff you don't like."

"Hmm. I'll eat almost anything, but if I had to say, I'm not big on pasta."

He gave a mock gasp. "What? That's just wrong!"

She laughed. "I know I'm weird, but I don't care for slimy food. Don't like calamari or escargot, either."

"Okay. Squid pasta it is." He loved the sound of her voice when she giggled. "Nah, how about chicken quesadillas? I grill my chicken and everything, don't use that precooked meat in the package."

"That sounds fabulous."

When they got to his quarters, he let them in and gestured to the phone as he led her into his living room. "Feel free to use my phone. I'll be in the kitchen to give you some privacy."

"Thank you."

Walking to the fridge, he opened the freezer door and got out a package of boneless chicken breasts, trying not to eavesdrop. Okay, trying not to *appear* as though he was eavesdropping. She punched in the number and waited for it to ring, and as she started talking softly, he felt guilty. She had no idea that while a normal human man would've had to strain to make out her words, Ryon had no such problem.

"Hey, Dad! Yes, I'm fine, I've just been— No, no, everything's okay." A pause. "No, there's absolutely no need for you to fly out here!"

He smiled at the hint of desperation flowing through their bond. His mate definitely didn't want her father rushing to the rescue. Taking care of her was Ryon's job anyway—even if she didn't know it yet.

"Just a few scrapes and bruises, nothing serious." Pause. "Yes, it was awful. I've seen death, but never anything like that. Nobody here knows for sure what killed that poor woman, but it was probably a grizzly."

An outright lie. Immediately, remorse flowed to him through their bond. She hated lying to her dad, but what was she supposed to say? *Yeah, she was torn to shreds by a wolf-tiger-bear-lizard-human monster and it's still on the loose.*

Right.

"So, other than the poor hiker, why were you trying to reach me? Has something happened?"

This time, Daria's pause was longer, and after a few seconds of listening to her dad, her gasp of shock and the emotion behind it hit Ryon hard. Whatever her dad had to relate, it was upsetting her. His wolf rumbled in displeasure, not liking his mate to be unhappy for any reason.

Daria broke in with one-word questions—When? How? Why? To his frustration there wasn't much he could glean except something had happened to someone she knew, and she wasn't saying enough to tell him who or what.

At last, she wrapped up the conversation. "All right, Dad, you take care, too. Call me if you hear anything else. Love you more."

When she hung up, he pulled the now-thawed chicken breasts from the microwave and began to rinse them. She came into the kitchen as he was putting the last one on a plate. "Everything okay?" he asked, reaching for a couple of shakers of seasoning.

"Just some news from home," she said evasively. "Mostly he was checking on me, worried about the body and making sure I hadn't run into the killer or something."

"You easily could have," he said. That was one horrible possibility that made him break into a cold sweat. "Promise me you won't go back out there until we catch this thing."

"I may be an independent woman, but I'm not a stupid one. There's a difference." Her tone was light, but she meant what she said—she wasn't about to be dumb and go off again by herself.

"So, you'll stay at the compound with us for a while?"

"This seems really important to you. Why?"

He shrugged, trying not to get too heavy. "I saved your bacon. I care about you, that's all."

"Thank you again for doing whatever it is you did to save my life," she said sincerely. But there was a light of curiosity in her eyes. "I'll stay, provided you tell me exactly how you did it and why I'm already healed."

Crap. Staring at her, he set the shakers on the counter. He couldn't tell her all of the truth. Not yet. But he did owe her the simple version. "Remember that I told you shifters heal fast?"

"It's not the sort of thing I'd forget."

"Right. Well, sometimes we can . . . pass along that healing ability. Through our bite."

She nodded. "I thought so. Is that what this is about?" She held up her good wrist that sported the two faded puncture wounds.

"Yes. I bit you," he said quietly, unsure how she would react. "If I hadn't, you would've died." And so would he have, eventually.

"Hey, it's okay," she said, laying a hand on his arm. "I understand, and I'm glad you acted quickly. If you hadn't, I wouldn't be here about to enjoy a fantastic dinner with a handsome man."

His face heated. It wasn't that he couldn't take a compliment. He'd just never had one offered so honestly, so matter-of-fact, from a woman. "Thank you. I think it was a selfish act on my part, because I couldn't allow a gorgeous lady like yourself to be taken from the world so soon."

Taken from me. He was glad she hadn't gone through her first shift. When she did, she'd be able to hear his thoughts. That was a gift reserved for mates. The other Pack members could only hear Ryon if he pushed his thoughts at them, and then they could reply. But mated shifters could mind-speak freely.

The silence threatened to grow awkward as they stared at each other. "Do you like red wine?"

"I do," she said, appearing eager at the prospect of a glass.

"Then how about I open us a bottle of Malbec? We can lounge on the patio while I grill the chicken."

"Quesadillas and wine? Why not?"

"There's never a bad time for vino. I catch some ribbing from the guys for liking it so much, but there's something about it I enjoy. It communicates a love of the finer things, creates a certain mood."

"And what mood is it you're trying to create now?"

She was teasing, and he liked that. Her fine black brows were arched over big brown doe eyes, her plump mouth curved upward. Just when he wondered how to read her, thinking she was so reserved, her passionate, fun side peeked out from behind the cool veneer.

"I want us to enjoy each other's company," he said, returning her gaze, making it clear that he was interested if she was game.

The spark in those whiskey depths, the flare of heat, made him want to shout. No celebrating, though. Not yet. He didn't want to give her the impression that this was some attempt at a casual hookup where they'd go their separate ways in the morning. No, his days of cruising Las Vegas with his single Pack brothers, letting his dick lead him to a cheap lay, were over. He couldn't say he was real sorry.

"Somehow I think we're going to get along with each other just fine."

Yes! His cock stiffened in his jeans, and he was glad his T-shirt was loose enough to cover the problem. He wanted to do this right, for everything to be perfect. From his black wine rack in the wet bar area, he selected a bottle of his best red and removed two glasses from the glass shelf.

"Do you bring your lady guests here often?"

He liked that she was blatantly fishing. That her teasing held an edge, as though his answer was very important. "I've never brought a woman here before."

She appeared pleased by that. Maybe she didn't know relief was written all over her face. "Because of the secrets about what you are and what you do?"

"That's part of it, but not all," he acknowledged. "Even if we could bring our hookups into the compound—which would never happen—I wouldn't feel right about bringing someone into my personal space who wasn't special."

Her lips parted and her eyes widened slightly. Had he said too much? He didn't think so, not if he wanted her prepared to hear the whole truth. He didn't elaborate further, nor did she seem to want to press. They both needed time to absorb being together, enjoying each other's company.

Taking the plate of chicken outside, he got the grill started while she sipped her wine and watched. While the grill heated, they made small talk.

"This is a nice setup. Each of your quarters is like a condo with its own private patio and a small yard."

"It's nice, but not too fancy, and I like that. It's home."

"I like it, but it's hard to imagine living among all of these people. You've almost got your own town right inside these walls."

Anxiety made his wolf restless. Would she reject living with him? What if she wanted to return to Missouri when she was finished with her studies? What the hell would he do then?"

He would move with her if she was determined to go. That was a given. But what if she didn't want him? God, he was borrowing trouble before it even began.

"It took some getting used to, but once I did, I fell in love with it here. Not just the compound, but the Shoshone. You won't find a more beautiful national forest anywhere in the United States, and my wolf loves to run for miles and miles without stopping."

"You're going to show me your wolf," she said. It wasn't a question. He could tell she still needed visual confirmation of his claims. Like Rowan had when she met Aric, Daria required tangible proof. But she was tougher than Rowan had been, even after meeting Blue.

"I'll show you after we eat, if that works for you." He wanted to at least savor a nice dinner before she rejected him and ran home to her father.

"All right." She gave him a tentative smile. "I can't wait to see."

She was trying, he'd give her that. "My wolf is anxious to meet his—to meet you."

Taking a sip, she studied him over the rim of her wineglass, and he sweated that she'd caught his near-slipup. If she had, and he thought she must've, she didn't say anything.

He laid the meat on the grill and tended it as they talked and refilled their glasses. He learned that she held degrees in fish, wildlife, and conservation biology from Colorado State.

"I'm part wolf and I'm not sure I even know what that means," he joked.

She laughed. "That's irony, I suppose. What it means is I studied topics like ecology, forestry, fish and fresh-water ecosystems, mammalogy. You know, easy stuff like that."

"Sure." He snorted.

"Then for my master's, we delved into more specific areas such as conservation biology and genetics, ecotoxi-cology, wildlife population management, and so on."

"I'm impressed," he said. "I like a smart woman."

Her bronzed cheeks flushed. "Thanks. But I'm just a regular person carrying on my father's work."

"What work is that, specifically?"

"He was a part of the government's conservation effort in the eighties to save the wolf population in the Shoshone from extinction. The program was a success, and now I'm a member of a small group that keeps track of the wolves' progress. We make sure they're still thriving all over the forest."

"You have a cool job. I'll bet you're good at it," he praised.

"I love animals," she said simply. "It's easy to be good at a job you love and believe in."

"True. I have one of those myself."

"I just protect wolves." She waved at hand at him. "You protect the rest of the world."

He started to protest, but she was right. "That doesn't make your contribution any less. What you do is so important," he said earnestly. "If the ecosystems fail, there will be nothing left for guys like me to protect. People like you have to prevent that from happening."

He'd struck exactly the right chord with her. But he wasn't simply trying to get into her good graces. He meant every word. He valued her work, and wanted her to know that. She did, and her elation trickled to him through their bond like liquid sunlight.

"Thank you for that," she said softly. "I can't tell you how many people, even friends, don't think that what my father and I do constitutes a *real* job."

"Well, they're assholes," he growled. "They're part of what's wrong with the planet."

Her expression became one of playful amusement. "So fierce. I think I like it when you get all rumbly like that."

That surprised a laugh out of him, and he had to remind his poor cock yet again to behave. "Then I'll make sure to do it often."

They chatted until the chicken was ready; then he decided to set the table outside. The weather was great, so they might as well take advantage of it. He brought out plates, utensils, tortillas, shredded cheese, and all the rest of the goodies they needed for their meal. Placing foil on the grill, he laid down some tortillas, loaded them with chicken strips, onion, and cheese, then browned them on each side. In moments, they were ready to eat.

"Mmm, this is fantastic! You could make me fat, feeding me like this."

"You've got a long way to go before that would ever happen. You're perfect."

"No, I'm not, but thank you. I love what I see, too." She took another bite and swallowed. "I have a thing for blonds."

"A thing?" His brows shot up.

"Yes, I know. How cliché, right? But I adore blond men."

If he had any say, her days of adoring any man but him, blond or purple, were over. "I like silky black hair myself. Just like yours," he murmured. "I'm partial to brown eyes and bronzed skin. A whole lot like yours."

After that, they pretty much rode a rising tide of arousal that simmered in the air between them. They cleared the plates, brought everything inside. They stacked the empty plates in the sink, and he told her he'd do them later.

"Right now, there's something I'm much more interested in doing," he said, turning her to face him.

"Is that so?"

"I want more of those kisses, because I'm a greedy man. Am I wrong in assuming you feel the same way?"

"You're not wrong at all." Her eyes searched his. "Kiss me before I go crazy thinking about tasting you again."

"Just kisses?" he asked, wanting to be sure.

"And more, if you want." She sucked in a breath. "I need you."

"You have me."

His mouth covered hers and gave her what she'd asked for. Delved his tongue into her heat, tasting spicy wine. All woman. She pulled back first.

"Oh, Ryon. Make love to me," she whispered. "*Now*."

He blinked, unable to believe his ears. What he'd done to deserve such a priceless gift, he didn't know, no more than he knew how to go about telling her the rest of the truth. Putting that out of his mind, he concentrated on his woman. Could he *please* her? Whether his experience was a blessing or a curse, he wasn't sure.

They only got as far as the living room before he stopped. Undressed her slowly, revealing each beautiful layer of Daria. In wonder, he eased her to the floor and then skimmed his palms down the graceful curve of her neck, to her slim shoulders, careful to avoid bumping her casted arm. The limb was probably okay, but he couldn't be too careful. He brushed his fingers across the swell of her breasts, her puckered little nipples. Marveled at the sensation, the pleasure of touching her at last.

Fascinated, he rolled the taut peaks between his fingers, pinching them lightly. Bracing her weight on her elbows, she leaned back, spreading those long, toned legs. Offering herself to him.

Her pink slit glistened, begging for his attention, and he groaned. Drinking in her natural beauty, his heart pounded at the base of his throat. She was all tanned skin, curvy breasts, and lean hips, a dark nest of curls at the vee of welcoming thighs.

He stood next to her, unzipping his jeans, pushing them past his hips. His erection sprang free, hot and hard. Throbbing to the point of real pain. Already, a drop of cum beaded at the head of his penis. He and his wolf strained, eager for fangs and cock to be buried deep, to shoot inside her heat.

But he couldn't claim her properly. Not until she knew she was his mate.

Smiling, she sat up on her knees and tugged his jeans to his ankles, pulling them as he stepped free. She laid them aside and wrapped her fingers around his erection, stroked and swirled the pearly drop around the head of his penis. He gasped at the wonderful, wicked bolt of desire sweeping him.

"Daria, I'm not going to last," he croaked. "I can't—"

"Shh, it's okay. Don't hold back."

Her tongue laved the tip, licking away the sticky wet-
ness as she continued to pump his shaft. He shuddered,
balls tightening, the heat rising in his loins, on the verge
of losing control too soon. Her other hand found his sac,
kneaded gently, and his breathing hitched.

Unable to help himself, he let his gaze drift down to
watch. The sight nearly undid him. Beautiful Daria,
kneeling between his spread legs. Working his cock
with her silky touch, her warm, wet little mouth. Taking obvious enjoyment in reducing him to a mindless
puddle. Demanding all of him.

Oh, yeah. She can have me. Whenever, however she wants.

She took his length deep, sheathing his cock to the
very base. He buried his hands in her hair, closing his
eyes in ecstasy. Hers now. All hers.

"Daria! Oh, God."

He pumped his hips slowly, in tandem to the pull of
her sweet mouth. She sucked eagerly, teeth scraping,
tongue sweeping the ridge of his penis. So damned
good. He wanted more. Harder, deeper. How could she
take all of him? He didn't want to hurt her.

Then he wasn't capable of thinking anymore. She
grabbed his hips, urging his thrusts. There was nothing
but the rising throb of heat threatening to burst him
into a million pieces. Blow him apart.

"Yes, baby, yes!"

He gave himself over. To Daria. Gave her what they
both wanted. Fucked her mouth, hard and fast. *Just like
that, fuck yeah, so good . . .*

With a hoarse cry, he stiffened. Shot down her throat,

pumping on and on. Riding the waves crashing through him until he stood trembling on legs that barely held him upright.

When the last of the aftershocks had faded, she released him and wiped her mouth with the edge of her discarded shirt. His rubbery knees folded and he sank down in front of her. She looked at him with a saucy grin, and his heart turned over. For a second, he'd been afraid of how she'd react to their lovemaking.

Unbidden, a surge of raw emotion took him by surprise. For the first time in as long as he could remember, happiness swelled in his chest. And a fierce protectiveness. His mate. *Mine.* He didn't want to try to examine the powerful feelings any further right now. But looking at the ominous cast on her arm, he knew he'd send the white bitch wolf responsible straight to hell.

"Mmm." She slanted him a sexy look. "I loved doing you. I think you've corrupted me."

"I hope so." He enjoyed her laugh. "It occurs to me that you didn't get any attention."

"What are you going to do about it?"

"This."

Taking her chin, he kissed her. Reveled in the dark flavor of himself on her lips. Him, and no one else. Ever again. The knowledge aroused him all over again, his half-softened cock waking anew. Thank God for shifter stamina.

He laid Daria back gently, following her down. Cradling her, he pressed butterfly kisses to her lips, nose, chin, forehead. She rested a hand on top of his head, running his hair through her fingers, and he loved the sensation.

Dipping lower, he turned his attention to her breasts. Capturing one tight pebble in his teeth, he groaned, sucking it. Feasting like the starving man he was. She arched into him, gripping his head, gasping encouragement. He swirled one peak, then the other, as one hand skimmed down her flat belly.

His fingers found the springy nest of curls, and lower still, to her wet sex. Her thighs parted for him, hips urging his touch. He stroked the hot, sensitive nub, the pouting lips, slick and ready for him. Suckled her breasts, teased her clit until she writhed, unable to take any more.

"Ryon, please," she moaned, yanking his hair. "I need you inside me."

He lifted his head, regret spearing his gut. "Shifters don't need protection for STDs, but we do unless you want to risk a small complication." He didn't add that a wolf shifter could not impregnate anyone but his mate—and that she was at risk.

"I'm on the pill, and I'm healthy," she insisted, eyes searching his.

Her words sent a thrill through him. "Daria, sweetheart, are you sure?"

"Yes! Please, just make love to me."

He needed no further encouragement. Positioning his body over hers, he guided the tip of his penis to her moist opening. Worked it in slow, making certain he wouldn't hurt her.

And in one long, delicious stroke, pushed deep. Her tight sheath gripped his cock with silken heat. She clutched his shoulders as he began to pump. In as far as possible, his balls rubbing against her bottom. Relishing the feeling of being buried inside her. Then out, inch by wicked inch. Skin deep, inside her again. Wanting to crawl in and never come out. Fusing their souls.

Never, ever anything like this. The power of their connection, that physical bond, shook him. Humbled him. She was a gift, a treasure. Mindful of her arm, he held her close, making sweet love to her right there on his living room floor.

Her nails dug into his back. "Oh, yes, yes. Faster!"

The feral wolf in him came undone, howled in triumph. *Mine*. He barely resisted sinking his fangs into her shoulder. Clutching her tight, thrusting hard, their bodies slapping together. Hot, blazing, burning him up. Higher and higher. *Going to freaking explode.*

"Come with me," he demanded.

Hips bucking, she cried out. Her release shattered him. Seated deep, he let her carry him over the edge, into oblivion. Her orgasm milked his cock as he spurted into her, harder than before. More than he'd thought possible.

Raising his head, he looked into her face and swept a damp tendril of hair from her eyes. She gazed at him, smiling dreamily, a woman well satisfied. A new emotion clogged his throat.

One he wasn't brave enough to name. Yet.

Seven

It was deliciously decadent, lazing on the floor with Ryon after making love. In the middle of the afternoon.

Her buttoned-up ex-fiancé had never committed a spontaneous act in his life. Much less anything that involved getting naked *and* messy.

As soon as the uncharitable thought crossed her mind, she felt bad. It really wasn't fair comparing two men who were so different. Ryon was an open book, his smile honest, his handsome face reflecting his love of life. Of laughter, his friends, the poor creatures like Chup who were displaced in a strange world. The exact opposite of her ex, who'd never had time for much of anything but his own career.

Head resting on Ryon's chest, she trailed her fingers through the crisp, dusky hair that was a darker shade than what was on his head. She teased each nipple, enjoying the way the brown disks puckered into tight points, then skimmed her palm lower, stopping at the intricate tattoo on his left hip. The artwork was a wolf's head, ears laid flat against his head, muzzle snarling fiercely in the direction of its owner's belly button. The ink appeared black at first, but upon closer inspection she saw it was actually a dark blue. Very, very fetching.

"I love the tat," she said, running a finger over it in appreciation. His abdomen quivered at her attentions and she smiled against his chest.

"Thanks. It was a moment of insanity, I suppose."

"Why do you say that?"

"Hurt like a bitch. I'll never get another one—that's for sure."

"You can fight vampires, nearly get gutted, then go back to battle again without batting an eyelash, but you won't get another tattoo?"

He made a noise of agreement. "Damned straight. Nothing like having to hold still for the torture when I'd much rather go down swinging."

"Well, it's nice. I'm glad you got this one." Sitting up, she sat and traced it. "I noticed some of the other guys have them, though they're each a bit different. Was it some sort of team thing?"

"Yeah." His voice got quiet. "All of us who were in the Navy SEALs together and got turned went out and got them when we first formed the Alpha Pack. We did it to remind us what we'd become, and as a solidarity thing."

Daria thought that was really cool, but from his tone

she guessed he might not, so much. It seemed like a serious occasion to his team, having the tats done. "Will you tell me the story of how you were attacked and turned?"

"One day," he said.

"I'm sorry. I didn't mean to pry, it's none of my—"

"No, don't apologize." Sitting up, he reached for her cheek, stroked it. "That's just a dark story for such a nice day. I don't want to ruin our evening."

"Well, okay. As long as I didn't overstep."

"Of course not." He was silent for a moment, then studied her thoughtfully. "You make the ghosts go away."

"What?"

"I mean literally. I told you we all have Psy gifts in addition to our ability to shift? Well, mine are that I can see spirits—sometimes communicate with them, though that's rare—and speak in peoples' minds. I'm a Channeler and a Telepath."

"Wow." She didn't know what else to say. "Do you see any ghosts right now?"

"No. That's what I meant before. You make them go away," he said in disbelief. "I just realized that when I'm with or near you, they don't hound me."

If she wasn't able to astrally project, she'd think he was one brick short of a load. "I'm glad about that. I can't imagine what it would be like to have ghosts following you everywhere like you're the Pied Piper."

"It's not easy. But it's better than being able to tell the future, like Nick."

"True." She studied him. "Can you speak to me tele-pathically?"

"Yes, but I doubt you could speak back to me that way, yet."

"What do you mean *yet*?"

"Never mind," he mumbled. "Want me to say some-thing in your head?"

"Sure."

Daria Bradford, I think you're the most beautiful woman I've ever met.

"Oh my God!" she cried out, clapping a hand over her mouth. "I've never—that was unbelievable."

He grinned. "Try to say something back. Think it re-ally hard."

She concentrated. *I think you're the sexiest man I've ever seen. I want you to make love to me again.* "Did you get that?"

"Nope, sorry. You'll get it down, eventually."

"What makes you say that?"

"You will, that's all."

She thought about that. Would she be around to learn how? She hoped so. She was coming to like this place. This man. More than like—he was fast becoming a necessity. At that thought, her skin itched again. It was puzzling how she seemed to need him more by the hour.

"Ryon . . . I'm ready."

"Ready for what?"

"I want to see you shift. I'm ready to meet your wolf."

"You sure?" He searched her face.

"Positive. You were right before when you said I wasn't ready, but that was before I met your team, Blue, and Chup-Chup. Bring it on."

She was rewarded with one of his blinding smiles as he rose to his knees. Without a word, he started the transformation. As she watched, stunned, his limbs began to reshape. Arms and legs became four canine ones. His face elongated, changing into a muzzle, and fur sprouted all over his body. In seconds, there was a full tail where none had been before.

Where the man had been crouched stood a big, gorgeous wolf. His fur was a rich silver and cream tipped with black on his back and shoulders, and the tips of his ears. His mouth was hanging open, tongue lolling like an oversized puppy. His blue eyes were the same.

"You're beautiful," she whispered.

You can touch me. Please?

Tentatively, she reached out and rubbed his broad head. Scratched around his ears, and laughed when he pushed into her hand to encourage her to keep going. After giving his ears a bit more attention, she scooted closer and ran her palm along his back. He was so soft, like down, not coarse or wiry like she had envisioned.

"You're amazing."

Thank you. Nobody besides my Pack brothers and the staff here has seen me like this, until you.

"I'm the first, besides them?"

You are.

"I'm honored."

It's your right, and your legacy.

"What do you mean?"

You'll see.

"That's your answer for everything."

He didn't reply this time. His wolf's body began to change shape again, and in seconds Ryon was kneeling there again. His eyes met hers, and he looked so hopeful. Happy.

"You weren't afraid?"

"No. It was still you, in a different form."

"God, Daria." He closed his eyes briefly. When he opened them again, he swallowed hard and touched her face. "I never dreamed anyone outside my Pack could accept me the way I am. Every one of us longs for it, but it's not a given."

"You never have to worry about me not accepting you. I can't believe you ever were."

Lowering his hand, he searched her face. "That means everything to me." He paused. "Can I ask you a question?"

"Sure."

"Earlier you seemed upset after talking with your dad. Is everything okay at home?"

She hesitated, wondering if she should get into the conversation. No man liked to hear about his partner's former lover. Then again, it wasn't like the news had any bearing on her life *now*. The man was called an ex for a reason.

"My dad has been trying to reach me because someone I know disappeared a few months ago. It's really strange, knowing Ben. He would never have just walked away from his career. He's a successful criminal attorney and is as married to his job as anyone I've ever met."

"This *Ben* is a friend of yours?" His voice had taken on a slight edge.

"Ex-fiancé." She shrugged. "We were good friends, once. We dated for over a year, but it didn't work out. He was so self-contained, so driven. Successful. Smart. But his career was his *entire* life, with not much room for spontaneity, or passion."

Ryon's expression took on a look of catlike satisfaction. Quite a feat for a wolf. "Unlike me," he said smugly.

"Very unlike you." She kissed his mouth. "For example, he wouldn't make love on mornings he was due in court. Said it would take him out of his *zone*, and he needed to be sharp for the jury."

Was that a growl she heard coming from his chest? The soft, ominous noise made her shiver.

"What an ass."

"He's actually a good man, just a tad self-absorbed. We weren't compatible as lovers."

"And you're worried about him, why? Who cares if he vanished."

Okay, that was tinged with outright jealousy. Possessiveness. If that was a shifter thing, she wasn't sure she appreciated it. "Cool your jets. I care because I know Ben. There is no way in hell that man would've left his practice and hopped on a plane to Bermuda or someplace, never to return."

"You hear of that happening. Men simply leaving

because they can't take the pressure of their lives anymore. This Ben guy sounds like a prime candidate for ditching his high-pressure world."

"That's what Dad said the police suspected, at first. But Ben's accounts are intact, checking and savings untouched. There are no records of him having purchased a plane or bus ticket, no credit card activity. Nothing. It's like the earth opened up and swallowed him."

"Why is your dad just now hearing about this if he's been missing for months?"

"Dad says Ben disappeared the day after we broke up. I didn't know anything about it, and honestly, although I thought it was odd for Ben to completely cut off all communication between us, I chalked it up to him changing his mind about us even being friends."

"You put it out of your head."

"Yes, and so did my dad. My work and lifestyle don't lend themselves to sitting around watching a lot of news, and none of Ben's friends thought I'd care, so they didn't contact me."

"The police didn't try to reach you, either?"

"No. My name either didn't come up, or they fucked up in their investigation. I'm thinking the latter, because I would've told them what I'm telling you—something bad happened to Ben. I know it."

"Even if it did, it's not like you can do anything. It's not even your problem."

She frowned at him. "This is a man's life we're talking about. Just because he and I didn't work out doesn't mean I'm not worried."

"I know that. It's just . . ." Raking a hand through his hair, he stared at her. "I don't like the idea of the woman I just made love to expending so much energy worrying about some guy who was too ignorant a jerk to understand what a good thing he had."

Her frown deepened to a scowl. "Ignorant jerks come in all shapes and sizes. The man is missing, possibly dead, and you want to be jealous that I'm concerned? Green is *not* a good color on you, Ryon. Doesn't go with blond at all."

"I can't help what I am," he ground out. "My wolf doesn't like you thinking about some other man, and neither do I."

"You know what? This jealousy thing from you is a little intense for me, considering we haven't known each other all that long." Standing, she started to gather her clothes and piled them on the couch. She pulled on her panties, and then started putting on her bra.

"Dammit, I'm sorry." Pushing to his feet, he held out a hand. "Please, don't go."

"I need some breathing room, okay? I'm not leaving, I'm just going to relax for a while and have some time to myself."

"If that's what you want." He looked so miserable she almost relented.

But she needed to get away, catch her breath. His emotions were battering at her, all of his joy, fear, hope, anger, and she felt like she was in danger of losing her mind. She didn't understand how his feelings were flowing to her like there was a superhighway between them, but she had to take a break.

Once she was dressed, she turned to face him. "I'll talk to you in a bit, okay?"

"Okay."

"Thank you for dinner. It was wonderful."

He looked away, not speaking. A wave of hurt and rejection poured to her from him, and she fled like a coward in the wake of it. She left, not risking another glance at him and was back in her own quarters in less than a minute. Once there, she paced the carpet.

She couldn't stop. There was something alive under her skin. That was the only way to describe the sensation that was driving her crazy. And this feeling seemed to be agitated by Ryon being upset. Daria regretted hurting him, but this was more. It was as if there was another consciousness making itself known, or trying to, and it wasn't happy. It wanted something.

Wanted out.

She gasped. What was that? She was losing her marbles. She—

During one of her passes by the window, she paused, her attention caught by movement outside. When she saw a silver and black wolf streak across the lawn toward the forest, her heart clenched.

The wolf was Ryon. In a compound surrounded by shifters, she wasn't certain how she knew it was him. But it was. The strange bond between them sang with fear, longing, and sadness. The desire to run until he was too exhausted to care.

Before she could question the wisdom of her actions, she was pushing open her patio door, exiting the small yard and running in the direction he'd gone. She tried pushing her thoughts at him, but whether any of them connected, she couldn't say.

Ryon! Please, come back. I didn't mean to hurt you.

Nothing.

Hey, let's talk. We can't do that if you're running.

She wasn't sure how far she'd gone or how long she'd chased him when she stopped and braced a hand on a tree. She couldn't run anymore. And there was a painful lurch in the pit of her stomach, like she had to vomit. That didn't happen, but sickness roiled in her belly. Spread to her arms and legs, which were now itching like mad, and became excruciating pain.

Crying out, she hit her knees, holding her casted arm over her stomach. Her skin and guts were turning inside out, and any second they were going to exchange places. All that would be left was a gruesome pile of muscle and bone, and they would all shake their heads in speculation of what could've happened. If she didn't know a creature had killed the campers, she might've believed there was a new disease going around, and she had caught it.

"Ryon!" Panting, doubled over, she clawed at the ground. Then she realized that her hands were tipped with actual claws. Black and sharp. "Shit!"

Her limbs began to move—and then one by one, they popped. Screaming, she could do nothing as the change she'd witnessed in Ryon just a short while ago took over her body as well.

The agony was horrendous. She continued to scream until her voice was hoarse—and then became a long, high-pitched howl. The pain ended as suddenly as it had begun, and she whimpered, frantically looking all around her. The cast that had occupied her arm was now split and lying in the grass. Clearly it was no longer needed, because her leg was fine.

Other than belonging to a wolf.

First she struggled to get free of her clothing. Then sitting, she looked down at herself, incredulous. She was covered in silky-looking black fur and had four paws. A tail? She tried wagging it, and to her surprise, it worked. It brushed the ground behind her, stirring leaves. Slowly, she tried to stand. That part went okay, but when she tried taking some steps forward, her legs got all tangled and she went down with a yelp.

Exhaustion prevented her from getting up, and so she curled into a ball and whined miserably. She couldn't walk back yet, and the sun would set soon. How was anyone supposed to find her? She didn't want to be out here alone, in a strange body, when the sun went down.

The memory of the screeching creature, not to mention Nick's rendition of what it might look like, made her shake. It had slaughtered two people, maybe more. If the beast found her out here, weak and defenseless, she'd end up as dinner.

Despite her fears, she grew sleepy. Staying awake wasn't an option. Before she went under, she could have sworn she saw a white wolf appear from behind a tree about fifty yards away. But when she blinked it was gone.

Daria, where are you? Hold on, honey. I'm coming.

She'd probably imagined that, too. But she was too tired to answer anyway.

In wolf form, Ryon raced through the woods toward the compound. Toward his mate. He had heard her cry out, and had immediately turned back when the pain felled him.

Her agony had ripped through him as though it were his own, and he'd actually stumbled and fell. Sitting on his haunches trying to figure out what had happened, the realization hit him.

Daria was going through her first shift. His mind reeled at the knowledge. Hadn't it taken Kira and Rowan a few weeks to experience their wolf for the first time? God, this had happened so soon, he wasn't ready.

She was confused, in pain. Alone. All of these horrible things should not have happened. If he'd been a better mate, he wouldn't have indulged in a moment of self-pity, leaving her by herself at the compound. Not even for an hour, not when he knew she would need him, and not over something as stupid as his jealousy of a man who was no real threat to his mating.

Because he was a selfish bastard, she was suffering. He called out to her as he ran, but she wasn't answering. The bond between them was blank, but not as though she was willfully shutting him out. It was as if she was asleep, or unconscious. He ran faster, frantic to find her.

He wasn't sure how long he searched, but he was starting to panic. Their bond would've helped him find her faster, but he was hindered. Maybe she hadn't even run in his direction.

The last thing he needed was to see the glowing form of a spirit step from behind a tree. Halting in his tracks, he recognized the woman who'd been mutilated. This time her image was whole, her skin unmarred by the atrocity inflicted upon her. Sometimes this happened, the victims reverting back to the state they were in before they died. Maybe they couldn't accept what had happened, much less that they were supposed to be dead.

As the ghost moved closer, eyes beseeching, Ryon shifted. Kneeling in the dirt, he shook his head. "I can't help you."

Monster, she mouthed.

Ryon shivered. The spirits were so seldom able to get their woes across. Leave it to this one to be different. "I know. I'm sorry for what the beast did to you, but we're going to catch him. I promise."

This time, her voice came through on a whisper. "My husband?"

"Everyone is looking for him. We'll find him." She didn't need to know they probably already had.

"Monster," she said sadly, the strange, dark eye sockets glistening with unshed tears.

Jesus. "I hope not. But one way or another, we'll find him."

From her bereft expression, she must have known he'd likely suffered the same fate. Why did the ghosts torment him when there wasn't a fucking thing he could do? What good was this stupid "gift"?

"Look for the light," he told her. "When you find it, keep going. Maybe your husband is there, waiting for you."

A look of hope bloomed, and she turned without another word. Began to walk away. In seconds, she vanished into the trees again, and he exhaled a shaky breath.

"I'll never freaking get used to that." If the woman's husband was dead, he prayed they'd find each other. It drove him crazy that he never knew if the spirits found peace.

Shifting again, he resumed his search for Daria. Scenting the air, he began to come undone. He couldn't locate her. Then a flash of white caused him to put on the brakes. In the path ahead, a small white female wolf stood with her head up, ears forward in a nonthreatening manner. She didn't snarl or offer any aggression. She simply turned, glanced over her shoulder once as if expecting him to follow, then took off.

Taking a chance, he ran after her. She could be leading him into a trap, but he didn't think so. Instinct typically served him well, and whatever this wolf's agenda was, Ryon and his mate were not a part of it. He hoped.

At one point he lost sight of the wolf, and bounded

around a bend in the path, determined to catch up. Instead, he found that the white wolf was gone—and a black shape was lying curled at the base of a tree. Torn and discarded clothes were strewn not far from the form. Approaching cautiously, he sniffed. Scented his mate.

She was a bit bigger than the white wolf, but not by much. His heart lifted at seeing her there, safe and sleeping. His poor baby must have been worn out from her first shift, and he felt bad that it had happened without anyone there to guide her.

Shifting back to human form, he knelt at her side and ran a hand over her silky black coat. "You're stunning," he said softly. "I'm so sorry I wasn't there."

His touch and his voice roused her, and she sat up, whining pitifully. "You're all right," he soothed. "Easy, now. I'm here."

Liquid brown eyes gave him a fearful stare. *How did this happen to me?*

His mouth fell open, and then he smiled. "You're doing it! You can mind-speak with me."

Not with anyone else?

"No." His smile faded with dread at the coming talk. He knew where her questions would lead, and he couldn't put off the answers any longer. "Just with me."

Why not? Is it because you bit me? And is that how I became a wolf, like you?

Her voice in his head was rising in anxiety. "You need to shift back before we have this talk."

Answer me!

"Shift and we will," he said firmly. "Imagine each part of your body. Your arms, legs, hands and feet. Your face. Make your wolf obey and step back."

I don't know if I can.

"It's not nearly as hard as shifting for the first time, and it isn't as painful from now on. Go ahead and try."

On her first attempt, her wolf remained stubbornly in the forefront, not pleased at all about being forced into submission again. It was out, and Ryon sensed that she wanted to run, play, and explore. Now wasn't the time, though.

The second attempt was a success. In seconds Daria was sitting on the ground, naked. Drawing her knees up to her chest, she glared at him, making him flinch.

"You deserve the whole truth," he began.

"Nice of you to think so." Her lips thinned.

"I want you to try to remember that ever since you woke up in our infirmary, you've had a lot to deal with. There was no way I was going to spring all of this on you at once."

She hesitated; then her posture relaxed a fraction. "I'll give you that. But I want the whole story now, not just what you believe I can handle. I'm tougher than I look."

"Fair enough." Jesus, this wasn't going to go well. "Yes, when I bit you, I knew that most likely you would turn into a shifter. Like me and my team."

"And you did it to save my life." A statement, not a question. She was working through it all in her head.

"Yes. As well as my own."

She tensed again. "What do you mean?"

"Remember when I said you could mind-speak with me, but *only* with me?"

"I remember."

He fumbled for a way to explain that wouldn't shock her too badly. "Well, only certain pairs of wolf shifters can do that who aren't Telepaths. Non-Telepaths can only talk in each other's heads if they are . . . mated. Or if you're a powerful born shifter, like Nick. He communicates with me really well. The others have to push their thoughts back at me if I talk to them first."

"Mated." She stared at him blankly, latching on to that word. "You mean mated, as in animals in the wild who pair off with their special other half? That kind of mated?"

"Or shifters who find their other half, yes." Hope rose at her calm questioning. It quickly crashed as understanding began to dawn, and a slow burn of anger simmered through their bond.

"When you bit me, you *mated* with me?" she asked, voice rising. "Like, *married* me, in a way?"

"Sort of," he said evenly. "I had no—"

"You had no choice? No other option but to let me die?"

"That's the absolute truth, I swear it."

"And it had nothing to do with your wolf half simply taking what he wanted? Excuse me if I don't believe that," she said flatly.

"I can't deny he wanted to claim you—we both

did—but I wouldn't lie to you. I honestly could not have done anything differently. Not unless I—"

"Save it." Her voice was cold as a winter's day. "Tell me about this bond I feel. It's not my imagination, is it? Now your possessive Neanderthal side when we were discussing Ben makes sense."

"No, it's not your imagination. We're bonded for life," he said, heart aching. "We won't be able to stand being apart for long. We can each feel the other's emotions, physical pain. I felt yours when you shifted, and that's how I knew to turn back. The white wolf led me to you."

She ignored the last bit of information. "That's just great, mate. I'm bound to a man I barely know. I didn't get a say. Maybe I would have chosen you, but now we'll never know."

"We won't?" Fear seized his chest. "Daria—"

"I can't handle this right now. I thought I could take about anything after what I've seen, after almost being killed and then recovering at warp speed." She laughed without humor. "But this? I don't know anything except I need for you to stay away from me right now."

Faster than he would've believed possible, she began to shift. It still took far longer than it would after she'd gained more experience, but she did an impressive job. It broke his heart that she was using her new skills to get away from him as fast as possible.

His mate turned and began to walk away. Her steps were a bit drunken as she figured out the use of her legs, but she did an admirable job.

"Daria!" he called "Please? I had to do it! I would have . . ." But she wasn't listening, or stopping.

Remaining on the ground, he sat with his head bowed for the longest time. Stared at the ground with his soul bleeding out.

"I would have died," he said to no one.

But he could fix that, sooner or later. There was always one more monster to fight. If his mate left him . . .

He'd just have to make damned sure he didn't win the next fight.

Eight

Daria walked back to the compound, anger and confusion riding her hard.

Sadness, too. Ryon's as well as her own. Every harsh word she'd spoken to him had hit his soul like a hammer blow and reverberated in her own chest. When she had walked away, she had left him devastated.

He had no choice but to bite her. She knew in her heart that was the truth, but that didn't make it any easier to deal with the fact that her life had changed forever.

Would that be so bad?

No. Contrary to what he or his friends might think, she wasn't angry about the actual mating itself—she could think of worse things than to be tied to the blond god of her dreams—or the fact that she'd been turned into a shifter. The crux of her frustration was that she didn't get a say in her own destiny. It had been served up without her consent, and presented after the fact with a big bow.

Congratulations. You can turn furry and you're tied for life to a man you don't really know. What if he leaves the toilet seat up? Leaves his dirty underwear on the floor? Is lying and has ten girlfriends, one in each part of the world? Too bad! He's yours.

Thank God no one was around when she approached the back of the building. The wing where her quarters was located seemed quiet, and she trotted to the private yard, glad she hadn't taken time to latch her sliding patio door. On the porch, she concentrated on her human form and shifted back, then hurried inside before anyone spotted her.

Padding to the bathroom, she decided on a much-needed shower. But when she got under the hot spray, the soothing effect of the water pounding down was eclipsed by how much she hated that Ryon's scent was being washed away. Her wolf wasn't pleased, either, and was becoming more vocal by the minute.

Out of the shower, she toweled off and dressed. After she'd dried her hair she felt human again—and she tried not to laugh hysterically at that expression that used to mean nothing. She was sitting on the sofa contemplating the waning light outside when there was a knock at the door.

Immediately her pulse started hammering, and she wondered what she'd say to Ryon. She should have known he wouldn't give up so easily. Secretly, she was glad. But when she opened the door, it wasn't Ryon who'd come to see her.

Two women stood there with warm smiles, one a small blonde she knew as Kira, Jax's mate, the other Rowan, Aric's mate. Trying not to show her disappointment, she let them in.

"Hello," she said. "Come inside."

"We're your welcoming committee since the guys are too dense to be social. I'm Kira Locke."

The other woman snorted. "They're not dense. Ryon scared them off, the possessive bastard." The tall, built brunette stuck out her hand. "Rowan Chase."

Daria shook it, then waved a hand at the kitchen. "I'm afraid I don't have anything to offer you guys to drink. I haven't gotten into town, or anywhere else for that matter."

"Not a problem," Rowan replied. "We just wanted to say hello, see if you're settling in, if you need anything."

"Other than a manual for how to deal with wolf shifters? Can't think of anything."

The other women chuckled as they followed her into the living room. "If any man should come with a manual, it's one of the Pack," Kira said. "Jax about drove me out of my mind before I really got him or his world."

"This whole thing is so hard for me to accept," Daria told them, taking a seat on the sofa. Rowan sat next to her. "I don't know how you managed to get used to it."

Rowan shook her head. "I was skeptical when I first met Nick and he started spouting shit about being a PreCog and how they were battling an evil Unseelie who was trying to create a race of super-soldier shifters. I thought he was about one delusion from a nice, long stay at the county asylum."

"Exactly!" The woman understood. "So how did you accept it?"

Rowan shrugged. "I'm a former LAPD cop. I grew up there on the east side, in one of the toughest barrios in the city. I've seen the weirdest stuff you can imagine, and I've handled plenty of dangerous criminals. For my part, present me with irrefutable evidence and I have to believe you."

"You're a *show me facts* kind of girl."

"Right. Kind of hard to refute a bunch of guys turning into wolves right in front of you, not to mention witnessing them battle demons from the Unseelie Court. Since I'm not crazy, it had to be true."

"My head knows that, but . . ."

"Your heart is having trouble catching up?" Kira guessed.

"Yeah. It's not even that I can't accept Ryon's world, it's just that I was thrust into this by fate, if you will, without any say in the matter."

"That's how it happened with us, too," Kira put in with a laugh. "You're not alone."

"Ryon's world?" Rowan asked. "So it's true, you and him are together?"

"I—I suppose. I mean, when he bit me to save my

life, he mated with me." She couldn't help the bitterness in her tone. "He knew biting me would bond us together for life, but he did it anyway. I hate not having a say in the outcome of my own existence."

"Let me ask you, what would you have done differently if you could? Would you have said no, told him to let you die?"

"Well, no. But that's not the issue!" she said defensively. Didn't they get it?

"Isn't it?"

Daria stared at the brunette. "What are you trying to get at? Because I'm not following."

Rowan sighed as she and Kira exchanged a knowing look. "Did Ryon tell you much about Bondmates?"

"Not a lot, except he *had* to bite me, and now we're bound forever."

"So, he didn't tell you what happens to a shifter if he meets his true mate and doesn't bite her?"

"No, he didn't." She thought back to earlier, when she'd been upset. "I think he was trying to tell me something else, but I wasn't listening at the time. I guess I should have."

"Yes, you should've." Kira's voice was soft, no hint of accusation in her tone. Only understanding. "Once a shifter meets his mate, scents her, it's all over for him. He can't become physically aroused by another potential sexual partner, ever. If he doesn't bite his mate, and claim her, within a certain amount of time, usually a couple of weeks, he becomes ill with flulike symptoms."

She scrambled to process what Kira was saying. "He becomes impotent for anyone else, and he'll get sick?"

"Exactly. "

"So, if Ryon hadn't bitten me?"

"Within two or three weeks, he would've been dead."

Daria reeled from the revelation. "No."

"I'm afraid so." Kira took her hand. "When Ryon told you that he had no choice, he wasn't just talking about saving your life. He saved his, too."

She had to know. "What if my injuries hadn't been life-threatening? Would he have turned me without my consent?"

Rowan shook her head. "Ryon is one of the most honorable men I know. He never would've taken that course of action unless it was to save his mate. If you hadn't wanted him, he would've let you go without saying a word."

"He would rather have died than force me," she whispered.

"Any of them would."

"That's probably how he feels now. Like I don't want him." She looked between the women in shame. "What happens to a mated shifter who feels rejected?"

"Eventually, he'd lose his will to live, I imagine," Kira said. "But don't worry about Ryon. He's made of stronger stuff than that. He won't give up easily."

"Take tonight for yourself," Rowan advised. "Give both of you the night to cool off. Then talk to him when he gets back from their search mission tomorrow."

She thought about that, then nodded. "Sounds like a good idea."

"Now, why don't I go back to our place and fetch stuff to make mojitos?" Kira suggested.

Rowan smiled. "Girl, I think that's the best idea I've heard all day."

Daria couldn't agree more.

"Jesse? This is Nick."

"If this is bad news, I'm hanging up," the man said gruffly. "I'm up to my dick in piranha."

"Don't get testy, I just have a question. You know that missing criminal attorney from Missouri that Daria's father called you about when he was trying to find her?"

"Yep. The guy's her ex-fiancé."

"What did you say the man's name was?"

"Hang on." A shuffling of papers sounded on the other end. Nick didn't have to be a PreCog to see the mess. "Here it is. His name is Benjamin Cantrell."

"Oh, *fuck*." Pinching the bridge of his nose, he stared at the piece of paper on his desk.

"Why? What does that mean?"

"It means we've got a huge goddamned problem, and now I have to ask a favor. I need something containing Cantrell's DNA and I need it here yesterday. A strand of hair from his bathtub, his toothbrush, anything."

"What the hell is going on, Nicky? If you got a body, tell me."

"Oh, we've got something far, far worse than that. And if my information is correct, we've got an ID on our beast that's ripping up campers."

Bring the wolf to OR-4. I want to try to splice his DNA with human subject 356 again. I'm on the verge of a break-through.

Human subject 356—a missing human named Benjamin Cantrell.

Ryon suited up, pulling on his fatigues, slamming a clip loaded with silver bullets into his pistol, sheathing a wicked knife in his boot. If those human weapons weren't enough, he had his wolf. If he couldn't beat the beast, in wolf form he could hopefully outrun the bastard.

Ryon's group consisted of Jax, Aric, and Micah. The others had split up as well, covering other quadrants. Ryon's group focused on the area where the husband had been found, two miles from his wife. They would work their way outward in widening circles, looking for any sign that something large had come that way. Ryon wished his group had Kalen in it, so the Sorcerer could simply do his magical thing and shrivel the creature to nothing like he'd done with Malik's batlike Sluagh. But Aric could always torch him if things got bad.

Or he could if Nick hadn't given the order to take the thing alive if at all possible. Nothing worse than searching for the Incredible Hulk of paranormal beasts, except attempting to subdue it with a *no kill* order over your head. There were hopes that the man trapped inside his beastly counterpart could be saved.

He wasn't holding his breath.

Ryon parked the Range Rover as close as he could to the site of the second body and they walked the rest of the way. Aric carried a heavy net over one shoulder, Jax a coil of rope. "Nothing like having to play rodeo star with an enraged lizard."

"No fuckin' shit," Aric muttered. "It'd be a lot easier if I could just fry his ass. Then we could get on home and get laid."

"That's got my vote," Jax put in.

Micah remained silent, and Ryon studied his friend in concern. He never had much to say these days, and seemed kind of spacey. But he figured Nick knew best, letting him begin to take assignments although he was actually worse off than Phoenix, who still hadn't been cleared for duty.

A thirty-minute hike later, they came to the area where the man's body had been found. Crime scene tape was wrapped around the trees to form a rough circle, but if it hadn't been for that, there wouldn't have been much to mark where another life had ended so horribly.

Except the odor. Ryon detected old blood, and a more rancid smell that must belong to the beast. It was strong here, more so than at the first scene, for whatever reason. He wanted to gag.

The reminder that Daria had discovered the first body, and could easily have fallen victim to this creature as she went about her job, had him breaking out in a cold sweat. He was glad she was at the magically warded compound, well away from danger. That was about the only point in this day's favor.

Just to the right of the area marked by the crime scene tape, Ryon saw the glow of a figure seated on the ground. He moved closer and saw that it was the spirit of a man with his arms encircling his legs, staring forlornly into space.

"Whatcha got?" Aric asked. "Another Casper?"

"Yeah. It's the male victim. He's confused."

Ryon was about to try to question the man when another ghost appeared beside him—the woman that Ryon had seen twice before. Looking up, joy bloomed on the man's face and he bolted to his feet, taking her into his arms. They held on to each other as though they'd never let go, and a lump formed in Ryon's throat. He never got to see happy endings, and guessed this one was as close as he'd ever seen.

The man spun his wife around, then kissed her soundly. Then, hand in hand, they walked toward the trees . . . and disappeared into thin air.

Ryon cleared his throat. "They're together now."

"Well, that's good," Micah said quietly. "I guess."

The others agreed halfheartedly. Ryon contacted his commander.

Nick? How's it going?

Not great, Nick pushed back to him. *We've found another body, six miles south of where Daria found the woman. It's a god-awful mess.*

Sheriff on the way?

Yeah.

Okay. Nothing here yet, except I saw the spirit of the man close to the site where he was found. His wife showed up and they were reunited.

Did either of them say anything to you?

No. They were too wrapped up in each other. Never noticed me.

Okay. I'll check in soon.

"Nick said they've got a body," he told the group. "Six miles south of where the woman was found. Said it's a mess."

There were several curses and expressions of general disgust. Aric was most likely about to pop off a smartass remark when he stopped and squinted into the trees ahead.

"Man, I think my vision is messed up."

Ryon looked in the direction his friend was staring. "What is it?"

"Over there." He pointed. "Do you see a big area where the trees look blurry?"

Micah piped up. "I see it. Looks like a kaleidoscope effect, only clear."

Ryon's eyes studied the big area, his brain slow to catch up with what he was seeing. And when he did, a roar shook the entire forest that sounded just as Daria had described.

"Fucking Christ," Micah shouted as the blur detached itself from the trees.

The *pum-pum* of the beast's feet slamming into the earth as it ran toward them reminded him of a scene out of *Jurassic Park*. Only instead of a T. rex, the creature bearing down on them was almost a dead ringer for Nick's drawing of it.

Except the fucker was almost invisible.

No wonder the thing had been able to sneak up on unsuspecting hikers. They couldn't see the damned beast until it was too late.

Nick! The beast is here, it's attacking! We're gonna try to catch it!

On our way, hang tight!

Whatever was going to happen, Nick couldn't prevent it. Ryon just hoped their commander wasn't forced to scoop up their remains with a shovel.

Ryon and his teammates formed a square around the creature as it skidded to a halt in the middle, bellowing. He watched in sick fascination as that maw opened wide, the outlines of two rows of jagged teeth visible if you knew just how to look. The beast snapped its broad head toward him and just stopped. Stared. Its bulky arms were held out slightly from its sides, long, razor-sharp claws deadly on the ends of its webbed fingers.

Ryon suddenly realized the beast was confused. It had obviously not encountered any sort of opposition from anyone in the weeks since it had escaped from the lab, and it didn't know what to do now. For a fleeting few seconds, he thought maybe the man inside the beast would take over, allowing them to take him in peacefully so the doctors could work on a cure.

He should've known it wasn't going to be that simple.

He held out a hand. "Hey, man. We want to help you. Why don't you—"

The creature let out another deafening roar and charged him. Scrambling backward, Ryon barely managed to escape a swipe with those deadly claws. Then the net was thrown over the beast's head, stopping his attack. It swiped and screeched, pissed off and trying to get out of the net. Jax tossed the rope, attempting to lasso its shoulders, but the creature managed to grab the rope, yanking it right out of Jax's hands and trampling it underfoot as he dropped it.

Rushing forward, they grasped the edges of the net and tried to wrestle the beast to the ground. If they could make him fall, all four of them might be able to hold him until he was tied up.

It didn't work out that way. The creature used the net to sling them with all his strength, the net flying off him. Ryon, Jax, and Aric were flung in different directions—

But Micah, the closest one to the raging monster, was now caught in the net. As the thing stomped over to him, Micah's eyes widened and he worked frantically to free himself. He shifted his hands into claws and sliced at the net, just as the monster seized his leg and started pulling him backward.

"Fuck! Somebody do something!" he yelled.

Ryon and the others bolted toward them, Ryon pulling his gun from his waistband. He squeezed off a couple of shots to the creature's shoulder, just as it raked Micah across the ribs. Micah screamed, then went horribly silent as it threw him down. The beast turned toward Jax and took two steps, but the others joined in, firing at it.

Apparently not happy with this development, it whirled and fled into the woods. As far as Ryon could tell, they hadn't even wounded the damned thing.

"Jesus. Come on, kid, hang on," Aric begged.

Ryon ran to where his friends were kneeling by Micah, worry etched on their faces. Jax stripped off Micah's shirt and balled it up, pressing the cloth into the wound in his side. The slice was long and deep, made by one of the claws. If the beast had struck with a bit more curve, their friend would've been gutted.

"I'm all right," Micah panted, pale and sweating. "Burns, though. Like acid."

He wasn't okay by a long shot. Blood was fast soaking the ground, and his eyes drifted closed. Though they kept talking to him, he was losing ground fast.

Jax put his arms under Micah's knees and back, and lifted him. "Let's go."

They made the long hike as fast as they could, jogging a good part of the way. Nick's group had just arrived at Ryon's Range Rover when they came through the trees. The commander jogged up to them, laying a palm on Micah's slack face—the scarred side.

"Dammit, we just got you on your feet," Nick said grimly. "Your sister is going to kill me."

The younger man didn't stir. Nick helped get Micah into the back of the SUV, and climbed in with him. Ryon jumped in the driver's seat and soon they were on their way, the other team racing behind them.

Nick spoke into his cell phone. "Melina, get the trauma room ready. We've got one coming in with an open wound to his side. Coming in hot."

Meaning he was in bad shape.

Gripping the steering wheel, Ryon sped up. This day had been a clusterfuck from the time the alarm went off.

It appeared things were going to get worse before they improved. One thing for sure, they needed to develop a different strategy to catch the monster.

Because that one sure as fuck didn't work.

Daria was losing her mind.

All she'd had to hear from Blue while sitting in the cafeteria was that one of the Pack had been badly injured fighting the creature, and she had almost fainted. How was she going to take this every time they went on an op? Always terrified that her mate would come home in a body bag?

She was waiting by the emergency entrance doors when the first teams poured in. Jax was carrying the hurt man in his arms—and it wasn't Ryon. The man had shoulder-length brown hair, not blond. Her knees nearly gave out, her relief was so great. Then she heard Rowan's stricken cry and realized it was her brother, and guilt flailed at her.

Rowan followed after Jax, and Daria could only stare at the doors and wait for Ryon.

When he walked through them, she ran toward him. The instant he saw her, he opened his arms and she ran into them, clasping him tight. He returned the embrace, holding her against his strong body. She could feel every muscle and ridge, and took joy in him being there.

Sweaty, salty, dirty. But alive.

"I'm so sorry," she whispered. "I was such a bitch to you last night, and if that had been the last time I ever saw you—"

"No, shh. I'm here, honey. I'm safe."

"This time."

"This is my life. There will always be danger, but I'll always move heaven and hell to come home."

"I was awful to you," she repeated. She couldn't get past that she could've lost him in the wake of her stupid pity party. "I would never have forgiven myself if something had happened to you."

"You've had a lot thrown at you, so give yourself a break." He kissed the top of her head. "Let's just move forward, all right?"

"Can we?"

"Good grief, woman." Pulling back, he gave her a mock frown. "Do I look like a man who gives up easily?"

"No. Rowan may have said something like that."

"Well, she's right. I'm a stubborn bastard and I like getting my way. Now, why don't we join the others and wait for some word about Micah?"

"Sounds good."

Ryon told everyone assembled about the doomed fight with the creature, and how Micah was injured. Rowan, eyes red from crying, sat huddled next to Aric, shushing his repeated apologies for getting her brother hurt.

"You didn't get him hurt," she snapped finally. "So knock it off, okay? He's a grown man."

"Sure, baby." They kissed gently, with such love, in their own universe.

Three hours later, Melina came out to inform them all that he would recover, and the relief swept through the group like a storm. But the creature's claws contained some sort of venom that was making his system and the gash slow to heal. It was a word of caution for future battles against the monster.

Ryon squeezed Daria's hand. "Now that we know he'll be okay, shall we go back to my place?"

"Sounds great."

On the way, she got one more confession off her chest. "I'm still not sure about the whole wolf thing, and I'm still angry at having fate decide my life for me."

"I understand," he said, and she read the truth in his eyes. He was an incredible man. "I've been there, Daria."

"God, I'm an idiot! Of course you have."

"You're not an idiot. You're doing the best you can, and no one blames you for being upset, least of all me."

"But I do care for you," she said softly. "I realize I don't want to miss out on something wonderful with you because I'm so busy looking backward."

"I'm glad to hear that." They came to his door, and he let them in.

"Make love to me?"

"With great pleasure." His gaze burned into hers. "You don't know the hell I went through back there, battling that monster. Do you have any clue what was going through my mind?"

"Um, if I die at least I'll be free of the old ball and chain?"

He laughed at her pitiful joke, but his blue eyes glistened with tears. The sight melted her heart, warming a path clear to her toes.

"No, baby. Not even close. I was thinking, What if she never forgives me? Then it wouldn't have mattered if I was dead or not. I'd never again have a chance to do this." Ryon cupped the back of her head and lowered his lips gently to hers.

Electric.

Daria's mouth moved under his, loving his soft lips. She twined her arms around his neck and pulled him closer, inviting him. His tongue swept inside, stroking, and she reveled in his warmth.

His hands skimmed her shoulders and down her arms. He helped her off with her shirt and bra, and she arched against him. The puckered tips of her nipples brushed the material of the shirt covering his chest, and a bolt of heat shot straight to her sex.

"Sweet, so sweet. I've gone to heaven."

Daria buried her hands in his hair, suddenly the aggressor. She sucked at his lips, exploring his mouth at will, making love play with her tongue. Her knees threatened to buckle.

Helpless, dying for this. For you. God, I want more.

He broke the kiss, panting. "If I don't stop now, I might not be able to."

"So don't stop."

He didn't need more encouragement. Pulling her to his bedroom, he pushed her gently to the bed and removed the rest of her clothing. Then he positioned himself between her thighs, began to ease inside. Holding her close he started to move, whispering words of passion in her ear, stoking the fires until they were both straining toward the precipice. It was raw, tender, honest. All too soon they cried out, hurtling over the edge together.

As he held her close, she pretended they were safe, that the danger was over. And for a while, they were given a reprieve.

It was a beautiful fantasy while it lasted.

There probably wasn't a more delicious sight than a bunch of shifters playing baseball. Or playing anything at all, really, but today they happened to be wielding bats and gloves.

From Daria's spot on the grass, sprawled on a blanket, she sipped a beer and eyeballed the tight tushes as they bounced around in an assortment of jeans, athletic shorts, and baseball leggings. She had to admit, when they blew off steam the results were lovely to watch.

All of that glistening male flesh, sweat dripping off the ends of their hair. Broad chests heaving, muscles bunching in exertion—

"Do you even have a clue who's winning?" a voice asked from her right.

Glancing over, she grinned at Micah. Forbidden from playing while he recovered, he was convalescing in his lounger. "Winning what? Is there a game being played right now?"

He snorted. "Figures. You're just like the rest of the lovesick mates around here." He jerked his head at the other mated women who were observing their men just as avidly as Daria had been.

Then the word *lovesick* lodged in her brain, and her smile dimmed some. The other women loved their mates to distraction. The emotion was etched on every one of their glowing faces, and shone in their eyes. *And Ryon is my mate.*

Do I love him? Can I, when I'm still not completely at peace with what I've become?

"Hey, did I say something wrong?"

"No," she assured him. "Just thinking."

"You looked really preoccupied for a few seconds."

"Oh, it's just . . ." She tried to think of how to explain.

"I know how hard this must be for you," he said softly. "Believe me."

Studying this man who'd been through such hell, she felt ashamed. "How did you deal with it? When you were turned, how did you cope?"

"I just did. I had no other choice. I woke up in a military hospital and I was changed. I had known for some time that I was a Dreamwalker, but now I was more than I'd ever been, with a wolf living inside me. I wanted to crawl out of my skin, or rip it to shreds with my claws, trying to get at the new beast that wouldn't let me rest."

"That's how I feel, too. She wants to run, to hunt." Daria gazed at her new friend, and saw complete under-standing. "She wants to be free, and it's so hard to rein her in. It's weird and scary to have all of that wildness inside me. Not to mention ironic, considering my job."

His brown eyes were sad. "As difficult as it is, re-member you have a mate who's a fine man to help you. We didn't, and learning all of that alone was tough. I mean, we're like brothers and we're there for each other, but it's not the same as having someone special to comfort you at the end of the day."

Her heart went out to him. "I *am* grateful for Ryon. He's been nothing but wonderful to me and I care about him very much." She paused. "You're going to have someone, too, one day."

"Who's going to want me?" he questioned, gestur-ing to the ruined side of his face.

"That's not who—"

"Who I am? Is that what you were going to say?" He laughed, the sound hollow. Aching. "Even if my mate could get past how I look, it's what's on the inside that's really fucked up. I don't remember much about my time in that shithole with Bowman, but from what the doctors tell me, that could change anytime. The point is, I'm more messed up inside than out. No mate deserves to be stuck with me."

"I won't believe that for one second," she said firmly. "You're going to meet your special someone, and then you'll eat those gloomy words of yours."

"Wanna bet?"

Before she could respond, Ryon came jogging over, looking sexy as sin in his tight athletic shorts and sweaty tank top. She almost swallowed her tongue as he beamed at her.

"Hey, good lookin'! Some of the guys suggested going out to the Crosseyed Grizzly in a bit. Want to go hang out?"

"Sure, sounds like fun. Anywhere, as long as I'm with you."

"Aww, how sweet." Leaning over, he gave her a big, sloppy kiss as Micah made a choking noise. Ryon pulled back and winked at his friend. "Jealous?"

"Not on your life."

But Daria knew the truth. Ryon missed the flash of pain on his friend's face, but she didn't. "Micah, are you feeling up to coming?"

Nick's voice broke into their conversation. "That's not a good idea. Micah needs to stay here and finish healing."

Micah frowned at the approaching commander. "Don't I get a say in the matter? I'm not ten years old, for cryin' out loud."

"Of course you do." Moving to stand by the lounger, Nick laid a hand on the other man's shoulder and gave him a kind smile. "But I have to discourage you."

"Why?"

"Because it isn't time."

"I won't drink if that's what you're worried about, boss. I know better than to do that when I'm still on meds."

"That's not it." The commander sighed. "You know I don't interfere with free will, but I'm suggesting you to stay here, just this once. You're not supposed to be at the Grizzly tonight."

Those cryptic words gave everyone pause. Nick was creepy like that sometimes, making statements that gave the hint that he knew much more than he was saying.

Micah stared at the older man for a couple of seconds. "Fine, I'll stay here," he said slowly. "Want to tell me what will happen if I go?"

"No. It doesn't matter now. And since we're both staying in, how about I trounce your ass on the Wii?"

"You're on, old man."

"Who're you calling old, pup?"

"It's true, isn't it?"

The commander smiled, the tips of his canines showing. "More than you know." He gave Micah a hand up, then turned to Daria and Ryon. "Have a good time."

"We will," she said. "See you later, Micah."

"Later."

As the two men headed back to the building, Ryon gave her a predatory look. "I'm all sweaty, and we're going out."

"So?"

"So, I need a shower first. Want to wash my back?"

A thrill went through her. "You don't have to ask twice."

Grabbing her hand, he took off, dragging her behind him as she laughed in pure happiness.

Nine

R yon decided there was a lot to recommend slippery, soapy shower sex.

Pressing his mate into the tiles, buried balls deep in her while hot water streamed over their bodies, was just about the best feeling in the entire universe. Any way he could have her was fine by him. How had he ever lived without this? Without Daria?

Groaning, he emptied his seed inside her as she shuddered under him, squeezing every last drop from his length. Then he kissed the nape of her neck and nuzzled the soft, wet skin there.

"Am I forgiven?" She tensed, and he instantly regretted bringing up a tender subject. Too late now. He eased out of her and backed off some, allowing her to turn and face him.

"It's not about forgiving you," she said evenly. "In fact, what I'm going through is not about you at all."

Hurt stabbed his chest. "I disagree. We're in this to-gether. You're my mate, and what causes you to be un-happy does the same to me."

Her expression softened and she touched his cheek. "I get that. And I don't blame you for what happened to me because you would've given me the option to be turned if you could have."

"That's true." He kissed her forehead.

"What I'm saying is you can't magically make me happy with being part wolf." Pausing, she searched his face. "Think back to when you were turned. Was there anything anyone said that made you accept it? Or did you just need time to get used to having your life turned upside down?"

"I needed time," he admitted. "But I hope that get-ting me as part of the deal isn't what's making you un-happy."

"Oh, Ryon," she breathed. Softly, she took his mouth in a lingering kiss, twining her arms around his neck. "I am *not* unhappy with you. On the contrary, I feel pretty darned good about us. Can't you tell?"

In truth, he'd been shutting off his awareness of their connection, afraid of being inundated with her scorn. Her anger. But her words encouraged him. Opening his senses tentatively, he found the golden bond stretched between them, thrumming with life. Some anxiety threaded through her emotions as she struggled with her wolf.

But much stronger was her affection for him, growing steadily into a richer connection. Every minute, she was falling deeper for him, and it both surprised him and took his breath away.

"Yes," he whispered. "I can tell. I feel the same way."

"Give me time to accept my wolf?"

"Anything you need." Quickly he rinsed away the evidence of their loving. Stepping out of the shower, he grabbed two towels and handed her one. As they dried off, an idea occurred to him and he grew excited. "How about we go for a run tomorrow, in our wolf forms?"

"I don't know . . ." Her brown eyes were worried.

Through their bond, he sensed her fear of the physical pain and hurried to reassure her. "The first shift hurts like a bitch, but it's never like that again, I promise. The more practiced you get, it's like breathing. And when you let your wolf out to run, the rush is like nothing you've ever experienced."

"Really?" She began to show some genuine interest.

Letting his towel fall to the floor, he pulled her to him. "Yes. We'll be together, too. It'll be fun, you'll see."

She bit her lip. "All right, you've talked me into it."

He gave her a sound kiss. "You won't be sorry."

"What about the creature that's out there, and the white wolf?"

"We'll keep an eye out and be cautious." He thought about the other wolf. "I don't think the white wolf meant to harm you when she pushed you."

"She did a good job of it anyway, even if it was an accident."

"She led me to you, after you shifted and were in pain," he said thoughtfully. "I think maybe she was trying to protect you the other day."

"From the creature?"

"It makes sense."

"But what's she doing here in the first place? If she's a shifter, why doesn't she simply approach the compound and request entry?"

"I don't know. But I have a feeling we'll find out, sooner or later."

"You're probably right."

Padding around Ryon's place, they took their time getting dressed. Daria enjoyed picking out his clothes, which consisted of a pair of soft, worn jeans, shitkickers, and a snug black T-shirt with a swirly gold pattern embossed on it that she claimed set off his blond hair. He rolled his eyes, but let her have her way. Whatever turned her on was fine by him.

Daria had brought over a pair of snug jeans and a button-up plaid shirt with a brown pattern that went well with her coloring. She looked like a yummy piece of chocolate, and shook her head, grinning, when he told her that she would make a tasty dessert.

Once he and Daria were dressed, they met the others at the hangar where they would take three SUVs to the Grizzly. Everyone was going except for Nick and Micah, and of course Zan and Phoenix, who were still on vacation.

As usual, Ryon took the wheel and motioned for

Daria to ride shotgun. Jax, Kira, Aric, and Rowan climbed into the back.

"Do you have your own car?" Daria asked as he pulled out, leading the caravan.

He glanced at her. "I've got a new Challenger, red with black stripes."

"Nice," she said. "I prefer the old ones, though."

"Me, too, but old muscle cars are for people who have a lot of time to tinker with maintenance, and I'm not that handy in the garage."

"You'll have to show it to me sometime."

"I will."

The six of them chattered all the way to the Grizzly, Ryon's friends asking Daria about herself. They were especially curious about her job, and thought it was cool that she studied real-life wolves. They stayed away from the subject of her being turned into a shifter, however, and for that he was grateful. He was working on getting her to embrace that side of herself, and didn't need them stressing her out.

The bar was hopping when they arrived, but not too crowded. Ryon and the other guys found an unoccupied corner and pushed several tables together to give them plenty of room, then seated their ladies and elbowed in. Ryon sat beside his mate and put an arm around her, pleased when she leaned into him comfortably. After watching three of his friends pair off and being nagged by envy for months, it was awesome to have his own woman at his side.

After ordering a round of drinks, they settled in, laughing and talking to those in their immediate vicinity. Ryon couldn't keep the smile off his face. His friends seemed to genuinely like Daria, and were very welcoming, making sure she was included in the conversation. She, in turn, got along well with them. Especially Blue and Noah, both of whom she seemed to be a bit sweet on. He wasn't bothered, though. He and his wolf knew Daria belonged to them.

They had a great time, eating, drinking, and making merry as one hour became two, then three. The evening out was a hit—until two seedy-looking men approached their table. The newcomers zeroed in on Kalen, eyes narrowed. Not everyone noticed them at first. But Ryon did, and he set the nacho he'd been munching on down on his plate, wiping his hands. Then he scooted his chair back a little, ready to spring into action if he needed to.

Jax and Hammer noticed the men, and did the same. One by one, the Pack became aware of the tension, and the lighthearted talk stopped. By now, Kalen was leaning back in his chair, sneering at the two rough, dirty men. Clearly, they'd met.

"Hello," Kalen said with deceptive pleasantness. "You guys didn't learn your lesson before? Back for more?"

Well, crap. Just what they needed, Kalen's hillbilly tormentors of a few weeks ago coming around to spoil their evening.

One of them spoke up, showing an unfortunate set

of bad teeth. "Our friend Billy seems to have disappeared off the face of the earth. We been lookin' for ya for a while now, figured you might shed some light on where he's at." For emphasis, he spit out of the side of his mouth—and the wad landed in the middle of Mac's salad.

Kalen's poor mate stared at the food, paling. Kalen's chair scraped on the floor, and he stood.

The Sorcerer was an imposing sight in his black leather duster, raven hair falling around the green kohl-rimmed eyes glittering with cool anger. Only an idiot would've messed with a man like him, and Ryon knew these two more than qualified.

"Why would I know anything about Billy?"

The two assholes had no clue that their stupid buddy had ended up as demon food, literally—Malik ate him. Kalen knew damned well what fate had befallen the town's most unsavory character, and he wasn't sorry.

"'Cause you fought with him right here in this bar. You had reason to want him gone," the man said in a nasty tone.

"From what I hear, so did half the county." Kalen cocked his head. "Billy was a thief, a liar, a bully, and he physically abused his family. I don't know anybody else who's all that concerned about him."

"I think you're a liar! Why don't you step outside so me and my buddy can kick your ass!"

At that, Ryon and his Pack friends stood. Ryon grinned. "Well, as long as you want to make it an unfair fight, you two can take on all of us. Sound good?"

The men stepped backward, not looking so eager in the face of those odds. Ryon knew how they must look, a wall of muscle against two scrawny dickheads.

"What the fuck is going on here?"

Ryon had never been so glad to see the sheriff. Deveraux stomped up to the group and took in the stand-off. Waving a hand at the two miscreants, he boomed, "You two? You're banned from the Grizzly, you idiots! Get the hell out of here before I haul you in for disturbing the peace, public intoxication, and anything else I can think of."

"But, Sheriff—"

"Get out!"

Muttering, the pair shot Kalen a glare before shuffling for the door. Once they were gone, Deveraux shook his head and frowned at their group. "Once again, you people are in the middle of the shit. I'm going to have an ulcer the size of a fucking watermelon in no time flat. And *you*." He pointed at Daria, then at a man across the bar before continuing.

"See that guy in the booth over there? He's a reporter for the local paper, and he'd love to interview you about the body you found, not to mention who your friends are and what the hell you're doing with them. You want my advice—and nobody fucking appears to—I'd get going before he notices you're here and he gives us all a buttload of publicity nobody can afford."

Immediately, Ryon felt stupid for bringing her out. "Sorry, Sheriff. I assumed their interest in Daria had died down enough that it wouldn't be a problem."

The older man looked exasperated. "It might have if mangled bodies would stop turning up. As it is, you might want to get lost. Because here the little buzzard comes."

The buzzard being the reporter, with a nice camera in hand and a gleam in his eye.

"Shit." Ryon held out his hand for his mate, and she took it. "Come on, baby. Anyone else leaving?"

"Me and Mac," Kalen said. "If my mate is ready."

Mac nodded and rose from her chair, giving her salad a glare of disgust. "I am."

"You guys go on," Jax told Ryon. "The rest of us will be back soon."

Ryon pulled Daria toward the door, ignoring the reporter's calls to wait. He wasn't about to subject his mate to any publicity, especially when it could harm her or his team in the long run. On the way out, he saw a flash, and cursed. That's all they needed, pictures of the Pack out there in circulation and perhaps ending up in the wrong hands. He hoped the sheriff or one of the guys confiscated them.

In less than a minute, they were on the road, heading back to the compound. Ryon threw his mate a look of apology. "I'm sorry, honey. I wanted you to get out and have fun."

"I did," she said, smiling at him. "It's nobody's fault that reporter was there, and we were going to leave soon anyway."

"I'm sorry about the two assholes," Kalen put in. "I had trouble with them and a friend of theirs before."

Daria glanced back at him and Mac. "People like them live to cause trouble, and they never learn. It's not a problem."

They talked the rest of the way, Kalen sharing some of his experiences as a Necromancer while Daria listened in rapt fascination. When the Sorcerer offered to let her sit in on a session sometime, she declined with a laugh.

"Oh, I don't think talking to dead people are my thing. I'd love to see some magic, though."

"Anytime."

At the compound, Ryon parked the SUV in the hangar and they said good night to the other couple, who walked off whispering quietly, Kalen's arm securely around his mate. Ryon took Daria's hand.

"Stay with me tonight?" His chest tightened as she weighed her answer. Then the band loosened when she smiled.

"I would love to."

And so, he ended a near-perfect evening with his mate wrapped in his arms.

He couldn't think of a damned thing that made him happier.

Daria awoke to two sharp points grazing her neck. Lips nibbling. As the fog lifted she squirmed and swatted at the minor irritation. A masculine chuckle rumbled in her ear, and the nibbling continued. More scraping. Awareness kicked in and she realized those were his canines, and little tendrils of pleasure began to spread through her body.

"Wake up, beautiful," Ryon sang. "Rise and shine."

"Ugh."

"Not a morning person?"

Giving up, she rolled over and peered up at his smug face. "Used to moving when I'm good and ready."

"Too bad. We have to eat breakfast. Then we're going for a run." He kissed her nose. "Unless you're backing out?"

"Are you kidding? I'm not a coward, my mate. I don't wimp out once I've made up my mind about something."

"Good for you," he said in approval. "Hungry?"

"I could eat."

"I've got a few MREs in the kitchen . . ." He tossed her a grin as he rose from the bed. Naked.

"Ha, you're a funny guy." She eyed his tight ass, disappointed when he pulled on a loose pair of shorts.

"Just teasing. I can cook, as you know."

"That you can, and you do a fine job. What am I getting?"

"Hmm. Omelets and toast?"

Her mouth watered. "That sounds great."

Forcing herself from his cozy, king-sized bed, she put on her jeans and shirt from the night before and padded after him into the kitchen. She observed her mate appreciatively as he went about getting out the stuff for their breakfast, shirtless and more scrumptious than any food.

"You like ham and cheese?" Opening a package of meat, he sniffed. "It's still good."

"Sure. I like just about anything that goes in an omelet."

"Then you're in luck, because I make the best ones in the whole compound."

He wasn't joking. Gesturing for her to sit on a stool at the bar, he got out bell peppers, onions, salsa, and mushrooms to go with the ham and cheese. Next, he poured two glasses of orange juice—which he then topped off with champagne.

"Mimosas?" she asked in delight. "You're going to spoil me rotten."

"That's the whole point. You deserve to be spoiled."

As she sipped her mimosa, he chopped the veggies and dumped them into a pan with melted butter. The delicious aroma filled the small kitchen and made her stomach rumble. He stirred them, refilled her drink, and then began beating the eggs, adding a bit of milk.

"To make them fluffy," he explained.

Yes, indeed. She could get used to having Ryon spoil her. In every way.

In two larger pans, he poured the eggs so he could make them both at the same time. Soon the sautéed veggies were added, then the cheese and ham. Slicing four thick pieces of sourdough bread, he shoved them in the toaster.

In minutes, he was ushering her into a breakfast nook seat at the table by the patio door, where he served their plates with finesse.

"My lady, your breakfast."

"Oh my God, this smells awesome."

"Tastes even better."

At his pointed look, she picked up her fork and took a bite. "This is wonderful. You're going to do all the cooking in this relationship, right?" Instantly, she realized what she'd said, as well as the significance—she was coming to accept their mating. What's more, she was truly enjoying her mate.

So did he, and he gave her a soft smile as he sat. "You bet. As long as you're mine, I'll cook whatever you want. Whenever you want."

"I'll hold you to that."

"I hope you do."

When they were finished eating, she helped him clear the table and wash the dishes. Finally done, he turned to her and wiped his hands on a towel.

"Since we're going to shift and go play, I suggest we shower later."

"Sounds good." Secretly she was dreading the actual shifting process, and he must've seen a hint of her sudden anxiety.

"Hey, I told you it would be okay, and I meant it," he said, taking her hands. "I wouldn't lie to you."

"I know. But what if I'm different? What if it hurts?"

"It won't. Trust me."

In the end, she did. As she followed him outside

onto his patio, she couldn't help that her knees shook. "What if someone sees me take off my clothes?"

"My patio is fenced, baby. The gate is open and we'll be able to come in and out without anyone seeing us naked. And if they did, nobody would think a thing of it."

"Really?"

"Yeah. Nakedness isn't a big deal here among the Pack and the mates. As the months and years go by, it will bother you less and less to strip and shift, until you're completely comfortable. Think of the Pack as your family."

"I wouldn't strip in front of my dad," she said, deadpan. "And he's family."

He laughed, amusement lighting his blue eyes. "All I can say is that it's different here. You'll understand it eventually."

"Okay." She blew out a breath. "What do I do now?"

"Strip. Then, like before, concentrate on your wolf. Feel her, and let her take over."

"I won't lose who I am, right? I mean, I'll still be me?"

"Exactly. You're you, the same intelligent being, even in that form. Your senses will be sharper, much more so than a real wolf's, and you'll feel her predatory instincts come to the fore, but you'll be able to control them. Your decisions will be conscious ones."

That was a relief to hear, especially since this would be only her second time in wolf form. Before, she'd been blindsided. Shocked, afraid, and upset. Today would be different, with Ryon by her side.

"I'm ready." She hoped that came across as confident.

Ryon pushed down his shorts and stepped out of them. Then the change flowed over his body, and in seconds his silver wolf was standing there, waiting. His voice came through their mental link.

I got better with practice, but the shift never happened for me as quickly or easily until you came into my life.

"Thanks," she said, pleased by the compliment.

Your turn. Just focus on your wolf. Let her free.

"Okay."

She got rid of her clothes and laid them on a patio chair. Then she concentrated, almost laughing when she found her wolf dancing in excitement like a pup. It was strange how they were different, yet one.

When the shift happened, it was so fast she barely had time to gasp in surprise before her limbs were re-shaping, her human body giving way to the she-wolf. Suddenly she was standing on all fours, tail wagging.

It didn't hurt!

Told you it wouldn't, he said smugly.

The shift happened so fast! Is that normal?

It's not the same for everyone. Like I said, I was always a bit slow. Walking over, he nosed her side. *Try to walk, baby.*

She wasn't too steady on her feet last time. But now she was definitely stronger, her legs moving as they should. It was weird that she knew what to do with four feet, and that she didn't fall. *I'm doing it!*

That you are. Ready to venture out?

You bet.

Side by side, they walked across the lawn. At the far

edge he led her into the trees via a well-worn path. For a while they simply enjoyed each other's company as she sniffed the air, taking in the scents all around. Some were familiar, like the plants and earth she was used to while camping. They were sharper, though, like a lens brought into high-def focus. Others were strange, gamey, and she wondered if they belonged to the wildlife she'd studied. It was neat to have the added senses giving her a clearer picture of what she'd known all her life.

After a half hour of walking, he broke into a lope. *Think you can handle this?*

She copied his movement, keeping up with him. *Easy!*

In her head, he laughed, but not in a mocking way. He sounded proud. Gradually, he increased their speed until they were running. Flying through the forest, the wind in their faces. His happy laugh echoed in her brain and joy rushed through her soul. *This* was freedom. Not the artificial trappings of man, the illusion of freedom that humans sold on a daily basis when hawking fine possessions and fancy vacations.

This was the real thing. She'd gladly remain out here with her mate forever. If they had no Pack, no responsibilities. No jobs to do. No people to protect.

She was so lost in the pleasure of their run, she almost ran right into Ryon's backside as he skidded to a halt. Barely missing him, she regained her balance and froze at the ominous rumble coming from his chest.

Ryon?

Stay back, baby.

Peering around him, she froze. On the trail ahead was the white wolf. *That's her! She's the one who pushed me into the ravine.*

His growl deepened as he glared at the other wolf, advancing slowly. *What are you doing here?* he demanded. *What do you want?*

The wolf merely lowered her head, a sign of submission. But if she offered an answer, Daria couldn't hear. Ryon bared his teeth, but the intruder didn't retreat, or seem afraid. She showed deference, keeping her posture small and nonthreatening as she turned. Then she glanced over her shoulder, took a few steps, and stopped expectantly.

She wants us to follow. Just like she did when she led me to you, Ryon told Daria.

Should we? Her worry sang along their bond, but her mate didn't echo it.

I think we should. She knows something, and I want to find out what.

Daria didn't necessarily agree that they should follow without a couple of other Pack members present. She wasn't sure she'd be much help in a fight, if it came to that. Still, she went with her mate, trailing him through the brush. They hadn't been following the wolf for long when she went still, and crouched low, staring into the trees with a soft whine.

Moving close to her, she and Ryon did the same, studying the dense forest ahead. Her mate was intent, nose sniffing the air.

Do you smell that?

She took a few whiffs. *It's like something . . . dirty. Like an unwashed body.*

Exactly. Do you see something over there? Look through those two trees.

At first, she didn't see anything. She was just about to tell him so when she caught a movement. A glimpse of something moving, so far ahead, so hidden it was hard to see. It moved again—and sat up.

From this distance, she could tell it was a human man. She couldn't make out his features, but his hair was shaggy, longish. It might have been brown, but that could've been filth.

Trembling started deep inside her, and she started to shake, but she wasn't sure why.

Could he be a victim? she asked her mate. *A lost camper?*

Maybe.

Then suddenly, horrifyingly, that question was put to rest. The man stood, naked. His head tilted back and he let out a bloodcurdling scream that caused the birds to take flight and made Daria jump. Then the scream became a roar. The deafening screech of a monster as the man's form changed. Enlarged to an astonishing breadth and height.

He appeared very much like Nick's drawing—just before he became translucent, all but vanishing.

Oh my God! That's the beast you're after!

Ryon flattened himself low to the ground. *Goddamn. I've never seen anything like that in my life. We tried to catch him the other day, but we didn't see him like that, as a man.*

The beast swung its head in their direction, and they held still, barely daring to breathe. They weren't equipped to take him on, and if he came after them, she wasn't sure whether she could outrun him. But luck was on their side. After a moment, the creature huffed and stomped in the opposite direction. The three of them waited a very long while, making sure he was gone before they rose from their hiding place.

Before Ryon could question the white wolf again, she bounded into the forest without looking back. Daria felt her mate's frustration at not getting answers from the elusive wolf, but they had bigger worries at the moment.

We need to get back, he urged. *Before that thing returns.*

There was something that seemed familiar about him— the man, I mean, before he changed.

He tensed at that. *How so?*

Not sure. Something about his scent seemed like I should know it.

Her mate's displeasure at that came through their bond loud and clear. She couldn't help what she'd noticed, and she couldn't understand why he'd be upset. But as they ran back to the compound, he grew more and more unsettled.

At last they made it onto his patio, and shifted. The change was much easier this time, and she figured she was over the hump and on her way to mastering her wolf. But her biggest concern was Ryon, who stalked into his quarters and waited, regarding her with his lips pressed together, blue eyes snapping.

"What the heck is wrong with you?" Crossing her arms over her breasts, she did her best to ignore the fact that they were having a serious discussion while naked. Probably wouldn't be the last time.

"What was familiar about that man?" His voice was cool.

"I don't know," she said, frustrated. "There was something underneath his odor, more than just a man who needed a bath. He smelled like . . . Obsession."

"What?" He blinked at her.

"Obsession for men. You know, that cologne that's been around forever. It was faint, but there. It's funny, I only knew one man who ever wore it—"

Instantly, she cut off that thought. It wasn't possible, so she refused to think it. But Ryon latched on to her words like a snapping turtle.

"What man wore it? Tell me."

"Ryon—"

"Who?"

She sighed. "Fine. My former fiancé used to wear it all the time. Happy?"

"No. I'm not thrilled that some man in the woods who's been turned into a murderous beast reminds you of your former lover," he growled.

"It's not like I can help how the guy smelled, for Christ's sake! I can't help it that the man's build even resembled Ben's . . . Shit."

Now her mate was pissed. She hadn't done anything

wrong, but at the mention of another lover, even a past one, he was going all alpha on her. It was annoying as hell.

And it was also a huge turn-on.

Ryon stalked her, pressing her against the glass patio door. "You remember how he smells? Not for long. Because I'm gonna fuck you, mark you with my scent until there's nothing left in your memory but me."

"Ryon," she whispered.

He claimed her mouth, kissed her senseless, tongue exploring. Tasting. Then he picked her up and carried her into his bedroom, where he proceeded to make good on his delicious threat.

Daria, his mate, recalled Ben's scent? His naked form?

Fuck that. Not for long.

Pulling her onto the bed, he tucked her into his side. The soft roundness of her breasts nestled against his arm, and he hardened, his length pressing into her thigh. She laid a hand on his bare chest, smoothing her palm over his pecs, the taut nipples. She journeyed to the curve of his jaw, stroked his face. One dainty finger found his lips, traced them as though she was remembering his kisses, perhaps thinking of savoring more.

His pulse quickened as she explored at will, and went a long way toward soothing his jealous wolf. Not to mention those lovely brown eyes shining with passion, just for him. She combed her fingers through his hair, sending exquisite little tendrils of pleasure down his spine, radiating to his fingers and toes. Heat surged between his legs, his arousal brushing her belly. He groaned, and Daria purred in his ear.

"Like that, do you?"

His body hummed beneath her hands. "Oh, yeah."

"That's good, because I *really* want to continue."

Before he could form an answer, her lips captured his. Gentle, urging. Her tongue found his, rasping. She sucked the breath from his lungs, the reason from his brain. He loved the taste of her, the wonderful feeling of her lithe form sprawled across him. Tender kisses nibbled his jaw, the base of his throat, and his chest. Her hot tongue worked its magic, circling each nipple in turn, teeth grazing them.

He had planned to be the one in charge, but he liked this. A lot.

She slid down his body, palm skimming his stomach as her tongue blazed a fiery path to his navel. Her hand dipped lower, fingers lightly stroking the hard ridge of his erection, and he nearly came undone.

"Ohh." He lifted his hips, seeking more.

"I see only you, my mate," she whispered. "Nobody else." Her hand slid down his belly, lower, finally encircling his shaft. Rubbing, stoking the fire.

"Daria," he breathed. His fingers dug into the blanket underneath him. He burned to touch her, to bury himself in her sweetness.

"Relax, let yourself go," she whispered. Her breath fanned against his groin. "You're mine and I'm yours."

Ryon was nearly robbed of speech. "For as long as you want. Anything you want."

She bent to him, long hair trailing across his lap, and rocked his world. With gentle strokes and kisses, laving him until he was mindless. Bodiless. She owned him, and he surrendered willingly.

"Daria, yesss!" He cupped the back of her head, near to losing control.

She pulled back, moved up his body. Captured his face in her hands and kissed him, the hardened tips of her nipples branding his chest. Blood pounded in his ears as his arms came around her. He smoothed her naked skin. Her bare back, the flare of her hips, and her small, firm round buttocks. She rolled to her back, pulling him with her. He took her mouth, licking his way inside. Their combined flavors maddened him, and he craved more.

Ryon kissed his way down the slender column of her throat to her breasts, returning the attention she'd given to him. He cupped them, enjoying her softness and how the perfect globes seemed to be made to fill his hands. He took the taut nipples between his thumbs and forefingers, not pinching too hard, but just enough to give that tiny electric shock that borders pleasure and pain.

"Oh, yes." She arched under his touch, inviting him.

He bent his head, suckling them, nibbling until his name became a murmur on her lips. Not nearly enough. *More*. He inched downward, parting her thighs. He skimmed her flat stomach, fingers delving into the curly thatch nestled below.

Daria's legs opened wider. He slipped a finger into

her slick heat, and she moaned. With a feral smile, he began to work it in and out. Slow, agonizing. He wanted to make her as crazy as she'd made him, send her flying apart. His cock throbbed, begging to be buried inside her. Not yet.

"Ohh! Oh, yeah."

God, she was hot and wet. Ready. His tongue joined his finger, tasting the soft skin. Reveling in her sweet honey. She bucked beneath him, pulling at his shoulders.

"Ryon, make love to me, *please*."

Trembling with need, he covered Daria, bracing his arms on either side of her head. Settling them together intimately, he sank into his mate. Grinding his hips, he filled her as deeply as possible. Their collective gasps rang in his ears, and she gripped his shoulders, urging him.

Ryon began to move, loving her. Never, never anything but this. She surrounded him with warmth, fitting to him perfectly. Never anything so fine, so right as burying himself in this woman. *My mate. Mine.*

"Baby."

Daria buried her fingers in his hair, rising to meet him. He pumped faster, harder, sealing them so tight he couldn't tell where his flesh ended and hers began. They were joined completely, one soul. One mind.

"Ryon!"

She wrapped her legs around his waist and met his thrusts with wild abandon, shredding him. He drove into her again and again, sending them spiraling into space. She stiffened with a cry, clinging to him, and he let go. Shudders racked them, gradually subsiding to a gentle rocking, like a ripple in a pond.

Ryon cradled her as the throes faded, and basked in contentment. He pressed a kiss to her forehead, then collapsed to his back, pulling her into his arms. She snuggled in, resting her head on his chest.

She sighed. "You're the one I want."

Contentment spread through his heart. Daria was his.

And he would never let her go.

Ten

That afternoon, Nick called Ryon and Daria into his office.

He was as serious as Ryon had ever seen him, and got swiftly down to business. "I wanted to talk to you both before I brief the others. I spent quite a bit of time after our conference the other day searching through the lab's files on test subject 356."

"The one Kalen mentioned," Ryon said.

"The same. What I discovered is not what I expected. But it answers a lot of questions, starting with the creature's human identity and why he's here, in the Shoshone."

Ryon exchanged a glance with Daria. "I was going to come and tell you on my own, but Daria and I saw the creature earlier today when we were on our run. Actually, we saw him as a man first and then he changed into the creature."

Nick leaned forward, brows furrowed. "Tell me what happened."

Quickly, Ryon related how they'd been on their run and encountered the white wolf. That she'd led them to the man, and how they'd watched him change into the beast.

"Were you close enough to identify him as a human?"

"No. I'm glad we weren't that close, because that was some scary shit and we weren't equipped to fight him."

"Just as well. Because I know who he is."

Neither of them had a clue where he was going. It sure wasn't where Ryon imagined.

"In the files, test subject 356's real name was recorded on a single document that took forever to find, and I almost missed it." He looked at Ryon's mate. "The name wouldn't have meant much if Jesse hadn't called the other day, telling me your dad had been trying to reach you."

Daria swallowed, growing dread on her face. "Please don't say what I think you are."

"I'm sorry. But subject 356's name was Ben Cantrell."

"Oh, God," she rasped. "Are you sure?"

"Unfortunately, yes. Jesse called in some favors, got us a DNA sample from hair in Cantrell's bathroom. Our own lab performed the DNA test, cross-referencing it with samples of the creature's saliva that was found on the victims."

"No."

"The creature is Cantrell," he said gently. "Daria, I'm very sorry."

Her voice wobbled. "I scented him today, in my wolf form. It *was* Ben, all along."

Part of Ryon hated that she was so upset over the ex-boyfriend. But she had cared for the man at one time, and she had a good heart. It couldn't be easy to hear this about someone she knew, so he forced down his irritation. Besides, he reminded himself, his mate had just spent an afternoon loving on him. Showing Ryon that she was his.

"Can anything be done to help him?"

"I think so, but it's going to be damned difficult to pull off." Opening a file, he slid it across the desk to her and Ryon. "I took the liberty of calling your father. I wanted some insight into Ben from his point of view, and I found out something interesting. Did you know that Cantrell once defended your dad's brother, August, in a criminal case?"

"Of course," she said, brows drawing together. "It was right after we started dating. But what does his defending Uncle August have to do with anything?"

"Plenty. I don't mean to be indelicate, but you do realize that your uncle was not innocent of the charges Cantrell got dismissed, that he's involved in a lot of nefarious dealings, correct?"

"That's why our visits to his estate tapered off over the years. He and my dad could never see eye to eye on that part of August's life. As interesting as this trip down dysfunctional family memory lane is . . ."

"Did you also know your uncle had dealings with a rich entrepreneur by the name of Evan Kerrigan?"

Ryon groaned. "Fuck, no. Say it ain't so, boss."

"Wish I could."

"Someone clue me in? Who's Evan Kerrigan?"

Nick answered. "Kerrigan was an alias used by Malik, the Unseelie King, in his human disguise."

It clicked, and Daria's eyes widened. "You're saying my uncle was in on all of that sick experimentation on the shifters? That—that he's somehow to blame for what's been done to Ben?"

"That's exactly what I'm saying," Nick told her. "When I delved deeper into your uncle's history, I learned that Dr. Gene Bowman was a good friend of his. Your uncle was a financial benefactor of his, along with Malik."

Ryon digested that. "So, you think her uncle had his eye on Ben as a test subject, bided his time, and then, when Ben and Daria broke up, he took the opportunity to snatch the poor bastard?"

"I'm pretty sure that's exactly how it happened. Now, what I've been able to learn is that August Bradford keeps all of his files on his computer at home. Never trusted leaving them at an office somewhere. They're much safer with him." He looked at Daria, who was nodding. "Tell Ryon why."

"Nobody who doesn't know the layout of my uncle's place could possibly hope to steal his files. His estate is only accessible by helicopter. There's no road in or out, and it's situated smack in the middle of fifty or so miles of forest in northern Virginia. The Shenandoah River isn't far from his place."

"How close are you to your uncle?" Nick asked.

"Not at all. And if he's behind what happened to Ben and so many others, I want to do whatever it takes to bring him down," she said fiercely.

"I'm glad you feel that way, because I have an assignment for Ryon. And the catch is, he's going to need you to accompany him."

Ryon bolted upright. "No way. My mate does not go with me on any mission. Ever."

"Um, hello. Your mate is right here, and she can make her own decisions," she hissed angrily.

"Daria—"

"We'll hear Nick out, but it's *my* decision."

She was not going to be swayed. His heart sank as he realized that winning this battle would cost him in the long run. If he left her behind, he'd damage important trust between them. Son of a bitch.

"Fine."

Nick went on. "I believe your uncle has in his possession a lot of important documents about more test subjects, shipments of designer drugs used on shifters, and lists of who's been in business with him. But I also believe that he never would have allowed these experiments without a fail-safe."

"An antidote," Ryon said. "Of course!"

"I believe it's on his computer with everything else we'll need. But we need Daria to get you two in and out. She knows the layout of her uncle's estate, his habits. She knows *him*."

"Just us? None of the others will go with us?"

"No. This has to be a quiet op. Aric and Jax will drop you off. You both get in, access the files, get out undetected. They pick you up again and we have the lab work on the serum. The next time you guys find the creature, he'll get dosed."

"That's a tall order." Ryon shook his head. "I don't like it. I want her to stay here."

"I'll make this simple—without *both* of you, the op will fail. You know I don't interfere with free will, but I'm stating the facts. The decision is up to you two."

"If we don't go?" Ryon asked.

"Maybe one day we'll get another shot at the antidote, and the rest of the files, but that day will be far into the future. In the meantime, lives will be lost without that information—some of them close to us."

"Jesus. You play hardball."

"Again, your choice."

He met Daria's gaze, read the determination there. She was fit, knew the outdoors, could handle herself in that environment as well as he could, probably better. If he left her behind, put their lives before others, it would cause a rift that might never heal.

"We'll do it."

The relief and gratitude on her face was his reward. He just hoped that information was there, as it was supposed to be. That putting his mate at risk was worth it when they saved lives.

"Thank you," she said quietly. "I won't let you down."

"I'm not worried about that. It's me letting *you* down that has me afraid. Stick with me all the way, okay?"

"You bet."

Nick rose. "You've got an hour to pack, and you'll study the map on the way. Take enough supplies for a two-day hike going and coming." He winked at Daria. "A piece of cake for our wildlife biologist."

She started out, and he caught her arm. "I'll just be a second."

"I'll wait down the hall."

Once she was gone, Ryon posed his burning question. "Will I come home from this op alive?"

"I don't know," the commander replied honestly.

"But you wouldn't tell me if you could?"

"Something like that." His voice was strong. "But I do know that you need her on this one. If she doesn't go, the op will fail. And you won't make it home at all."

"Christ," he muttered. "Better get moving, then, right?"

"I'll help you as much as I can from here. You need me, just speak to me."

"I will." He shook his boss's hand, then gave him a slight smile. "Until I get home."

"You bet."

Yep, it must suck to know the future.

In that moment, Ryon wouldn't trade places with Nick for all the money in the world.

Aric and Jax had dropped them off miles from August Bradford's estate with the promise that Ryon would keep in touch, and promise to contact them the instant he knew they were ready for extraction. In advance if possible.

The plan was to pick them up in the same spot. But plans had a way of going FUBAR.

Ryon thought Daria endured the helicopter ride pretty well, considering her white-knuckled fear of flying. She'd gripped his hand tightly the whole time, face ashen, but never commented. After they'd been dropped off, they had hiked the rest of the day, slept that night. Got up and hiked again. While hot, sweaty, and itchy, the trip was uneventful. Scarily so. That should have been his clue that things were about to go tits up.

Getting onto the estate was nerve-racking but surprisingly simple. Daria knew the secret places to hide, the guards' routine. She knew the best route inside, and that the best time to breach the premises was around two in the morning, when the men on watch were sleepy and complacent from guarding such a remote place where nothing ever happened.

Positioning himself in the shadows beside the French doors of the bedroom where she had stayed as a child, he used a claw to cut the glass. Reached inside and unlocked the bolt. Then he gave her a kiss.

"Be careful," he mouthed.

"I will."

And then she was gone. The wait stretched out, interminable.

Dammit straight to hell and back again.

Daria hunched over, intent on the computer screen, fingers tapping a staccato rhythm on the keys. If her uncle or one of his minions caught them here, in his private study, they would make certain she and Ryon disappeared without a trace. It wouldn't be the first time he'd gotten away with murder—but these days August didn't have Gene Bowman to plot with, and the Pack was on to him.

August was going to pay for his part in what he'd done to Ben.

On the heels of that thought, a pair of sad blue eyes haunted her, steeling her resolve. She had resisted Ryon, denied their mating in the beginning, causing them so much grief before she understood—hurting her mate was the same as hurting herself.

She hadn't believed she had a place in his world. Hadn't wanted to accept that she had no say in her own life and he had taken that as rejection.

But she would make it up to Ryon now by helping him and his team see this through. And then August, the bastard, would hang. Beaten at his own despicable game.

Even better than a bullet to his brain.

Right. She'd keep telling herself that, and one day the lie might wash.

"Come on, come on . . ."

The annoying security box popped up again, demanding the correct password. Obviously her dad had been wrong about which one would get her inside. They needed her uncle's medical research notes, his "black book" with the names of his contacts, quantities and dates of massive drug shipments. Drugs that were harmful to shifters, caused addictions of all sorts—and some that created mutant horrors like what Ben had become.

Enough evidence to put August away for good, at her fingertips. And she couldn't get at it.

Ryon's urgent voice pushed into her head. *Baby, get out of there!*

I'm coming, she answered. *Five minutes.*

Hurry.

She glanced out the window at the lightening sky and had to resist pounding her fist on the desk in frustration. She needed more time, and they had none left.

Any moment the estate and surrounding compound would stir to life. Disheartened, she removed her thumb drive from the computer. *So close.* She put it back in the waterproof bag, then zipped the whole thing inside her backpack. After tidying the desk and taking one last look around to make certain she'd left the area exactly as it had been, she eased into the corridor.

Voices and heavy footsteps drifted from the far end around the corner, heading her way at a brisk pace. As fast as she dared without making noise, Daria spun in the opposite direction. Thank goodness they weren't between her and the escape route. Still, she wasn't out of danger.

She wound her way through the maze of corridors, listening as the estate began to awaken. Tonight they would finish the job if it was the last thing they did. Twenty-four hours from now, the information they needed would be in the hands of the Institute's lab people, and a cure could be found for Ben and any other humans and shifters who were out there suffering. God, what she wouldn't give to see the shock on August's despicable face when he realized what she'd done.

Perhaps she would leave her uncle a taunting note guaranteed to give him an even nastier surprise. With this gratifying thought, she let herself back into the guest room and closed the door, leaning against it to calm her jumping nerves. Shoving back a strand of long black hair that had escaped the confines of her ponytail, she blew out a deep breath.

Then she headed for the French doors. She got halfway across the floor before it hit her.

Something was different.

She froze and listened. Nothing moved. The bedroom appeared empty and yet the atmosphere had thickened like the gathering of a storm, morphing into a very real sense of presence. Menacing. Precise as a laser beam, the feeling centered between her shoulder blades.

The closet?

Too late, Daria planted her feet and tensed, ready to confront the unseen threat. A disturbance in the air fanned against her back and before she could turn, a muscular arm snaked around her middle just under her breasts, jerking her back hard. Her breath left in a rush as she slammed against the unyielding form of a massive body. A familiar body, along with the mascu-

line scent of earth and sweat that made her wolf howl
with delight.

"What are you doing?" she hissed.

"Came to get my mate out of here." Kissing her tem-
ple, he grabbed her hand and yanked her toward the
French doors. "Let's go."

Daria hurried to match his stride as he hauled her
out into the morning. He skirted the back of the house,
making his way to the most secluded area of the compound, then stopped. Standing still, he listened for a
long moment, his eyes narrowed. The morning had
lightened enough that she could make out his profile
and the concerned frown pulling down the corners of
his mouth.

"What's wrong?"

He held up a hand to shush her. One minute crept
by. Two. Daria began to grow impatient and started to
tell him so, but he interrupted in the barest whisper.

"What do you see? Hear?"

"Nothing. Why—"

"Shh."

Complete silence. Even the forest ahead, which
should have been coming to noisy life with the chatter
of birds, stood mute as if someone had flipped an off
switch.

"Ambush," he breathed, palming his pistol. "*Run.*"

The import of his words hardly had time to register
when all hell broke loose. Ryon yanked her around the
corner of the house, setting off at a dead run with her
in tow as dozens of men with rifles materialized from

behind the wall they would've scaled. Shouting and cursing, August's security force opened fire.

Long legs pumping, he ran full out, never letting go of her wrist. Daria stumbled, heart in her throat, as more of August's goons rounded the opposite side of the house to intercept them. He veered off and cut through the gardens, using the lush greenery as a cover of sorts from the bullets pelting around them.

Panic washed over her. She and her mate possessed special abilities, but even they would stand little chance against dozens of bullets. How had August learned they were here? For now they were forced to abort their mission. But if they survived this crazy scenario, she'd find a way for them to double back and finish what they'd come for.

Ryon hesitated, scanning the wide expanse of cultivated lawn in front of the estate. Surely he didn't mean to do what it appeared.

He did. The man sprinted across the yard, heading straight for the imposing iron gates at the end of the lawn. Beyond that was nothing but forest. They couldn't have been more exposed if they'd posted targets on their backs, and there was no time to liberate a copter from her uncle.

They skidded to a halt at the gates next to the keypad, and he thrust her toward the panel.

"Do you know the code?"

Men streamed around the house, rifles poised, closing the gap.

"Dad gave it to me, but there's not enough time—"

"The code, Daria!"

Daria punched in the numbers as he dropped to a crouch, tucking the pistol in his waistband and whipping the M16 off his back. So many of them. It struck her as pathetic, one lone man against August's force. Like an ant biting an elephant.

Her mate fired several rounds and they responded in kind. She hit the ground with him, praying as the pop and groan of the mechanism began to swing open the gates. Tiny puffs of dirt kicked up by gunfire came much too close.

"Go! Go!"

Daria shot to her feet and slapped the button to close the gates again, then he hurled her toward the opening. The gates began to reverse direction, and he just managed to slide through after her before they clanged shut.

Clasping her hand, he dragged her through the dense forest, changing directions several times. Once, he halted at the base of a tree, grabbing a heavy backpack he'd left hidden close to the estate. He shrugged it over his shoulders without missing a beat. His pace never faltered, save when the thick undergrowth hampered their progress. Eventually the yells of August's goons faded and disappeared. She'd always stayed in good physical condition, but she thought her lungs might explode if he didn't slow down.

No matter. She'd die before asking him for any favors because she'd practically forced him to allow her to come. He might've read her mind. Where the foliage gave way to a tiny clearing, he stopped and turned to face her, his broad chest heaving.

Sweet Jesus. He affected her like this every time.

Her mate was a sexy beast. Camouflage pants hugged his long thighs and a matching T-shirt with the sleeves cut out displayed the ropy muscles in his arms. Tousled blond hair fell into his blue eyes. He stood with his booted feet planted apart, his gaze like twin lasers raking her in kind. Two hundred pounds of powerful male.

All mine.

Yes, yours, he agreed. His sculpted lips turned upward in his handsome, angular face. A mocking smile, rife with challenge.

Then the reality of their tenuous situation intruded. "That was an epic fucking fail," she groused. "August knew we were coming, or discovered our presence after we arrived. Now what?"

"We retreat, have the team pick us up. We'll have to figure out some other way to get what we need." His face, however, reflected bitter disappointment.

"Absolutely *not*. We can't give up now."

Ryon studied his mate's reaction with fascination. Whether she knew it or not, her whiskey brown eyes were windows straight to her soul. They brimmed with righteous indignation, and no small amount of fear. She looked so lost standing there, so disconsolate, as though she took their failure personally. The idea didn't sit well.

"We did the best we could."

"That's not good enough."

She stood, fists clenched, holding his gaze. Clearly she hated backing down.

"I'm proud to have such a brave mate," he murmured, curling a hand under her chin. "But it's not worth the risk."

"Yes, it is!" Angry, she jerked from his grasp. "Ben is worth the risk! He's a good man who doesn't deserve what they did to him!"

His gut churned. Ben again. Always that goddamned Ben Cantrell, standing smack between him and his mate.

Did the man have any idea of the gift he'd so carelessly lost? Her long raven hair was pulled back into a serviceable ponytail and hung halfway down her back. Her large brown eyes were set in a face that would put any angel from heaven to shame. Tiny laugh lines at the corners of her lips evidenced a passionate woman who often found much joy in her world. The coldness in her stare right now made him loathe the argument that had recently wounded it.

"You know, Ben is part of your past," he said stiffly, striving to keep the hurt and jealousy out of his voice. And failing. "Keep looking into the past and your future just might pass you by. Didn't someone say something similar to me recently?"

She stilled. "You're going to throw that in my face now?"

"Maybe you should figure out once and for all what it is you want, that's all. Let's go."

God, this was going to be a long hike. He could feel Daria glaring holes in his back.

Arrogant jackass!

"What did you say?" he called over his shoulder.

"Nothing." He could practically hear her grit her teeth in annoyance.

No. He wouldn't let her anger get to him. Better that she was mad at him than to have her uncle's men catch up with them.

"How far do we have to walk? I assume you'll do your Telepath thing and have the team pick us up?"

"Eventually. We're off the route we took coming in. From the map, we've got thirty miles to go, give or take."

Daria's protest was swift. "Thirty miles? That's sheer lunacy!"

"What other option do we have? Our wolf forms could handle the trip better, but we have to forgo that because we need our supplies. Besides, you're fit," he pointed out. "You spend half your year in the Shoshone doing research."

"Yes, but I'm not typically fleeing through it at a breakneck pace."

"Need I remind you that you insisted on coming along?" A huff of annoyance was his only answer. "When we reach the rendezvous point, I'll contact the team and they'll pick us up. And for the record, I don't like giving up any more than you do."

Silence, thick and heavy.

He wasn't capable of forcing her to talk any more

than he was able to make her see retreat was for the best. So he started walking, keeping the pace brisk but making certain she was close behind. As they went, he reached out to his commander.

Nick? The op was a bust. We got inside, but somehow August knew we were there.

You two okay?

Yeah, but it was a close call. We're using the alternate escape route, but it will take us a day or more to get to the rendezvous point.

All right. Let me know when you get close and we'll be on our way. And Ryon, be careful.

He smiled at the real concern in Nick's tone. *Will do.*

He wasn't sure how long they'd been under way, but it must've been hours before her breathless voice cut into his brooding.

"Can we rest for a minute?"

He stopped and turned to face her, wry amusement tugging at his lips. "And give August a chance to catch up? Sure, why not. Maybe he'll be so overjoyed to see you that he'll just kill me and spare you. It'll be a regular family reunion."

Ignoring his teasing, Daria shrugged off her backpack, snatched her canteen from inside, and took a draw, careful to conserve the precious water. When finished, she replaced the cap and squinted up at Ryon, who watched her without comment.

"Tell me the story of how you and your SEAL team were turned in Afghanistan," she said quietly.

He sucked in a breath, wondering if this was some

new strategy to prove her point. But he sensed no deception, just an honest desire to know his beginnings as a shifter. "I'm not sure you're ready to hear—"

"Stop protecting me! Trust me to know when I'm ready." Her eyes narrowed, her jaw set.

"All right. When we make camp, I'll tell you everything you want to know."

"Fair enough."

Ryon tensed, then narrowed his gaze in the direction from which they'd come. "Break's over. We'd better get going."

The heat and humidity of the day escalated as they walked until there wasn't a dry thread left on either of their bodies, which didn't do much for their already touchy dispositions.

Ryon pushed on, indifferent to her temper. They stopped only once more for a quick drink of water. "You hungry?"

"Unless you have a T-bone steak hidden in your pack, I'll pass."

"Nope. But I have dried beef, MREs, and energy bars. Or we could always skin a lizard." He waggled his brows, and with a snort, she grabbed her pack and started walking again.

That was the end of the subject of lunch.

Daria was visibly relieved when he announced they'd better find a place to make camp. His chest swelled with pride as he studied his brave mate. She was making the best of an unavoidable—but temporary—situation.

"Right here," he said, pointing.

Ryon led the way into a gnarled mass of vines and overgrown foliage. About twenty yards in, he located a spot where the grasses on the forest floor and the surrounding plants had formed a bowl-shaped bubble perfect to hide them.

Leaving the M16 slung across his back, he swung the large pack to the ground and retrieved a rolled-up piece of canvas strapped in a side holder. He popped it open with a snap and in short order had a small tent in place just big enough for two.

Ryon looked at her and nodded. "It will be hotter than Hades with the thing zipped up, but we should be relatively safe from things that walk, crawl, and slither."

"We could just sleep outside in wolf form," she noted. "It would be cooler."

"It would, but if your uncle's men catch up we'll have to run and leave all of our stuff behind." He shrugged. "We could do that, I suppose. We'd just have to drink out of streams and hunt like real wolves to eat."

She wrinkled her nose. "As much as that idea pleases my wolf, the idea of tearing into raw animal flesh doesn't do a thing for me."

"Then we camp like humans."

She glanced around. "Shouldn't we start building a fire before it gets dark? To keep the other critters away."

"Not unless you want to post a message in neon lights telling August where to find us." He gave her a considering look. "Or maybe you want to have it out with him."

"I do, but not out here, like this."

A flicker of remorse went through him. Heaving a weary sigh, he strode to his pack without a word. He fished around and brought forth two silver packets of MREs, followed by two small metal bowls and spoons used for camping. Placing the bowls on the ground, he knelt and tore the tops off both packets, then poured one into each bowl. Last, he added a bit of water to each and stirred. Finished, he sat cross-legged and held out one of the bowls.

"Your dinner awaits, madam."

Daria walked over and sat beside him. "It only looks slightly better than freshly slaughtered rabbit."

"Sorry. The Four Seasons seems to have misplaced my reservation for this evening."

Sitting beside him, she laid a hand over his. "I don't mean to sound like such a bitch. You're doing the best you can under the circumstances and I've given you a hard time. I want you to know that *you* are the most important thing to me."

He swallowed hard, trying not to appear as vulnerable as he suddenly felt. "Am I?"

"Yes." She paused. "Tell me what happened that day."

"This is hard for me to talk about." Encouragement shone in her whiskey eyes. After a long moment, he began his story as the shadows lengthened in the forest.

"There were six of us on the SEAL team together—me, Jax, Aric, Zander, Micah, Phoenix, and Raven. It was so hot that day, we were about to melt." He laughed softly, the pain always there, under the surface.

"Little did we know that more than half of us were about to die. But not at the hands of any enemy we'd ever seen in our worst nightmares . . ."

6 years earlier . . .

"Jesus Christ, I'm rank," Raven bitched, scratching at his crotch. "When I finally get to change this underwear, it'll probably walk off."

Micah grinned. "With assistance from the crabs you caught from that woman in the last village."

"Shut up, needledick. She did *not* give me crabs."

A few of the guys chuckled but Ryon wasn't paying much attention. He was thinking about his mom and sister, wondering whether he'd make it out of this godforsaken hellhole to see them again. Forget sex. Sweet baby Jesus, what he wouldn't give for a huge bowl of his mom's peach cobbler smothered in vanilla bean ice cream.

Would he be home by Christmas? As they trudged onward, he dreamed of how great the reunion would be. If he got leave, he'd surprise them. Just show up at the house and watch Mom and Lisa screech with joy when he came through the door. He'd bring lots of presents, champagne, and—

"Hold up," Jax whispered, coming to a halt. Tensing, he studied the mountain forest around them, and frowned. Somewhere hidden in the greenery, a footstep crunched to their left. Another to their right. And one from behind.

Ryon and Micah exchanged a fearful look. This area was supposed to be clear, and they couldn't have reached their target's stronghold already. God, they were surrounded!

Then, the forest went silent. Those few heartbeats that followed the utter stillness, those seconds before their lives changed forever, as he locked gazes one by one with Aric, Raven, and the others would haunt him forever.

Thud, thud, thud.

The ground trembled and the leaves shook. When a deep-throated roar split the air, Aric jumped, pointing the muzzle of his M16 into the trees, hands rock steady, a bead of sweat dripping off his nose.

"Fuck," Micah whispered. "What the fuck is that?"

Ryon stared in horror. The thing that broke through the foliage to their left stood erect on two legs, and was more than seven feet tall. Covered with a thick mat of grayish brown fur, it had a long torso, two arms, muscular shoulders, and a head sporting two upright ears and a long, snarling snout full of sharp teeth.

It looked like a creature that was half man, half wolf. He and his team stared, mouths open, fingers frozen on their triggers.

How things might have been salvaged, disaster averted, they'd never know. Because their buddy Jones started screaming, pumping bullets into the beast's chest. After that, everything went to shit.

The creature staggered backward and then rallied

quickly, rushing Jones. With a swipe of a paw the size of a dinner plate, the big bastard ripped out Jones's throat, tossing him aside like a twig. Then it pounced on Raven, biting into the vee of his neck and shoulder as the man screamed.

They opened fire just as several more of the beasts emerged from the forest. It quickly became apparent that while their bullets could wound, it would take something with far more power to kill them. Aric dropped into a crouch and desperately palmed a grenade as his friends fell all around him, waging a battle they couldn't win. The one who'd killed Jones shook Raven like a rag doll, released him, and ran toward Aric, who let a grenade fly. It hit at the target's feet and exploded, sending the damned thing to hell. But it wasn't enough.

Micah went down, his knife in hand, slitting one's throat. But another jumped on him, and his struggle was short-lived, his scream terrible. Jax fell next, then their CO Prescott, Zan, Nix, and so many others. All of them, one by one. Dead or dying.

Unsheathing his own knife, Aric spun to face the beast coming up on his flank. "Come on, bitch," he hissed. "Let's dance."

Ryon lost track of the battle around him as one of the creatures rushed him. Barreled into him like a freight train and took him to the ground. His M16 was knocked into the air, raining a spray of bullets into the trees. The weapon landed several feet away, useless.

Frantic, Ryon called on his gift as a Telepath. It was all he had. *Help me, somebody! Oh, God—*

Razor-sharp claws tore into Ryon's stomach and his agonized screams joined those of his comrades'. There was no one to help. Nothing to be done. The creature jerked him up and tore into his neck with those massive teeth, blood soaking them both. Dimly, he became aware of Aric shouting his rage at the beasts.

"Take that, cocksucker!"

As the creature dropped Ryon, he saw the impossible—Aric unleashed a blast of fire from his palms. The flames shot out and engulfed one of the beasts, which dropped to the ground, screeching and writhing as it burned. Aric torched three more wolves, then more still, until the fire was depleted. Suddenly the flames died, and one of the remaining beasts advanced, wearing a sinister expression that could pass for a grin. Aric faced it head-on, without flinching.

"Come on, you ugly fucker. Come to papa."

Whether it understood, Ryon couldn't have said. But it ran at Aric, and his friend braced himself. The beast took him to the ground and his back hit hard as Aric pulled the pin of a grenade.

The wolf brought its nose to Aric's, mouth open, fangs dripping with bloody saliva. Seizing his opening, Aric rammed his fist down the beast's throat, pushing his arm as far as it would go. Immediately, the thing gagged and jerked backward reflexively, clawing at his shoulder and arm to dislodge him. Aric scrambled back as far from the beast as he could.

The grenade detonated, spraying fur, blood, and entrails everywhere.

Ryon lay there, his lifeblood flowing from his body. Strange that in this place of soul-searing heat, he could feel cold.

As his vision faded, his body growing heavy, he heard Zan move to Aric, begging their friend to hang on. What in the hell did Zan think he was going to do? Fetch a needle and thread and stitch their mangled limbs and torsos back together?

Ryon couldn't see at all and could barely hear by the time a hand touched his shoulder.

"Ryon, hang on," Zan ordered from somewhere far away. "I'm a Healer, and you're going to be okay."

Warmth began to spread throughout his limbs. But despite his friend's healing ability, it would be a very, very long time before any of the survivors of this horror were all right.

The Christmas reunion that he'd dreamed of, the promise of which had urged him over every rock and around every tree in that godforsaken country, never did happen.

It would be months before he was well enough to learn that his mom and Lisa had died in a car accident on the way to the airport. They'd been trying to reach Ryon's side.

He was alone in the world, and couldn't help but think it would've been better if he had died, too.

"I'm so sorry," Daria whispered.

Jerked back into the present, Ryon gave her a small smile. "That was years ago, and Mom and sis would both kick my ass for thinking like that. It's what got me through."

Scooting close, she cupped his face in her hands. "I love you, my mate. You're not alone. Not anymore."

His breath caught. "You mean that?"

"Yes. More than anything. I know we haven't been together long, but I *know*."

He crushed her to him, pulling her into his lap. "I love you, too. So much, baby."

Right there, he peeled away her top. Freed her breasts and tossed the bra aside. He moaned as she leaned into him, nibbling his jaw and neck, hands exploring his chest and stomach.

Her fingers found his pants and freed him. Grasping his hard, needy flesh, she pumped him slowly, driving him insane. He growled as she moved off him briefly to rid herself of her own pants and underwear, but he took the opportunity to remove his, too. Then she was straddling his lap facing him, the warmth of her sex nestled against his throbbing rod.

Her mouth met his in a clash, their desire rising like a red tide. She smelled so damned good to his wolf, and when she wiggled on him, he nearly came like a teenager. Their tongues tangled and tasted, and he moved against her, making his intent clear.

Reaching between them, she guided the head of his cock to her entrance, and sank down on his shaft. He closed his eyes in pure bliss as her heat gripped and stroked his sensitive cock. The fire built steadily, threatening to send him over the edge much sooner than he wanted.

But any hope of holding back was lost when she urged, "Claim me, the way it should have been for us the first time! Please!"

His fangs lengthened, and with a low, feral snarl he struck, sinking them into the soft skin of her shoulder. She cried out as her sweet essence flooded his mouth. So much more mind-blowing than the bite he'd given her to save her life. His senses detonated, along with his release.

He shot into her, and his pleasure was increased when she tightened around him, clinging as she found her climax. They shuddered together endlessly, breathing hard when they finally came down from the incredible high.

For a time, he simply held her. Pressed tender kisses to her neck, lips, everywhere he could reach. Then he gently sat her aside, cleaned them both as best as he could. Then he took her inside the tent and spooned her, never wanting to let go.

Daria loved him.

That was all he needed in this world. At peace, he fell into a deep sleep.

A finger of guilt pricked at Daria's conscience. She loved him to distraction, and that's what made her decision so difficult.

Like his Pack friends, Ryon was stubborn to the core.

Once he'd set his path, there was no straying from it. He was taking her out of her uncle's territory, to meet his team. They would leave here and she would never get another crack at stopping August's nefarious practices.

She would be tempted to give up, let the Pack handle what to do next—if Ryon had never told her the story of how his team was turned. Everything for the Pack began there. Because of whoever had made those rogue wolf shifters, her new friends had suffered. Just as Ben now suffered because of what her uncle, Bowman, and Malik had done.

She could not, in good conscience, leave and go on about her life knowing that August was getting away with crimes worse than murder. She would not risk him coming back to haunt her family and friends.

Ryon rolled away from her, grumbled a bit, and fell silent. Daria's guilt ate at her conscience long after his breathing had evened out in sleep.

Long after she left his side and slipped into the night.

Eleven

R yon's curse knifed through the pitch-blackness as he patted the empty place where Daria had been.

Cool to the touch. He raked a hand through his hair in frustration. How long had she been gone? Five minutes or five hours? It took a matter of mere seconds to meet with death in the forest, especially at night.

Sweet Jesus. Since his wolf's night vision didn't work well unless he was in that form, he fumbled and located the flashlight he'd brought inside the tent. Because the light could alert any of August's goons camped nearby, he'd saved it for emergency use only. The thought of Daria stumbling across a band of men armed with assault rifles, or Ben in his bestial form, more than qualified.

He checked his watch. Half past midnight. She had as much as two hours on him. When he caught up with her, he was going to shake her teeth loose. What was she thinking? She wasn't, plain and simple. She'd let emotion overcome good judgment and escalated the danger they were already in.

Working quickly by flashlight, Ryon broke camp and tidied the area, making sure that he'd left behind no trace of their stay. A fleeting worry that she'd come back here to find him gone niggled at his brain. What if she'd only stepped away to take care of personal needs? He reached out through their bond.

Daria? No answer.

He tried again, waited ten more minutes, then dismissed the possibility of her absence being temporary. She'd left with no intention of coming back until she'd returned to August's estate and taken care of unfinished business. He had to give her points for having the temerity to see their op through. Unfortunately, he had to deduct them for lack of good sense.

Grinning now, he dug in his pack. His mate wouldn't get far, even armed with her own flashlight. Because of his secret weapon, she'd lose ground fast. He dug some more and the grin began to fade. No. She couldn't have—

"Dammit!"

The night vision goggles were gone. They would make traveling much easier for her. If she had a big head start, they were in deep trouble. Glancing at the compass on his watch, he got his bearings.

Ryon gambled that she'd circle around to the north, then west to stay on the left of August's goons and keep the river on her right. Hundreds of miles of untouched forest spread to the south, so it seemed reasonable that she wouldn't take that route.

Unless she'd figured he would see it that way. He muttered another curse. Christ, what a mess. In the end, he settled on the northwest route. His gut told him that she would choose the quickest, safest way to reach her goal. She wasn't stubborn enough to risk getting lost just to throw him off. He hoped.

The trek was slow going. His flashlight, though powerful, could illuminate only a few feet in front of him due to the dense tangle of plants that served as a barrier between him and what might be waiting beyond them. The world ended in darkness five feet in front of his body and slid at his back. It was a creepy sensation he could've done without. Even his wolf whined.

Ryon pushed on until daybreak. By then he worried that the security force had found her, or he'd missed her altogether. If August hurt her, Ryon would take the man to hell with him. His sharpened eyesight and smell had picked up a faint trail , but what if he was too late? Three hours past sunrise, fear had replaced worry. Without the cloak of night to hamper his tracking, he should've run her down by now.

What if thrummed in his brain. His nighttime jaunt had left him tired and desperate. Stopping for a drink and to decide where to go next, he was reaching into his pack when he saw it.

There, hardly visible through the trees. A sliver of black T-shirt and long black hair.

Daria sat on a rotten log not twenty yards from where he stood, his night vision goggles resting beside her. She was so perfectly still on her perch, she had to have heard him approaching. The woman had planned on letting him march right by! His rare temper exploded. He stomped through the trees toward her, thinking it odd that she didn't turn around.

"That's right, it won't do you any good to run!" he yelled. "You'll be lucky if I don't handcuff us together, *mate*."

Daria didn't react. Ryon stepped over the log, continuing his tirade and reaching out to grab her arm at the same time.

"Jesus Christ, do you have any idea how stupid—"

"Snake," she whispered.

Ryon's hand—and his blood—froze. Her brown eyes were wide with terror, her face ashen. He didn't move and for a few seconds, didn't breathe. *Calm, stay calm.*

"Where?" He had to strain to hear her answer.

"In my shirt."

Son of a bitch.

"Front or back?"

"Front. I think it's asleep."

He studied the front of her shirt and noted the barely perceptible bulge at her stomach. The snake must be small, but in nature, a creature's size didn't matter at all. In fact, the smaller the animal the more venomous nature seemed to have made it in compensation. Even her wolf might not be able to recover from the poison.

"I'll be right back," he said, keeping his tone soft and even.

Ryon straightened and backed away, making as little noise as possible. Her eyes locked with his, frightened and beseeching. God, he might've startled the thing into biting her if he'd jerked her arm. He berated himself for an idiot. He should have known better when he'd seen her frozen like a statue.

He retrieved his pack and returned to stand behind her, agonizing over what to do. They couldn't wait out the serpent, that much was obvious. It had found a nice, comfy nest to sleep away the day and most likely wouldn't move again until nightfall. Daria would pass out first, either from exhaustion or fright.

"I'm going to cut your shirt off. It's the only way."

"Okay. Ryon, I—"

"Shh. Stop talking."

"Hurry."

Slipping a hunting knife from his boot, Ryon fought to quiet his racing heart. Hands trembling, he pushed her ponytail aside, grasped her T-shirt at the collar with one hand, and positioned the blade of the knife pointing downward. Slowly he began to cut, splitting the shirt open at her back. Her lacy white bra peeked at him from beneath, hugging perfect bronze skin. His gut knotted and he forced himself not to think of what would happen to that perfection if he failed.

Next he made a cut from each armhole in order to let the garment fall away from her skin without jostling the snake. Last, he tugged the shirt from her waistband, inch by torturous inch, until all that remained to be done was lift it away—hitchhiker and all.

Moving around to her front, Ryon knelt between her splayed legs. Sweat trickled into his eyes. He swiped an arm across his brow, then began to pull the shirt off, gathering it at her stomach. He looked into her white face and nodded.

"I'm going to put my hand underneath the snake to support it as I lift it away. Here goes."

Ryon carefully slid one hand under the bundle, the other on top. He had to resist the strong urge to lurch to his feet and sling the creature. A sudden move, however, would result in one of them getting bitten. Legs shaking, he stood with agonizing slowness. As he did, part of the mutilated material slid off the creature to reveal its head and color pattern.

Red and yellow kills a fellow, red and black, friend of Jack. His heart slammed painfully against his ribs. Death rested in his hands. Awake now, the coral snake raised its head to stare at him with cold, beady eyes, tongue flicking. Never taking his attention from the serpent, Ryon continued to back away from Daria until he was positive she was out of danger.

With all his strength, he flung it far out into the forest.

"Oh God!" Daria's voice broke and she buried her face in her hands, elbows on her knees. "I sat down to rest and that thing crawled up my arm and into my shirt. I couldn't move."

Ryon reached her in two long strides and sat on the

log beside her. Without thinking, he wrapped his arms around her and gathered her against his chest. His body leapt to painful awareness of hers pressed close, trembling, her skin smooth as silk under his roughened palms. Her dark head was tucked under his chin, one hand clutching the front of his shirt as though she'd never let go. Fierce protectiveness swelled around his heart, making his chest ache.

"It's all right," he crooned. "You're okay. I'm here, baby." He murmured other things too, lilting words he knew she didn't catch—but she didn't have to know their meaning to allow them to soothe her. She began to relax.

"Never run from me again," he rasped. "Never. Swear it to me."

"I swear."

For a while she was content to let him hold her, accepting the comfort he offered. At last, she drew away and wiped at her face. He felt the loss of her warmth, immediate and disconcerting.

She heaved a deep, shaky breath and Ryon tried not to stare at the ample swell of her creamy breasts. The lacy scrap of material posing as a bra didn't do much to hide them, and now wasn't the time to indulge in some afternoon delight. With an effort, he moved his gaze north and kept his attention focused on her face. Mostly.

"Thank you." She sniffed.

He cleared his throat. "You're my mate. There's no way I'd let anything happen to you."

"I'm sorry I left without telling you." She stared at the ground, miserable. "But I can't give up, Ryon. I can't just leave without getting the information we need."

Ryon gaped at her. "Are you kidding me? Daria, meeting up with a poisonous snake is only one of a hundred dangers you could've run up against. You promised me you wouldn't run again."

"And I won't. But what August is doing is terrible, and stopping him will save lives. I need your help to bring him down."

"To help Ben, you mean," he said bitterly. Instantly, he regretted letting out the green-eyed monster, but she took his hand, shaking her head.

"Not just him. Everyone who's been ruined by him, Bowman, and Malik. This might be our only chance."

Exasperating woman! "I'll think about it, but that's all I'm saying." Ryon stood and offered her his hand. "Do you have an extra shirt?"

A flush colored her cheeks and anger flashed in her eyes, but she nodded and took his hand, allowing him to help her up.

Daria fished through her pack for the garment. Ryon was disappointed when she brought forth a camouflage T-shirt and slipped it over her head, covering her beautiful skin. He didn't know what he wanted to do more—strangle her or make love to her. Then she walked the few yards to where her mangled black shirt rested on the ground, poked it with her foot, stooped, and retrieved it.

"Never know when a rag might come in handy," she speculated, stuffing it into her pack.

Ryon didn't answer. Had he detected a sound to the west? A movement? The hair on the back of his neck prickled, but it could be his overwrought imagination, nothing more.

A flash of metal through the trees caught the corner of his eye a split second before he spun, bracing the M16 at his shoulder.

"Daria, go!" he shouted.

To her credit, she didn't hesitate. She swept the pack onto one shoulder and bolted in the opposite direction as the forest came alive with bodies.

The figures seemed to detach themselves from the forest wall like demons from the underworld, come to claim his soul. And he should know.

But not today, dammit. He sprayed the area with a round of ammo to buy them precious seconds. The men fell back, ducking behind cover, giving Ryon an instant to whirl and sprint after Daria before they returned fire.

She negotiated the undergrowth like a swift deer and he had to work to catch up. He barely heard the rhythmic tap of the gunfire over the blood rushing in his ears. He'd almost reached her when she stumbled over a root and went sprawling with a cry. He paused a beat long enough to grab the back of her shirt, yank up hard, and drag her in his wake.

Branches and vines tore at their faces and clothing, scratched their arms. Wouldn't matter much with a bullet in each of their backs, though, especially if the men were using silver. But that paled in comparison to the horrors August was capable of should they be captured alive.

Ryon pushed harder. Taking a detour south, he hoped to throw the men off the trail. They would look for him to stay close to the river, so he'd do the opposite. After a while, the shouts and curses disappeared, so it seemed to have worked.

He stopped, holding fast to her arm, and listened.

Time stretched out and the whistles of the colorful birds all around them resumed. Ryon let out the breath he'd been holding. Thank God, they'd lost the goons.

Daria tugged her hand free of his and put her hands on her hips, shooting him an annoyed look. The stance made her the very picture of a perturbed dark angel and he had to resist the urge to grin.

"Well, I hope you're happy with yourself."

Ryon's jaw dropped. "Me? You're the one who—"

She stepped close and touched his right arm. "You're bleeding."

Ryon glanced at himself. A gouge marred his biceps where one of the bullets had grazed him. Blood trailed in a thin line down his arm and dripped off his fingers. He shrugged. "I'll heal. Let's get moving."

Giving her a quick kiss, Ryon caught a glimpse of the exasperation that flashed across her face before he took her hand, turned, and strode through the trees.

Ryon pushed them east as fast as he could hack through the dense undergrowth. Daria had been silent for several hours, holding her own without complaint or asking him again to consider turning back. They'd stopped only twice for a quick drink of water and a brief rest.

By the second break, he could see exhaustion taking its toll on her. Long strands of dark hair had escaped from her ponytail, and floated around her face in disarray. She sat on the spongy earth, legs drawn up to her chest, and hugged her knees, staring into the forest with an expression that had taken his breath away. The look went deeper than grief, more eloquent than tears, and it had cut Ryon to the bone.

She hated to give up. He was forcing her to abandon finding the cure for Ben, at least temporarily.

"When are we going to turn north?" Daria asked.

"Tomorrow we'll head that way gradually, and make our way toward the rendezvous point at an angle. If we push hard, we can still reach the team before August intercepts us."

"How long will it take us, at this rate?"

"By the afternoon, maybe sooner. Provided you don't lead me on any more wild-goose chases."

A soft groan sounded at his back. They'd have to haul ass to stay one step ahead of August and reach the Pack that fast. Still, she offered no complaint.

Ryon had to admire her courage, and he understood her need to bring down August all too well. Yeah, he'd get the sonofabitch even if he had to come back here alone to do it. The last few years had been about healing, then starting his new job with the Pack.

He'd tried to keep his mind off the nightmare of his past by diving into one dangerous assignment after another. Rebuilding his life, securing his future. Then disaster had blindsided him yet again when his team had been ambushed months ago, and he'd driven himself even harder.

"When will we make camp?"

"As soon as I find a good spot. It'll be dark shortly."

She muttered, "About time." He couldn't help smiling to himself. That his mate allowed the smallest gripe to pass her lips testified to how wiped out she must be.

He wasted no time finding a secluded area similar to where he'd pitched the tent last night. Working to beat the coming darkness, he quickly erected the shelter, making certain the material couldn't be seen easily.

"Looks good," Daria approved. "I don't think anyone passing by could spot it."

"Let's hope we don't have to find out."

"Yeah. Hungry?" She waved a hand at the ground behind her. The two metal bowls had been placed on a blanket, along with a strip of jerky for each of them. "Instant beef stew. I'm starving and somehow getting less picky by the hour."

"Me, too," he admitted. His stomach grumbled as he joined her. "I appreciate it."

They sat cross-legged on the blanket facing each other. Daria picked up her bowl, sniffed, and wrinkled her nose.

"You know, this stuff isn't that bad and I'm used to it, but there's something mildly disturbing about food that poofs out when you add water. How do they *do* that?"

Ryon laughed, and she smiled back. His heart did a funny leap in his chest. "One of life's great mysteries, I suppose."

"I'd say you're one of those mysteries," she retorted, waggling her spoon at him. "Every bit as interesting as old, dried up beef, and twice as tough."

He barked another laugh, nearly choking on his stew. "Gee, you'd better stop with the compliments before my ego explodes my brain."

"Sorry. Guess I'm getting punchy." She hesitated, then observed him thoughtfully. "Tell me about you, or your family."

"What's to know?" He stared, admiring the way the corners of her eyes crinkled with tiny crow's-feet when she smiled. Her full lips, the graceful curve of her jaw.

"Where did you grow up?"

"Atlanta, Georgia, armpit of the South." He didn't offer more, and she put down her bowl, throwing him an exasperated look.

"You're not going to make this easy, are you?"

"Nope. You compared me to dehydrated meat. I'm still recovering."

"Jeez, we're touchy." She leaned forward, peering intently into his face. As she did, Ryon tried not to stare at the perfect roundness of her breasts pushing against her T-shirt.

"What?"

"You told me some about your mom and sister. What about your father?"

His throat tightened. "He was a Marine lieutenant.

He was killed in action in Operation Desert Storm when I was a boy."

Daria laid a hand over his. "I'm sorry," she said softly.

"It was a long time ago. And I had Mom to put up with me, bless her." He smiled. "Lisa came along later, from her marriage to my stepdad."

Daria cocked her head, an odd look on her face. "Do you ever see him?"

"Not often. We call once in a while, send Christmas cards. I really should make more of an effort since the man helped raise me, but we were never all that close. What about your dad? Your father must be a special man."

"He's the best. When he retired from studying wolves, I couldn't wait to take over where he left off. We're very close, but we don't get to see each other as much as we'd like."

"After we've put Ben to rights, we'll visit him." *If we aren't forced to destroy Ben first* went unsaid.

Daria gave him a wan smile. "I'd like that, and so would Dad."

Neither of them felt much like talking after that. In silence, they cleaned their bowls and utensils with leaves, which they buried to avoid attracting unwanted nighttime guests. With nothing else to do, they readied themselves to bed down. Daria changed into a pair of shorts, muttering that it was too hot to sleep in her pants.

Ryon tried not to stare as she emerged, and failed.

Her long legs were slender, toned, and tanned. He could imagine them wrapped around his waist while he pounded into her with precision. He never tired of fucking her. Not tonight, though. They needed rest.

"God, I wish I could risk even one ounce of our water supply to wash off." She spared a longing glance for the canteen next to her pack.

"I'll try to find us a safe place tomorrow. With any luck, we'll run into one of the tributaries branching off of the river."

"Ohh, that would be *fantastic*."

Idiot! Had he lost his mind? Facing a firing squad would be less torture than guarding Daria while she bathed. They'd never reach his team if he banged her all the way across the forest.

They settled into the shelter, lying on their backs, neither one speaking. The quiet between them was companionable.

If only he could silence the chaos in his mind so easily. If he had to kill Ben, she would hate him forever.

You don't know for sure! She'd forgive you. Right?

Ryon couldn't handle the truth. Not now. He shoved it away, but it loomed. As deadly as the coral snake, waiting to strike, to poison his blood. His soul.

Damn you, Ben Cantrell. He slid into fitful dreams, the echo of Cantrell's screams winging him into the darkness.

Ryon surfaced by slow degrees. He couldn't move. Pressure on his legs, his chest. The waking dream collided with his nightmare. He called out.

Daria? No!

But the cry reverberated only in his mind. His lips wouldn't move.

Where was his mate? Trapped. Blood. Soaking his clothes, his hair. Drowning in a crimson river.

Ryon!

Forgive me, forgive me . . .

"Ryon!"

He came awake with a jolt and the nightmare broke apart, the tendrils of unspeakable terror receding into the gloom. The pressure on his body remained, and he realized that someone was half draped across him. A hand was clamped over his mouth.

"Shh," Daria whispered, urgent.

Ryon tensed, listening. Nothing at first, and then . . . The distant call of a night bird to the north, and an answering call to the west. The rest of the forest had gone unnaturally still. A chill of fear zinged down his spine. Christ, August had his goons searching for them before dawn!

They were so close his wolf could practically smell them. Waiting. Footsteps crept through the brush around them, so furtive the slight movements might never have awakened him. Sweat streamed down the sides of his face. Daria removed her hand from his mouth but remained motionless on top of him, breasts crushed against his chest through the fabric of their T-shirts. The thundering of her heart matched his own.

Ryon stretched out an arm and felt for his M16. His fingers found the stock and closed around it, but the weapon's presence gave him little relief. They were sitting ducks. If their hideout was discovered, he'd take out as many of them as he could, but he'd be firing blind. No doubt, they were well equipped with night vision goggles, and his pair was stowed in his pack. He didn't dare risk making noise by digging for them.

The footsteps receded and the calls faded, melting into the returning blurbs and shrieks of the forest's nocturnal inhabitants. Long, agonizing minutes inched by, became an hour. Finally, Daria slid off him, slow and careful. When the first gray streaks of dawn began to lighten their view, Ryon put a finger to his lips and motioned his intent to take a look around.

Daria gave a small nod and mouthed *be careful*. He sent her what he hoped to be a reassuring smile, then palmed the rifle and crawled from the tent opening on his belly. Bracing the rifle against his shoulder, he half expected his appearance to draw fire.

Nothing.

Only the busy chatter of day creatures awakening all around them. The men had probably moved on. He waited several more minutes, then rose to one knee. Still nothing. He stood, then made a quick sweep around the area. Satisfied, he returned to the shelter.

"Come on out. It's clear."

Daria joined him, glancing around. "Are you sure?"

"Yeah. They've gone. The problem is, they're fanned out, moving in a straight line in the same direction we want to go—toward our rendezvous point. And now they're *ahead* of us, or at least this squad is, rather than behind."

Her brown eyes widened. "Oh, God. That means we're literally surrounded."

"We can assume so. The good news is they don't know that, or we would already be dead."

"Somehow, honey, I don't find that very promising."

"We're breathing. For now, that will have to do." Ryon paused, considering the wisdom of his next move. "You need a weapon."

"I'm not exactly a marksman."

"Desperate times." Bending, he retrieved the handgun strapped to his ankle. Straightening, he held it out to her, butt first. "Three fifty-seven SIG. Can you handle it?"

Daria took it from him, mouth falling open. "You're trusting me with this?"

"I'm not worried about your abilities. Just point and shoot if you have to, but watch the recoil."

She studied it dubiously. "All right. I'll do my best."

"That's all either of us can do," he said quietly. "Ready?"

"We're keeping to the plan? This would be the perfect time to turn back and get the evidence we need," she said eagerly. "August would never expect it."

Grabbing his pack, Ryon stood for a moment, thinking of the pros and cons. With the majority of August's men out searching for them, she was right. He just didn't want to admit it. After a long moment, he let out a sigh. "You make a really good point."

Her eyes widened and she stepped into him, placing her palms on his chest. "You mean that?"

"Yeah. I do." At last, he forced himself to swallow his pride and jealousy. It was a bit rough going down. "Ben is important to you, so he is to me, too. I want to help him and anyone else out there who's been hurt by those experiments."

She flung her arms around his neck and kissed him soundly. He had to force his mind from taking her then and there, no matter how badly he wanted to do it. Reluctantly he let her go and they got ready.

Daria changed back into her dark fatigues for the day's hike, tucking the gun into the waistband. Then she took two protein bars from her pack and handed one to Ryon.

"Here. Quick energy before we go."

"Thanks. Until now, I can't remember when I've ever looked forward to eating compressed sawdust." He unwrapped the bar and consumed half of the nasty thing in one bite. "I'm so hungry, I'd give my firstborn for a plate of bacon and eggs."

"Think about something else. How's the arm?"

Ryon glanced at the scratch. "A little sore, that's all. I'd nearly forgotten it."

She stuffed the rest of the bar into her mouth, then peered at his arm. "Looking good. No sign of infection."

"Thanks, Doc." His lips turned up. "You are a woman of many talents, my mate."

"You have no idea," she teased, hefting her pack.

"Oh, I think I do."

As they headed back, making a wide berth to avoid any of the goons that might've been behind them, he reached out to Nick.

Change of plans, boss. Most of August's men passed us, so we're going back to take one more crack at getting that evidence.

All right, but be careful. There's been a development.

Ryon tensed. *What's going on?*

The creature isn't here in the Shoshone anymore. We don't think he's anywhere around, in fact.

He let that sink in, and his blood chilled. *You think he's coming here?*

I'd say it's highly possible.

How fast can he possibly get here on foot?

Pretty damned fast if he was given any Tracing abilities during the experiments. The park rangers here have reported three more kills that are less than a day old—and each kill is more than twelve miles apart. No way could he have covered that wide an area on foot in one night.

Shit! But why would he come here?

I'm guessing he's going after August, or you and Daria. Perhaps he senses that Daria is gone. Keep your eyes open.

Very funny, boss. He's fucking invisible!

Not totally, Nick reminded him. *Watch for irregular patterns around you, like a clear kaleidoscope effect. You can spot him.*

Thanks for the pep talk.

Hang in there. Shoot us the information the second you break into his files. If there's a cure present, we'll give it to

the lab and have them get right to work on it. Then, when we
get the word from you, we'll go wheels up and head out to
retrieve you both.

Thanks, Nick.

Talk soon.

"Daria, hold up." She stopped, looking at him questioningly. "Bad news—Ben is on the move."

"In his beast form?" she asked in a quiet voice.

"Unfortunately, that's likely the case. Nick thinks he might be headed this way, maybe coming after us or your uncle."

Her face paled. "Now we've *got* to get that cure. We're running out of time and we've got nothing effective to fight him with."

He nodded. "Seems you were right all along and I've been a fool."

"Give yourself a break. We were being pursued and shot at. You were protecting me."

"Thanks, sweetheart. Ready?"

"As I'll ever be."

As they started off again, a shadow passed over his soul. This was a suicide mission.

And even Nick wasn't saying whether Ryon would make it home alive.

Twelve

For hours, Daria trudged along behind Ryon, staring at his perfect backside. How wonderful was her mate for seeing this through? She craved justice against August for what he'd done to Ben, and she'd have it. Ben had been a fine man, a good friend. As lovers, however, she and Ben were all wrong for each other and the parting had been painful.

But she'd done her share of grieving, and had come out the other side. After a long, desolate stretch, Ryon had awakened the longing to be touched, held. Wrapped in Ryon's arms, she finally knew what it meant to find the other half of her soul.

"Check this out."

Ryon halted in his tracks, staring ahead. The trail had led them to a small pond about a quarter of the size of a football field. The thick foliage surrounding the banks made it seem much smaller, more secluded. Sunlight filtered through the forest canopy, causing lovely dappled patterns across the greenery and glassy surface. Huge old trees stood sentry at the perimeter of the bank, their dark roots extending into the water like bony fingers. Several azure butterflies floated on the air, some drinking from large flowers.

"Oh, wow! It's gorgeous!" Daria tugged on his arm, as excited as a child. "I'm *so* hot and grimy, could we cool off? *Please?*"

"I don't know." He scowled, taking in the area. "Let me try something first. Give me a bit of your jerky."

"What for?" Curious, she wasted no time setting down her pack and fetching the beef, especially if it meant a bath. She opened the bag, tore off a piece, and handed it to him.

"Watch."

Ryon tossed the dried meat into the center of the pond. Nothing happened at first, but gradually, tiny ripples broke at the surface of the water, like a pot beginning to boil. The action, however, never became frenzied. The fish nibbled at the treat until nothing remained, then disappeared. All was calm again. Nothing else moved.

"You were testing the pond for dangerous critters," she remarked. "I'm impressed. I probably wouldn't have thought to toss out bait."

"Just a precaution. We're close to the estate again, and getting eaten by something mutated that August helped create would ruin my day. It appears safe enough, but I'll go first. Pull up a tree root and try not to get into any trouble." He gave a lopsided grin. "And no peeking."

"Huh. Don't flatter yourself."

From his smirk, he knew she was teasing. She didn't turn away as he peeled off his dark T-shirt. When he tossed it aside, sent her a smoldering look, and went for the zipper on his fatigues, she did moan. A low, deep laugh rumbled from his chest, warming her like a shot of the whiskey she wished she'd brought along.

Daria sat on a big root, eyeing him as removed his pants and rustled through his belongings. The water swirled invitingly as he waded in. Dear Lord, Ryon belonged on one of those hunk-of-the-month calendars. The man possessed a body to rival a Greek god. Silky blond hair brushed his neck. The lean muscles of his back and arms bunched under golden skin. His chiseled butt cried out for her hands.

He waded out until the water lapped at his hips and turned so that she had a great side profile. Then he leaned back and dunked his head, giving her a tantalizing view of his chest and ripped abs. *Whoa, baby!*

Ryon straightened and began to lather his hair with a bar of soap she hadn't noticed in his hand. He repeated the procedure all over his upper body until she actually began to feel envious of the bubbles. He dunked himself twice to rinse, then swiped the water out of his face with his free hand. Without warning, he spun and grinned at her.

"Enjoying the show, baby?"

"I was just scouting the area for danger," she quipped.

His grin widened into a blinding smile. "Your concern for my safety is heartwarming, but the only dangerous animal around here will be me if you keep eyeballing me like I'm a steak."

"Deal with it."

Laughing, he finished up. Then he got out, used the blanket to pat dry, and got dressed. Too bad. She rose from her gnarly perch as he was pulling on a clean shirt, still favoring his side. He donned clean fatigues as well.

"I'd like to wash our dirty clothes before we leave so we can lay them out tonight to dry," she commented. "No telling when we'll find another good place to get clean."

"Good idea."

Daria discarded her clothing as fast as humanly possible, grabbed the soap, and dashed for the water. She plunged into the pond and faced Ryon, making sure her breasts were well within his appreciative view.

"Oh, it's so warm!" she called to him. "This feels terrific."

"Doesn't it?" He didn't look like he was thinking about the water as he eyed her.

"I'll never take my shower at home for granted again."

He laughed once more. She loved the rich sound. As she scrubbed herself from head to toe, she spent the time contemplating how to get him to do it often. And that voice, made for a darkened bedroom and tangled sheets on a hot summer night? Made her wet.

Rinsing the last of the soap from her body, she pushed her wet hair back and opened her eyes to see Ryon grinning at her like a fool. "Nice show."

"Hey, no fair!" she squeaked playfully. She smiled back—and then a strange thing happened.

Ryon's grin withered, and he rose slowly, frowning, looking past her.

"What is it?"

His expression bloomed into a mask of horror, and he yelled at her. "Get out of the water! Get out!"

Ryon stooped, retrieved the knife from his boot and broke into a dead run as Daria spun about. Nothing but a weird ripple in the water, no more than fifteen feet away. No, not just a ripple. More like something gliding, but she couldn't see what. At first.

"Daria, get out!"

Ben was here. And the beast was in control.

She barely caught the distorted outline of the creature's huge bulk, then turned and lunged for the bank, too terrified to scream. Her feet slipped on the slimy bottom and she went down. Scrambling, she dug her toes in and shoved forward, heart pounding in her throat. Frantic, she glanced back to see the beast sloshing through the water now, right at her back, jaws gaping. Snaggled, ugly teeth were ready to tear into her skin. She found her voice.

"Ryon!"

He plunged into the water and leapt at the creature, landing on top of it just as it reached her. Daria stumbled onto the bank, panting in fear. Ryon was straddling the monster's back, his arms wrapped around the large head. The thing had to be more than twice his height, its strength incredible. The beast tried to pull him off, then twisted in a violent roll, over and over, moving Ryon into deeper water where it would attempt to drown him. Or tear him apart.

"Oh my God! Ryon!"

The water churned with the force of their battle. Each time the creature would roll, it held Ryon under longer, wearing him down. Toying with him, it showed a keen intelligence that was more frightening than if it had been blindly slashing at its prey like before. As it flipped Ryon upright, he'd emerge gasping, arms straining to hold on to the beast and the knife.

Desperate, she considered his rifle. No good. She couldn't shoot the creature without perhaps hitting Ryon. And the bullets would likely have no effect anyway.

The knife flashed in Ryon's hand. With one mighty lunge, the beast thrashed, dislodging Ryon from his back. And disappeared. Treading water, Ryon sucked in gulps of air, casting about for the beast.

"Are you all right?"

"Yeah. I stabbed it," he sputtered, chest heaving. "It went under."

It couldn't be that easy. Terror rose, for her mate and for Ben. "Hurry and come out of there." He glanced at her, nodded, and began to swim without a word about her state of undress.

Daria had slipped into a pair of panties and was

reaching for her bra when he stopped swimming. "What on earth are you doing?"

Ryon's body jerked in the water. His eyes widened in disbelief just before he was slammed. He threw back his head and screamed in agony, flailing. Then he was yanked downward, and the water closed over his head. This time he didn't resurface.

"Ryon? *Ryon!*"

Daria stood immobile, unable to comprehend for a moment what had just happened. Bubbles rose from the depths, along with a bright stain of blood. So much of it that the entire area where he'd gone under ran completely red. Her stomach clenched, and she fought back the sickness, clamping a hand over her mouth.

"Nooo." A sob welled in her chest, then another.

Ryon was gone. He'd suffered a horrendous death, and it was her fault for insisting they stop here. For keeping after him until he agreed to help her save Ben—her ex-lover. The man, the creature, who'd murdered him.

My mate. Tears streamed down her face.

Shoulders shaking, she stared out over the water. She didn't care if Ben came back and ate her as well. Not now. Then, abruptly, the water swirled and Ryon exploded to the surface, choking.

Numb with fear, she ran to meet him as he swam to where he could stand. He staggered toward her, limping badly. She waded out to him, draping one of his arms around her neck and grabbing him around the waist.

Ryon made it to the bank before his knees buckled. She sat beside him, patting his back as he knelt on all fours, coughing and gagging. Ironic, but she'd never beheld a more welcome sight than her mate hacking up his lungs.

"I was scared to death," she murmured, wiping at her tears. They wouldn't seem to stop. "I thought you were dead."

"Me, too," he rasped. "But I think you would've known for sure if I was gone, because our bond would've been severed."

Pausing, she realized the golden thread was still there, humming with life, energy. Letting out a sigh of relief, she nodded. "You're right. I wasn't thinking straight or I would've felt that it was still intact."

"I lost my knife during that round."

"All that blood in the water," she said, shuddering.

"Most of it was his, but I think he still got away. Or he came to himself enough that he let me go."

"What do you mean, *most* of the blood was his?"

His strength spent, Ryon slumped to the ground. Daria rolled him to his back, and he grimaced in pain, closing his eyes. His head listed to the side and his body went slack. He'd passed out.

Daria brushed his sunlit hair out of his face, and love welled in her heart. Ryon had placed himself on the line for her again, and this time, his bravery had nearly killed him. The truth she had already accepted and voiced to Ryon seeped to every corner of her soul; she loved this man and would not accept life without him.

She dressed quickly, then began a thorough inspection, making certain all of his limbs were intact. Then she spotted the holes in his fatigues, high on his right thigh. Dread consumed her, and she bent close. Blood darkened this area of his wet pants, and wicked bite marks were visible through the tears in the fabric.

She scooted to kneel by his shoulders, and shook him gently. "Honey, wake up. Come on, big guy." After several more tries, his lashes fluttered open, much to her profound relief. Which was short-lived.

"What . . . happened?" His eyes were dazed.

Daria's fear escalated. She prayed that his wolf could fight off the creature's venom and that he wasn't going into shock, because she'd never tended to anyone severely injured. "You duked it out with Ben's creature. Remember?" She took one of his large hands and rubbed it between hers.

"Yeah. God, that shit burns." He gazed at her through half-closed lids. She let a thread of steel creep into her tone.

"I know it does, but you *cannot* check out on me. It's going to be dark in a few hours, and we need to finish what we came here to do so we can get the hell out of here and head home." She pulled at his arm. "Get your ass *up*! I need to get you somewhere so I can see about that leg."

To her amazement, he rose, pushed to his feet. "My pack. And the rifle." His voice was breathless, heavy with exertion.

Her mate's wolf must have the strength of ten men. And the heart of a lion. Her admiration grew exponentially as she retrieved both, and assisted him in shrugging the pack onto his back. "I'll get the rifle," she offered. He surrendered the weapon without a fuss, and her concern mounted.

They set out, but Ryon managed only a few miles before coming to a halt. He stood swaying, then braced an arm against a tree for support. With a wave of his hand, he indicated a temporary place to stop.

"Over there."

Daria led him to the spot, hidden well off the trail. He looked dangerously close to passing out again, but gritted his teeth and carried on. She spread the blanket on the ground, then ordered him to take off his pants.

Under normal circumstances, the Ryon she'd come to know would've given her a disarming grin and made good use of their privacy. But he merely complied, his face gray. That scared her more than anything.

Leaning against her for support, he eased the fatigues past his hips, and off. Daria sucked in a sharp breath. "Lie down."

Ryon settled down on his back, eyes fixed on the trees. He hadn't looked at the wound and Daria didn't blame him. Lord have mercy, how was he going to be able to walk? At best, they had a day left to travel before their job was complete and they reached the team.

"How bad is it?"

She touched his shoulder, dreading what she had to say. "Let's put it this way. Your part in this op is over. Starting now."

*   *   *

Ryon propped himself up on his elbow and squinted at the wound. A vicious oath sprang to his lips, but he suppressed it. Two rows of bloody punctures marched horizontally across his right thigh. The creature had attacked from the side, clamped down on the leg, and pulled him to the bottom of the lagoon. Their struggle had been brief, but vicious.

Daria's brows furrowed, her eyes soft with worry. "Bend your knee. I want to see underneath." He did, hissing between his teeth. "Easy. Oh, boy. You have a matching set on the back of your thigh."

"Terrific," he muttered, lying on his back again. "A human pincushion."

"Hey, you're darned lucky he didn't crush the bone, or worse, hit an artery. As it is, keeping your leg from getting infected before we can reach your team will take a miracle."

Ryon shrugged. "We're only losing a couple of days total by doubling back to get the evidence on August. I'll keep." In truth, the acidic poison from the creature's bite was a slow burn in his tissue, seeping toward the bone, making him sweat.

She gaped at him. "Didn't you hear what I said? You're done. I'm taking you to meet the guys, and you're going to let them get you to a hospital."

"I'm the one who knows where August's computer room is located. Without me, you're done, too."

Daria frowned. "What do you mean? What computer room? Is there another— Oh, no. I'm not going to like this, am I?"

"I got a message from Nick a few minutes ago that he received some intel on August's estate. The office and the computer you were trying to hack is supposedly a decoy. August keeps the real computer setup in a secret room underneath the house. It's made of solid concrete walls, and the entry door has a keypad. You have to know the code to gain access."

"Please tell me Nick was able to get the code."

"He passed along what he *thinks* might be the code," he muttered. "Let's hope it works."

"Plan B if it doesn't?" She knew the answer before he said it.

"There is no Plan B. If it fails, we're going to die together."

"I won't accept that. I'll take one of the Pack with me to finish the job."

Another man. One of his friends, taking care of his mate while she went into danger. Stupid as it was, a hot spurt of jealousy stabbed his gut. "No."

"Be reasonable. That wound is going to get infected, and with you sick out here, the op is endangered. I'm the one who knows my uncle's estate best, secret room or not."

The leg could damned well fall off before he'd allow her to come back into this hellhole without him. The very thought of having to wait days for word of her safety was enough to make him sick. And if August caught her, she'd die horribly. Disappear without a trace.

"We finish this *together* or not at all," he emphasized. His tone left no room for further argument. "End of discussion. Now, patch me up and stop harping at me."

"Harping?" Daria fisted her hands on her hips and glared at him. "Stubborn, hardheaded idiot!"

She looked like an angry goddess with her shiny raven hair falling around her shoulders. He couldn't help but manage a tired smile.

"And you are my angel. I'd wrestle all the beasties in the universe for you."

"Oh, Ryon," she said on a sigh. The irritation on her lovely face vanished. "You're impossible."

"Kiss me," he said in a hoarse whisper.

"I think I can handle that."

Cupping his cheek, she bent and covered his lips in a slow, tender kiss. So good, so right. A warm, fuzzy haze descended over him and he became weightless. Daria's touch had a way of banishing the ache in his body, his heart.

As he watched her clean and dress his wounds, he prayed that they would survive this and go home.

Where they both belonged.

Afternoon light penetrated Daria's eyelids and she stifled a groan as she awoke from the brief, unplanned nap. Much more pleasant was the weight of warm, solid male draped across her. Too warm. Obviously, he'd needed the rest.

"What am I going to do with you?" she whispered, combing his hair out of his face; then she touched his forehead and uttered a curse. He had a fever. Carefully, she wiggled out of his hold.

Ryon's lashes fluttered open. For a couple of seconds he seemed confused. Then it passed and he pushed up to a sitting position and gave her a boyish grin.

"Hey, beautiful. I woke up to find my arms empty. Now, why is that?"

"I had to breathe, for one. You were squashing me."

In an instant, his expression turned sorrowful. "Sorry. Come here and allow me to check your sweet person for bruises." The predatory gleam in his eyes made her pulse race.

"Oh, you are *so* bad."

"I'm trying. A little cooperation, please?"

"Take it easy, hotshot. You're already getting a fever."

"Yes," he growled meaningfully. "I am."

Ryon patted the blanket beside him and her gaze dipped south. He was gloriously naked, and not a man to let an injury get in the way of his desires. "I can see that."

"See what you do to me?" He cupped the back of her head and drew her to him.

Her mate captured her mouth, tongue sweeping inside, devouring. Hot and demanding, it speared her, darting in and out. Tasting, igniting the flames. He wasn't asking. This was 100 percent pure male, taking what belonged to him, and it sent a thrill of joy straight into her soul.

He took her hand, guided it to him. "Only yours, angel."

The smooth texture of him was wondrous. Satin and steel. She was glad she'd undressed before joining him for their nap as he bent and captured one delicate nipple in his teeth. He grazed it, sending little circles of delight through her belly.

His fingers crept along the inside of her thigh until they found her center. They flicked the little nub until she moaned, spreading her legs wider. He dipped two fingers inside, stroking, driving her mad.

"You're so beautiful," he whispered. "So hot and wet."

"Ryon, please."

He gave a wicked laugh, rubbing the sensitive mound with deliberate slowness. Any second, she would fly apart.

"Please what?"

"I need you inside me," she panted.

Ryon hauled her into his lap facing him, her legs straddling his thighs. He hissed in pain as she bumped his bandages. Before she could scoot off him, big hands encircled her waist. He lifted her slightly, then seated her atop him, burying his shaft deep.

Linking her arms around his neck, she looked into his face, and began to pump her hips. Lips turned up, he gazed back, the raw sexual heat in his eyes threatening to burst her into flames.

"That's it, ride me. I'm yours," he murmured.

Daria thrilled at his words, as the two of them joined together. The slick hardness of him, filling her completely. Sliding up and down, she moved slowly at first, needing to become familiar with every inch of him. Every decadent sensation. She leaned into him, stroking her bud along his shaft, flirting with making them both lose control.

"Daria, baby, you're killing me."

Ryon's breathless plea pushed her over the edge. He'd closed his eyes and tilted back his head, cupping her bottom. This big, strong man had given himself over to her seduction. A powerful, feral beast, tamed in her arms. She'd never seen anything so totally erotic.

Her control shattered and she rode Ryon hard. She clasped him tight, hands splayed on his back, enjoying the play of his muscles as he met her thrusts. Molten waves crashed over them, carrying them on a red tide. He went rigid, his cry of fierce, savage pleasure mingling with hers, merging their souls. Spasms rocked them as his release poured into her.

They held each other for a while, unmoving. A tendril of fear snaked its way into her heart that this happiness was fleeting. That she would lose him before this was over.

"We should get ready to go. The day is almost gone," Ryon pointed out.

"Wish we didn't have to."

"There's nothing I'd like more than to blow off this whole thing." He sighed. "Sometimes it sucks being the good guy."

"I wouldn't have you any other way."

He winked. "Really? Because I'm saving my bad boy side just for you."

"Sounds good to me."

They began to gather their things and finally headed out for her uncle's estate. If they managed to escape him a second time, it would be a miracle.

The scent of his mate on his own skin was driving him out of his frigging mind. He wanted to throw her to the ground and make love to her again. And again.

The woman had turned his heart inside out. Like a little boy playing with matches, he hadn't been able to resist her spark. The flames would burn out of control, consume them. And it would be worth the burn.

He wasn't sure whether he'd tasted heaven or had been cast into hell. Probably both. Pausing, he wiped the sweat from his brow. Her nearness wasn't the only reason he was about to spontaneously combust.

"Are you okay?" Daria asked, touching his shoulder.

He turned and gave her his best reassuring smile. "No worries."

She wasn't buying. Feeling his forehead for the hundredth time, she scowled. "I think your fever is getting worse, and you're limping."

"I was nearly the main course for lunch. Of course I'm limping."

"Men can be such idiots. Here, let me take your temperature again."

She slung her pack off, but he laid a hand on her arm. "I am *not* putting another one of those paper thermometers under my tongue. Put it away, will you? You're starting to freak me out."

"You've had worse things in your mouth, my wolf. And last time I checked it was one hundred point three."

"From being near *you*, angel."

She scowled. "Insufferable man."

He sighed in exasperation, but he had to admit it was nice being fussed over by his beautiful woman. "You've cleaned and changed the dressings. There's nothing else to do, so stop worrying."

"The wounds are red and angry, Ryon. We need to get you out of here."

"And we will, as soon as the job is done."

Daria uttered a ripe curse, and he laughed. "Come on, my stubborn mate. Let's go."

The rest of the day passed uneventfully, except for Daria's occasional poking and prodding. They talked about trivial subjects, mostly growing up, families, and school. He learned that Daria had been valedictorian of her senior class, while he'd been the guy voted most likely to wind up in the Marines, like his father, though he'd taken a different path with the Navy. He'd had a bit of wandering spirit, even in his youth.

Close to dusk, they made camp as close to August's estate as he dared. He found a secluded spot in the foliage for them to await their next move.

Daria checked his wounds and temperature again, clearly unhappy. "Nearly one hundred and two. Your wolf isn't fighting this off."

"We'll be inside August's complex tonight, right after dark, get what we came for, transfer those files to the compound, and then we're out. By this time tomorrow, we'll be on our way home. I'm good."

"Getting away will be twice as dangerous as before, and you're getting sick. Why don't you wait outside and save your strength while I go in and—"

His patience snapped. "Not a fucking chance. Don't push this."

"Fine, be an ass." Daria fell quiet.

Ryon studied Daria from under his lashes. She sat on the ground with her knees drawn up to her chin, arms around her legs. He thought she planned to ignore him until it was time for the job, but he was wrong.

"I love you," she said quietly.

"I love you, too, baby." He met her gaze, throat tight. "Listen. If I don't make it, get the hell out and get to the team. Don't look back."

"Forget that. I won't leave you." She paused. "What if neither of us makes it?"

"Then try to hold my hand so we're not alone." He reached out to her and she clasped her fingers in his, their previous argument forgotten in light of the danger to come.

"I promise."

By nightfall, she hadn't let go of him. Saying a quick prayer, he nodded at her. Cautiously, they made their way to the very edge of the property.

The estate stood eerily silent. A few lights were on inside the grounds, the glow reminding Ryon of multiple eyes on a huge poisonous spider, crouched and waiting in the darkness.

Time to slay the beast.

Thirteen

Only a couple of armed guards were visible, hovering near the corners of the main house. Looks, however, were deceptive.

"Where is everyone?" Daria whispered, palming the SIG he'd given to her. "He always had several more guards posted whenever I visited."

"Many of them are still out looking for us. The rest are around. If they spot us, it'll be like kicking a fire ant mound."

"I vote we hit while they're full and sleepy from dinner and booze. August doesn't allow them to drink on duty, but that hasn't ever stopped them from sneaking a few rounds after he goes to bed."

"Good to know. Stick close to me."

Crouching low, Ryon led them from their post at the front gate around to the back. Hugging the wall, he located the approximate place he'd entered the estate a few days before. Using the thick vines as handholds, he hauled himself up and over the wall, then dropped to the ground on the other side.

Blazing fire shot through his injured leg, and he gritted his teeth to keep from making a sound. With an effort, he fought down a wave of nausea and dizziness. Daria had been right. He was fast becoming a serious liability. If they were forced to make a run for it, he wasn't sure he'd make it to the pickup point. For Daria's sake he had to try, and if she had to go on without him, at least the mission would be complete.

Daria dropped beside him with a soft thud, and he caught her around the waist to steady her. Once the guard on the other side of the swimming pool turned to amble in the other direction, he readied the M16 and headed for the pool house. At the moment, it was locked tight, windows dark. They crept across the porch to the door, which sported nothing more than a simple lock. Ryon picked it easily with his pocketknife and let them inside, shutting the door behind them.

He walked past the wet bar and into the tiny storeroom. Once inside, he shut them in pitch blackness before turning on his penlight. Daria's anxious whisper sounded beside him.

"What are you doing? There's nothing in here, unless you're planning to get back at him by drinking all of his guests' wine."

Ryon flicked the penlight at the modest wine rack that covered the left wall of the room. "That's what you're supposed to think. Nick told me where to look, remember? Watch this."

Striding to the rack, he braced the rifle on one hip, and slid his hand along the right edge until his fingers found the latch and pressed. The rack gave a pop and he swung it out to reveal a hidden door.

Daria was suitably impressed. "Well, I'll be damned. The wine rack serves as a fake wall. Does this lead where I think?"

"Even better. The stairs behind this door descend straight underground to a lighted corridor, which travels toward the estate for about forty yards. At that point, it branches off. The left corridor continues to the main house, the right one to his computer room."

She arched a brow. "That's damned good intel your boss has."

"I'm sure being able to see the future helped a bit."

"True," she agreed.

"I wonder why he built access through the pool house. That's pretty risky."

"Nick said August likes to have a hidden route out of the main house in case of emergency, like a raid or a house call from a dangerous enemy. Besides, nobody knows it exists except his current right-hand man, August, and now us."

"Is the corridor monitored by camera?"

"Motion sensors. No cameras, unless he's added them recently. Getting inside isn't the difficult part, if you know the route. Once we're in, though, if they discover us, the danger of being trapped down there is pretty high."

"I don't like this."

He linked their fingers. "Me, either. Personally, I think the whole deal stinks. Do you want to quit? Whatever you decide, it's now or never."

"I want to get the rest of those files and watch him hang, but you're—"

"Then it's settled." He pressed a kiss to her lips, cutting off further protests about his health. Releasing her, he turned and went to work on the door. In short order, they were standing at the top of a steep, narrow staircase. He left the exit behind them open a slight crack for their return trip.

"Follow me. When we get to the bottom, stay to the right," he instructed. "Don't stray toward the center of the hall. The motion sensor beam runs straight down the middle. August likes it positioned that way so he can make a quick escape without worrying about setting off his own alarms and alerting the enemy as to which direction he's taken. Anyone else wouldn't know not to walk down the center and they'd get busted."

"And if he's changed the sensors?"

"We're screwed. But if we make it to the computer room, I think I've got us covered."

With that mysterious pearl of wisdom, he started down, weapon ready. Once at the bottom, they followed the corridor to the intersection, then veered right. So far so good. No shouts or pounding footsteps rushing to intercept them.

A massive metal sliding door dominated the end of the corridor. A control panel mounted on the wall to the right resembled the cockpit of a small plane with its array of buttons.

"Terrific," Daria muttered. "How do we get in?"

Ryon smiled grimly. "With the override code Nick's security contact was able to provide, since August uses one of the same systems they serve. What's more, the code deactivates the sensors until the doors close again. Brilliant, huh?"

She peered over his shoulder and frowned. "I wouldn't get too cocky if I were you."

"Why?"

"Because the room is empty."

Ryon spun and stared in disbelief. He walked inside, fists clenched. Solid concrete walls and nothing else.

"Son of a bitch."

"No telling how long ago he cleaned it out. Apparently Nick's all-seeing eye isn't foolproof. Any other brilliant ideas?" She waited, glancing around nervously.

"I'm open to suggestions," he bit off. He felt like a fool. Of course August would've moved his files the instant he learned that his estate had been breached. Ryon's mistake had cost him and Daria time they couldn't afford to lose.

"I think the files in his office are the real ones," Daria speculated. "Dad said he's been really preoccupied with some sort of construction off the far wing. He told Dad he was adding on to the estate, but now I think it's possible that he's building a better headquarters for his transactions."

"Makes sense, but why wouldn't he just leave the files down here until the new facility is ready? His data is more secure here than upstairs."

"He's a spider waiting to spring his trap. The million-dollar question is, do we take the bait?"

Every instinct he possessed was urging him harder than ever to get Daria the hell out, forget the whole thing. But he longed for August to roast for what he'd done to Ben, and to other humans and shifters. If nothing else, he could give Daria that much.

Ryon waved a hand. "We've come this far. Let's do it."

"Wait," she said softly. Stepping close, she laid her palm on his chest. "I'm sorry I pushed you into coming back here, especially now. You're sick and I don't want anything to happen to you."

"It's all right, baby. If I didn't want to try again, you couldn't have made me." He gave her a quick kiss. "We're going to accomplish what we came to do and get out of here, trust me."

Daria looked deeply into his eyes, as if trying to discern his sincerity. After a minute, she stepped back, satisfied. "All right. So, did Nick say what part of the house the corridor leads to?"

"The kitchen pantry."

Her jaw dropped. "You're kidding."

"Nope. What better place to hide the other entrance than behind a wall of food? We can restock our packs, too."

"Clever," she admitted.

"We've got to hurry."

Every cell in his body alert, Ryon padded toward the house, Daria pressed to his back like a second skin. The narrow confines of the bright corridor made him more uneasy than before. He half expected the passage to be booby trapped, then dismissed the notion. A man like August would prefer to mete out pain himself and witness the results.

They reached the stairs and ascended slowly. Ryon found the latch, and the mechanism emitted an audible pop, the wall creaking when released from position. He tensed. After a minute, he used the tip of his rifle to inch the gap wider. Light from behind them flooded the large walk-in pantry. Quickly, he stepped inside and motioned for Daria to close the panel behind them. If anyone in the kitchen had seen the strange light below the door, he and Daria would soon find out.

Nothing. Breathing a sigh, Ryon used the tiny penlight to scout for food to replace what they'd consumed. Being a man of finer tastes, August didn't allow the cook to buy a lot of junk. However, Ryon did locate several packages of crackers, jerky, and a few granola bars. With a grimace, he stowed them in Daria's pack, thinking he'd give his small fortune for a juicy steak and a baked potato. An open case of bottled water rested on the floor and Daria put several bottles in his pack. Ryon figured he'd rather collapse from carrying the extra weight than to starve or dehydrate. What a choice.

This done, he flicked off the penlight and opened the

pantry door an inch. All was quiet. A clock on the wall revealed the hour to be one thirty in the morning. His tired, aching body felt every minute of it.

They made their way from the kitchen into the open, airy living room, placing their steps carefully, keeping to the perimeter. Moonlight filtered in through the floor-to-ceiling glass windows overlooking the pool on one end of the room, the front lawn on the other. A burly guard stood next to the patio door with his back to the glass, facing the pool, shifting restlessly.

August's office wasn't far, just across the living room and a few feet down the hallway. Ryon barely made the safety of the shadows in the hall and turned to beckon for Daria to hurry, when the guard suddenly pressed his face against the window. The big man jerked upright in surprise, shouldering his rifle.

Shit, he'd spotted her!

Daria saw him, too, and froze, the SIG trained on the man's broad chest as he strode inside, stalking her. His cocky smile flashed in a sliver of light. Totally ignoring her gun, he lowered his own weapon and pressed his body against hers.

"Well, what do we have here? August's sweet little do-gooding niece can't shoot, so what are you going to do? Shall we work out a trade for my silence?"

Ryon's wolf snarled in rage, and he barely kept the sound from escaping. The claws on his hand lengthened, and he waited.

Daria didn't answer, but began to back away, bringing the guard closer to Ryon's hiding place. *Good girl.*

Just a bit more. Ryon clenched his teeth as the dirtbag crowded her and cupped a breast, confident in his ability to overpower her. A sloppy fool, smelling faintly of whiskey. And groping his mate. It would be his last mistake.

"Very nice," the man laughed, low and nasty. "You're going to come with me, open your pretty legs, and learn how to treat a real man. Then I might be persuaded to forget you were here—"

Ryon had heard enough. Moving silently, he came at the goon from behind, reached around him, and delivered a vicious, lethal swipe to his neck. Blood sprayed over the pristine floor, and he could muster no sympathy for the slimy bastard.

Working fast, he lowered the huge man to the floor, laid the rifle on his chest, took him by the ankles, and dragged him away. The living room offered no place to stash the body, so he secreted it inside the pantry. Next, he grabbed a couple of kitchen towels and quickly wiped as much of the blood as possible from the floor. A hurried inspection would pass in the darkness, but the guard would be missed eventually. After relieving the man of his shirt, pants, handgun and bullets, he rejoined Daria.

She hadn't moved, but stood like a small, pale ghost with wide, fathomless eyes that he couldn't see in the dark. Only the firm line of her unsmiling mouth gave voice to her thoughts. He touched her cheek.

"I had no choice, baby. He would've killed us both."

"I know."

But her tone was dull. She was coming to terms with the fact that the man she loved was a natural-born killer. He wasn't some romantic commando from a Stallone movie, but the real thing, and he had other abilities tacked on for good measure. Knowing that and witnessing it were different matters. Heart heavy, he dropped his hand and turned to head for the office.

Daria swept in ahead of Ryon, and he left the door cracked a bit before joining her at the computer. She settled into August's black leather chair, retrieving the thumb drive case from her pack. She wiggled the mouse to wake up the sleeping machine, then stuck in the thumb drive. The password box immediately appeared on the screen.

Fingers flying, Daria tried the last several codes. Access denied. "Damn. Have any more secret access codes up your sleeve?"

"Try *Project Malik*, no spaces."

She clicked out the word, pressed enter. They were in! "Another safety net, mate? My, you and Nick were busy boys," she commented without looking up.

Intent on her purpose, she leaned forward. His affirmation fueled her desire to get that final piece of evidence, the ace in the hole. Ryon didn't interfere. Her computer skills matched or surpassed his, and he knew she would've eventually broken into the main screen, even without Nick's help.

Conscious of the minutes slipping away, he peered into the hallway. Still clear, but not for long. Any minute one of the guards would stroll to the pool to check in with the missing man. He and Daria might have a few more minutes before they realized the man wasn't in the restroom, or in the kitchen pilfering a late-night snack.

Sweat beaded on Ryon's forehead and neck, and not just from nerves. The room was unbearably hot, his leg killing him. Not a good sign. Forcing the discomfort from his mind, he walked back to Daria.

Hunched over, she punched in another series of numbers. Waited. Then, like a miracle, a spreadsheet filled the screen. All the information they needed, at their fingertips. Smiling, Daria raised a fist in victory.

"It's all here. The drugs they used on the shifters, names of their victims—or *test subjects* as the assholes called them—names of doctors and others in their employ. All sorts of damning evidence."

"God, this is so much more extensive than what we recovered from Bowman's last testing site." Something caught Ryon's eye. "Look there. It says *Medicinal Countermeasures for Morphing Agents*, and it looks like a recipe. Does that mean what I think?"

"It's an antidote," she breathed. Typing fast, she opened a window and, following Ryon's direction, began to send the all-important files to the Pack compound's server.

He contacted his commander. *Nick, we've got it! All the files are coming your way, and it looks like there's a reversal drug for the shit they did to Ben and the others.*

After a couple of seconds, the man answered in relief. *Great job. As soon as it's sent, get the hell out. Time is short. I'll get our lab people working on the antidote and try to have it in hand when we fly out to pick you both up.*

All right, and thanks. For everything.

Just go, and hurry.

A box flashed with the words *Transfer Complete*. Ryon kissed the top of her head. "I'm impressed, angel. Now let's get going. I never want to see this place again."

"I couldn't agree more."

Daria removed the thumb drive and secured it in the case again, hands trembling. Ryon could imagine what a monumental occasion this was for her, because it meant as much to him. Now Ben at least had a chance. She zipped the pack, logged off the computer, and turned to him.

"I can't wait to see the government come down on his ass like a bad case of clap."

A deep, taunting laugh reverberated against the walls, startling them both. August Bradford stepped into the office and flipped on the lights, a pistol trained on them.

Oh, Jesus.

Ryon froze and Daria pressed herself to his side. He didn't dare glance at her. Sweat trickled down the side of his face. Swallowing his sickness and anger, he met his enemy's black gaze without flinching.

August was a handsome man, with few lines on his face to hint at his age. He carried himself tall and straight, and wore an expression of faint amusement. He looked and acted the part of a spoiled, entitled man who must have very much enjoyed playing God along with Malik and Bowman.

"They wouldn't be the first ones to try, dearest

niece." August looked from her back to Ryon, his smile chilling, voice dripping with meaning. "Place your weapons on the floor, nice and slow."

They did, keeping their hands in sight, then straightened. Ryon didn't respond right away, but took in the rest of August's appearance. He was dressed in blue silk pajamas, his hair shooting in several directions, mussed from sleep. They'd surprised him, which might work in their favor. The fact that the guards hadn't followed on his heels meant he had yet to alert them. That might prove their only chance for escape.

"You might want to play nice with us, old man," Ryon said flatly.

"All right, I'll bite. Why would I want to play nice?"

"Because we just sent all of your files to an arm of the government that is very interested in stamping out every last trace of the heinous experiments you were involved in with Gene Bowman and the Unseelie, Malik, whom you knew was masquerading as rich entrepreneur Evan Kerrigan."

Though the man maintained his smile, it tightened noticeably. "The government, you say? Well, there was your first mistake."

"Now *I'll* bite. How so?"

August cocked his head, studying Ryon. "You're a shifter. Cat? Wolf?"

He saw no reason to lie. "Wolf."

"Made, not born."

"Yes." He exchanged a quick look of confusion with Daria. Where was this going?

"Since you're with an *arm* of the government, as you put it, I'll assume it's black ops. Am I correct in also assuming you were military before you were turned?"

"Navy SEAL," he admitted, a cold ball forming in his stomach. This man was getting at something very bad, and they were about to learn what. "So, what does any of that mean?"

"Ah, Ryon Hunter, you've been wondering that for *years*, haven't you?" August almost whispered, a clever light in his eyes.

A cold shock went through him. "How do you know my name? What are you trying to say?"

"Must I do all the work here? Connect the dots, boy. Haven't you and your fellow SEALs who were attacked in Afghanistan and turned six years ago wondered *why*?"

Ryon stared at the man, his heart pounding in dread.

August chuckled, stepping closer. "Why did you all survive, when so many others died? How is it that a group of human men, each with Psy powers unbeknownst to the others, ended up in the same unit? How did it happen that they were attacked *that* day, thousands of miles from home, and *no one* but the men with the Psy abilities survived the slaughter? At some point, each of your team must have wondered *why, why, why.*"

Ryon groaned as the full import hit, and he nearly collapsed. "Mother of God. It's true. We were set up."

"Yes, young wolf. You were set up from the very beginning, down to the last man." Glancing at the computer they'd hacked, he shook his head. "You might be able to help my niece's hapless former fiancé, but in the end it won't matter. Where do you think all of the information you've gone to so much trouble to obtain will go? In whose hands will it finally rest?"

"Someone high up," he said desperately. "Someone who'll stop you, maybe put you behind bars for the things you've done."

August studied him for a long moment. Then he spoke quietly. "Did your team honestly think that Malik and Bowman were the end of the line? That we could possibly have put in place an operation of such a large scale without someone *high up*, as you say, calling the shots?"

"No," Ryon whispered. "I won't believe it."

"Believe what you will. Malik had his own agenda and his own God complex. But the truth is, the tentacles of this thing go all the way to the top. To the fucking Oval Office. Are you following me, boy? It's not one person, but several in key positions of power in the United States government."

Ryon gripped the edge of the desk, sweat dripping onto the surface. Horror consumed him, robbed his speech.

August nodded. "Everything was planned. Your team pulled together beautifully, and afterward we focused our research on other areas, such as how to create an even stronger, more lethal shifter. A legion of super-soldiers. Until things began to go wrong."

"You mean until the Alpha Pack turned on its creator, and began to dismantle the project."

Nick! Nick, did you know? Please, tell me you didn't. The commander remained silent.

"Exactly. Thanks to someone of power who's helping the Pack, guiding them from afar." As though suddenly remembering the gun in his hand, he leveled it at them more squarely. "And you're going to tell me who it is, or I'll kill you both."

August doesn't know. He has no idea General Jarrod Grant is our ally.

"I don't fucking think so, you sonofabitch!"

Moving fast, he launched himself at August.

The deafening blast of the gunshot, and Daria's terrified scream, tore into Ryon as he fell.

Fourteen

Ryon yelled, throwing himself at August, and all hell broke loose.

A gunshot blasted the air, and the two men crashed to the floor, grappling for the weapon. They rolled, and Ryon landed a punch to August's jaw with his free hand. Daria bent and snatched the SIG off the floor, hoping to get a shot at August.

"Daria, go! There's no time!" Ryon shouted.

She hesitated, but knew he was right. A crash sounded somewhere in the house, followed by pounding feet. If she distracted him by not following his order, he'd lose focus on the fight and they would both die for nothing. She hated leaving the pack with their supplies, but they had no choice now. Speed was everything, and all they had to do now was make the rendezvous point. Praying Ryon would follow, she turned, released her wolf and shifted, and dove headfirst through the plate-glass window.

Daria's first thought was that that stunt always looked so easy in the movies. Her second, that she'd probably scalped her hide on the glass even through her thick fur. She rolled to her feet, shaking off her clothes and the shards of glass that rained like confetti, and hit the ground running as though the hounds of hell were on her heels.

Shouts. Curses. Rapid-fire gunshots.

The security floodlights bathed the compound, bright as daytime. Any second she expected a bullet to plow into her back and end her life. Or Ryon's. God, where was he?

Two men were closing in fast on her right, shouting, "Stop!"

No freaking way was she going to do that, so why did the bad guys always yell something so stupid? She saw them raise their rifles. A scream welled in her throat, but came out as a pitiful whimper. Her head-long flight, along with sheer terror, had sucked the air from her lungs. The back wall loomed near, but she wasn't going to make it. They were going to kill her.

Daria braced herself, but no bullets ripped through her body. Swiveling her head as she ran, she saw Ryon coming across the lawn after her, half-limping, rifle trained on the two goons. Their bodies jerked, and fell. He stopped, spun, and sprayed more bullets toward the shattered office window.

Reaching the wall, Daria's wolf had no trouble scaling it in about two seconds flat, and she flung herself over. Three steps, and she was plunged into total darkness. Chest heaving, she halted and tried to figure her next move. A thud and a crunch of leaves alerted her that someone had come over the wall. She swung around in terror.

"Daria?" Ryon called.

Thank God. She shifted and held out a hand. "Right here. Take about three steps."

"All right," he said, breathing hard. "Let me put on the night vision goggles and I'll come to you. Are you hurt?"

"I—I'm not sure. Maybe my head, from the glass. Lost my clothes when I shifted and ran, too. What about you?"

A hesitation. "I'm fine. Okay, I see you." He stepped up and grabbed her hand. "I've got on the goggles, and I'll lead the way. You're going to have to trust me to be our eyes, but I promise I won't let anything happen to you. Hang on tight to the strap on my pack. If you accidentally lose your hold, yell and I'll get you."

"Wouldn't it be better just to ditch our stuff now, shift, and run to meet the team in wolf form? We're done with the op, and we'd make better time."

"I'm sorry, but I can't hold my shift, baby," he rasped. "I'm too sick."

"It's okay," she reassured him. "We'll make it."

"Here, put these on." Rustling in the pack, he threw a spare set of clothes at her, and some shoes.

They were hers, and she realized he'd grabbed her

pack as well as his, plus the weapons. Bless him. Ryon muttered an oath and moved around her, placing her left hand on his pack. She found the strap and locked it in a death grip, the SIG in her right hand.

Daria tugged on the strap. "Ready."

Ryon starting walking fast, beating a path through the forest. She couldn't see a damned thing, and had to console herself with the fact that he could see just fine. If they ran into August's men or some other vile creature, Ryon would know.

Daria stumbled upon occasion but managed, for the most part. He was careful to move slowly and tell her when to step over a fallen tree or duck to avoid a branch in the face. Even so, having her movement restricted by hanging on to him proved a tedious way to hike. Before long, her arms and shoulders ached. Better than getting lost, however.

The tough trek helped focus her attention away from what she really longed to do—find a nice, soft bed and sleep for a year with her mate curled around her like a second skin.

Then she became aware of something. "Ryon, stop and listen."

He did, and they stood, drinking in the usual nighttime symphony.

"They're not following us. Damn."

Dread pricked at her. "And that's a *bad* thing? What're you thinking?"

"My best guess is that August's calling in his men who are already out there looking for us. If I were him,

I'd have them form a dragnet around us. That's why they aren't giving chase. He's not worried about catching us."

Ryon let out a deep breath, which ended on a slight wheeze. He coughed a couple of times, then slumped sideways. When he didn't fall, she reached out with her gun hand and came into contact with bark. He was leaning against a tree.

She frowned. "What happened back there between you and my uncle? Are you really all right?"

"I wanted to send him to the devil where he belongs, but his men were storming the house. I had to either let him go and run, or stay to finish him, and die."

His voice was thick and strange, not like Ryon at all. She didn't like it one bit.

"How's the leg?" she pressed.

"Still holding me upright."

Okay, but not for long. "Are we stopping here? You need to rest."

"We're not making camp tonight. Have to . . . keep moving." Another cough, and a shudder.

Daria stuck the SIG in the waistband of her fatigues and reached for him. Her fingers found his neck, and skimmed up to his stubbled cheek. "You're burning up!"

"No help for it." He straightened, relaying his plan as though he wasn't about to collapse. "Listen, we have to divert from our course in a major way, or they're going to surround us."

"How about turning just to the south?" she suggested.

Ryon nodded. "When we locate a suitable place for the helicopter to lift us out, I'll tell Nick, and the guys will be on the way. Shouldn't take them but a couple of hours to get to us."

"Sounds like you've got us covered. It's your show."

Indeed, it had been, from the second he exploded into her life. Ryon, infuriating her, capturing her heart, then wringing it like an old dishrag. If he didn't get help soon, she'd lose her mate. It was that horribly simple.

After a few hours, the forest began to lighten enough to see. He took off the goggles and she no longer had to hang on to him. When she was finally able to study Ryon from behind, even her limited view couldn't hide his condition.

Sweat dripped off the ends of his blond hair, making it appear darker, and his T-shirt was soaked. She wasn't so dry herself, but she didn't have a sky-high fever. He walked stiffly, stumbling now and then, boots dragging as though every step caused agony. And he never once complained.

Around midmorning, the banks of the river appeared. Ryon, however, kept to the cover of the trees, pushing them hard and not stopping for a break until nearly noon. When he did, he slung his pack and rifle to the ground, backed against a tree, and slid to the ground without a word. He removed two bottles of water from his pack and offered one to her.

Daria took it gratefully, forcing herself not to gulp. Ryon drained his in a few swallows. Her stomach growled, and she fetched a couple of the stolen granola bars, holding one out to him. To her dismay, he shook his head and closed his eyes, tilting his head back.

She ate hers, worried about the lines of strain on his face. He had purple smudges under his eyes, and his cheeks were flushed. Finishing the snack, she wiped her palms and scooted next to him.

"Drop your pants, honey. Let's have a look at the leg."

With a heavy sigh, he worked them down to his calves and leaned back again, not even bothering to make a joke about her need for him to get naked. Her gaze dropped to his right thigh and she received a violent shock. A small, neat hole marred the flesh about three inches above the bandages.

"You've been shot!" she exclaimed. "Dammit, Ryon, why didn't you say anything?"

"Because there's nothing you can do. It hurts, but it's not bleeding much, and I can walk."

"Yes, I can do something, even if it's not much. You're going to take some aspirin, even if I have to shove them down your throat. Do you understand?" she insisted.

In his weakened state, he wouldn't win this one, Daria told herself as she dug for them. Shaking out four pills, she handed them to him, along with her water. He scowled, and she returned it. As she predicted, he gave first.

"Well, I guess they won't kill me any faster."

"That's not funny."

Next, she unwrapped the bandages around his thigh. Her triumph over the medicine was short-lived. The wounds were infected, no question. Each puncture oozed fluid. They should've healed over by now, given his special abilities, but the surrounding flesh was swollen and red. Angry crimson streaks brushed his leg. *Poison.*

Daria had never felt so helpless. Ryon was in terrible danger, and she couldn't do a thing to help him. She rinsed the bite marks with the remainder of her water, then wrapped his leg in fresh bandages. There wasn't anything more to do.

Ryon pulled his pants up and closed his eyes. He was still for so long, she thought he'd fallen asleep. God knows he needed the rest. She'd almost given in to her own fatigue when he spoke in a low whisper.

"Never forget I love you. More than my life, more than anything."

She touched his face. "Never. Same goes for me. You're my world now, and I won't rest until we're both safe."

He looked away, staring out over the river for several minutes, unblinking. Daria had never witnessed such misery. He was close to giving up, and she could not let his spirits dip that low.

"Say, do you realize you haven't been tormented by your ghosts much lately?" she asked.

"They haven't bothered me in a while. I think that's because of you." He smiled at her. "You ground me. Now I only see them if I need to—which I hope won't be very often."

"That means you're strong. You're not going any-where, you hear me?"

"Yeah. I do, baby."

They sat together for a time, collecting themselves. When he was ready to leave, he simply stood next to her and waited. She rose and shrugged on her pack, glancing at him. His expression was calm, accepting. That scared her almost more than she could handle.

The rest of the day, Ryon didn't speak. He'd disap-peared inside himself. This wasn't the smiling, confi-dent man she'd first met. She wanted that man back. She loved him.

As horrible as the day had been, the evening was much worse. She pitched the tent for them because he could barely stand any longer. He accepted the help in silence, face drawn. Usually, they would sit outside the tent and talk. Or make love. Tonight, he crawled inside, period.

Determined to at least try to cheer him, she went in after him. He lay on his side, eyes closed, an empty bottle of water beside him. She reached out to touch his shoulder, then decided not to push too hard.

"Can I fix you one of those instant dinners?"

Silence.

"You haven't eaten all day. You need to eat if you're going to have any strength to finish the hike. How about some jerky?"

Nothing.

"God, Ryon, try to shift! Please!"

"Don't," he said hoarsely. "Baby, just don't."

Grabbing his shirt, she forced him to his back and shouted right into his face. "*You* don't! Don't you dare give up on me!" She smacked his chest as he stared at her, wide-eyed. "Shift, you pussy! Shift now, goddammit!"

The effect was instant. In less than five seconds, Ryon's silver wolf was struggling to free himself of his clothing, snarling and pissed as hell. If the situation wasn't so dire, she would've smiled. As it was, she put a calming hand on his broad head.

"Calm down, big guy." He stilled and then whined, nuzzling her hand and scooting into her side. "Let me get these clothes off you. Stay in your shift as long as you can. Then I'll help you get dressed again."

The longer he could stay in wolf form, the better for his healing. At least he might be able to make it to the transport. Carefully, she removed his clothes and examined his back leg. She couldn't see the punctures for all the fur, but she hoped the wounds were improving at least a little.

Despite his earlier protests, he managed to hold his shift for almost half an hour before he morphed into human form again. Beside her, he was completely down for the count. But she thought he was breathing a tad easier, his color a bit more natural. On examination, she found the wounds on his thigh to be not quite as angry, and that sent a wave of relief washing through her.

Her mate had bought himself some time. Hopefully just enough.

Daria wasn't sure how long she sat beside him,

watching and worrying. Eventually, she gave in and slept.

By dawn, Ryon was shaking with the chills, teeth chattering, yet scorching heat radiated off his big body in waves. Alarm kicked her in the gut. The shift should've bought him more time, and if they didn't get moving he'd be out of what little he'd gained.

She'd have to wake him. Laying a hand on his arm, she shook him gently. "Ryon? Wake up, we have to go."

Several attempts later, he opened his eyes and stared at her with a dazed expression. For a few seconds, he had absolutely no clue where he was, and it scared the hell out of her. Then, awareness returned.

"Daria," he croaked. "Take the spare water from my pack."

"Why?"

"You're going to meet the helicopter alone, then send the guys back for me."

"No. No way," she said in a steely tone. "That is *so* not going to happen. Get up. Now."

"Listen." He coughed and shuddered, taking a deep breath as though talking cost him. "I'll slow us down, and we'll get caught."

"If you stay, August's men could find you before help arrives."

"Just do as I ask, all right? I don't want to argue with you."

"I won't argue with you, either," she said firmly. "I'm not leaving here without you and that's final. If you can't go on, my uncle will find both of us."

A few minutes later, he rose with a great effort, gathered his things, and stumbled out of the tent. Daria sagged in relief. Thank God. Now she just had to keep his sexy ass moving.

A lot of the fight had gone out of him, but she intended to keep pushing.

No matter what, he wasn't going to give up.

Somehow, Ryon put one foot in front of the other. He'd never been this low. Ever. Not even when he'd awakened in a hospital overseas with a raging wolf for a brand-new companion. Not in the months afterward, when he'd fought to control his other half and retain his tenuous hold on sanity.

Nick's voice broke through his thoughts. *Ryon?*

Yeah, boss?

The lab has a batch of the serum ready, so we'll bring it, see if we can find Ben. Where are you? We're about to leave.

That's great! Um . . . I'm not sure. A few miles south of August's estate, following the river. We're looking for a good clearing.

On our way. Hang in there, all right?

Sure thing.

He wasn't sure at all, but he kept moving. "Nick contacted me," he said hoarsely. "They're coming. They've got some serum for Ben."

"Best news I've heard all week!"

Daria attempted to speak to him again, but he didn't really hear her. Couldn't. He just walked until a weird buzzing noise made him stop, cock his head, and listen.

Daria said something else. He couldn't understand her over the noise, like thousands of bees in his head.

The forest began to dim. His head tilted back and he saw blue sky as his knees buckled. Sky?

Then nothing but darkness.

"Ryon, look!" Daria exclaimed, pointing. Just ahead, the forest ended and a flat river delta widened before them for at least a mile. Plenty of room for a helicopter to land! "Better contact Nick and tell him about this place. Ryon?"

He'd stopped and was looking up, his head cocked— then he folded and slumped to the ground.

"Shit!" She knelt at his side, slapped his face. "Come on, don't do this! We're almost home free, so you can't quit."

Ryon's breathing was harsh and labored, his color gray beneath his tan. Rolling him to his side, she worked the pack off his shoulders and laid aside the rifle. After settling him on his back, she fished through the pack and retrieved a bottle of water.

Cradling his head in her lap, she placed the opening between his lips and poured a tiny bit of the liquid into his mouth. He sputtered and coughed, but opened his eyes to slits and raised his head, seeking more. The next swallow went down without difficulty now that he'd regained consciousness.

"That's it, easy now," she crooned. "Hang in there, okay? We're at the edge of a clearing. Perfect place for them to land. Couple of hours, maybe, and we're home free."

He tried to smile. "That's good. Nick will send a small team in to find Ben. They'll help him."

She was beyond touched that he'd think of Ben at a time like this—especially when it was Ben's creature that had put him in this condition. "I'm grateful they're willing to give it a shot."

For a while, Daria sat running her fingers through his hair. His skin was hot and dry as a desert, a sign of dehydration. The infection had spread through his body and was running its course. If he didn't get medical attention soon, shifter or not, he would die. Fear threatened to overwhelm her.

"Drink more water." She helped him, and he didn't resist. Still, his beautiful blue eyes were dull, his sensual lips unsmiling.

"Daria, if August gets here before my team and I can't stop him, don't let him take me alive."

"God, Ryon, don't even say that," she gasped.

"I won't fall into his hands and become one of his experiments, not if I can prevent it. I saw what they did to Aric, Micah, and Phoenix. Ben, too. I won't let him do that to me."

She was spared from responding to his awful request when he fell asleep. If August caught them, she knew she wouldn't take Ryon's life, or her own. Not because she was a coward, but because she wouldn't give up hope that they would get out of this mess. His team would come. They always did. If he wasn't so sick and was thinking straight, he'd know it, too.

Daria combated the boredom by dozing lightly,

keeping an ear open for Ryon's breathing, as well as any sounds that didn't belong. A friggin' helicopter would be nice. A big one or two loaded with wolves—and one panther—and armed to the teeth.

One hour came and went. Two. Cramped, Daria had to shift Ryon off her lap, stand and stretch. She made a tour around the immediate vicinity to work out the kinks, not straying far from him. Strolling to the edge of the tree line, she admired the pretty green delta, the river snaking away in the distance. An odd oasis smack in the middle of the rain forest.

She started to turn, then froze. *That sound*. Could it be?

Whump-whump-whump.

The distinctive pumping of rotor blades, and just there, a tiny speck in the distance. Then two specks that grew progressively larger.

"Yes! Ryon!" she squealed. Pushing through the tangle of vines, she ran back to him and dropped to her knees. She shook him hard enough to rattle his teeth. "Wake up. They're here!"

Ryon sat up and blinked at her. "What?"

"The Pack is here! Hurry, get up."

Blinking, he struggled upright. "Thank Christ. Where's our stuff?"

"Right here."

A sharp crack split the air, followed by more. Bullets were suddenly pelting the trees around them, men shouting.

Ryon staggered to his feet and shoved her pack into

her hands. "Run to one of the copters and don't look back!"

The *whump-whump* from the big Hueys filled the air as he pushed her forward and dove for his rifle. Daria ran into the clearing, across the flat ground. Her heart slammed in tempo with her feet as shouts drifted after her. Bullets kicked the dirt beside her, plucked at her pack.

The helicopters loomed over the horizon, coming in fast and low. The first pilot slowed, hovered, and set down about fifty yards away. She saw that it was Aric, and he left the blades whirling and ready to take off. Jax was sitting in the open side door, holding an M16 like Ryon's, yelling and waving her on. The second Huey landed not far from the first, Pack guys spilling out and sprinting to back up their endangered comrade.

Almost there. Twenty feet, ten, five. And then she was in, Jax yanking her clean off her feet. She landed inside hard, but didn't spare him a glance. She spun about to see Ryon making a magnificent stand halfway between the tree line and the helicopter. His muscles bunched as he sprayed the forest with a steady onslaught of bullets, pinning down the goons to cover her flight. His team was coming up fast behind him.

One of the men coming to his aid, Micah, grabbed Ryon and pushed him in the direction of the helicopters. Ryon whirled, half-running, mostly limping, toward her. Strain etched his face, but he kept coming. Aric held their position as Jax fired past Ryon and the others into the trees. The fight heated up as the two forces continued the gun battle—and then something horrifying happened.

At the edge of the trees, August's men began to pour from their cover, straight into the Pack's sights. A few took hits and went down before the guys realized something wasn't right and ceased fire. Looks of confusion at their enemy's actions were replaced by shock as a body came flying out of the brush, mangled and torn. Then another.

"Aw, fuck me!" Aric shouted.

A huge section of the trees shook from side to side. Split apart and was hurtled away. Then the unmistakable translucent outline of the creature became visible, and it paused just inside the clearing. Ryon looked back at that moment and stumbled to a halt, mouth dropping open.

And as the creature advanced on them all, throwing its head back to roar, Ryon turned and began to limp right back toward danger.

"Nooo!" Daria launched herself toward the door, but a strong arm wrapped around her waist.

"Stay here! I'll get the serum and help them!" Pushing past her, Jax leapt from the copter and ran, presumably to the other aircraft to fetch the medicine.

August's men were panicked, the survivors fleeing the scene as fast as possible. The Pack let them go and concentrated on the beast, firing on its massive bulk. That accomplished nothing but turning its attention on them, and pissing it off.

More than half of the men shifted, including Kalen into his panther form. They ran circles around the beast, keeping it occupied by taking turns running at it, snapping and barking, staying just out of reach of its deadly claws.

She couldn't help them. Ben wouldn't recognize her in this state, so she could do nothing but watch, hand over her mouth, heart in her throat.

Ryon stripped and shifted, joining his friends in battle. Then Jax ran toward the fray, legs pumping, a large cylinder clutched in his hand.

When Ryon made a flying leap and attached himself to the creature's back, the thing went nuts. Grabbed and swiped, trying to reach him, and when that failed, spinning his body in an attempt to shake him loose.

Ryon was going to get himself killed. And there wasn't a damned thing she could do to stop it.

Fifteen

R yon jumped onto the creature's back, sinking his fangs into the tough, leathery hide. It roared and tried to claw him off. Twisted and turned.

"Shift and catch!" Jax yelled.

Ryon saw his friend run up, holding a large tube. The spike on the end was long and silver, and if it was a needle, it was the thickest, most wicked one he'd ever seen. Then again, it would have to be to penetrate the creature's hide.

The shift was difficult, especially while riding an enraged mutant lizard. In human form, he wrapped an arm around the thing's neck and held out the other. "Throw it!"

The first try missed, and he cursed when the tube sailed past them and landed on the ground. It narrowly missed being crushed by the creature's webbed feet as it stomped around, oblivious to the fact that they were trying to save its life. Or rather, Ben's life.

"We're trying to save your ass, you fucker!" he yelled.

Jax threw the tube again, but it bounced off Ryon's fingers. The next second, he was thrown to the ground, rolling to avoid being stomped or eaten. As he scrambled, he saw the cylinder lying just a few feet away. He went for it. Just as his fingers closed around it, he was yanked backward.

The creature's claws dug into his shoulder as it dragged him to its hungry, gaping maw. Fetid breath wafted in his face and he had an up-close and personal view of those rows of deadly teeth that were ready to tear out his throat. Flipping the tube in his grasp, spiked end toward the creature, he drove the business end into the vulnerable skin of its belly. The beast let out a roar as Ryon quickly pushed the handle all the way in. He didn't know if that was the best spot, or even if it would work, but he'd done his job.

It would have to be enough. He was finished.

The beast flung him away and he landed in the dirt hard. Unable to move, he took in the monster standing in place, shrieking in agony, no longer aware of anyone else in his vicinity. Ryon felt a pang of sadness, knowing the creature was not really evil. It didn't possess that sort of thought process. All along, it had simply been ravenously hungry. Angry. Confused.

But never evil. Because the man underneath was good.

Incredulous, he saw the creature begin to shrink. Scales became flesh, webbed feet and hands human ones. The knobby skull returned to its regular shape, and a full head of chestnut hair appeared. The distended torso became taut, the stomach flat. In less than a minute, a man stood swaying where the beast had been, blinking as though he'd never seen them before. And indeed he hadn't.

Ben Cantrell was tired, shell-shocked, worse for the wear, but a man all the same. He crumpled to the ground.

Some of the team ran to Ben, and the others toward Ryon. Nick and Jax appeared, looking down at him, smiling.

"You did it, buddy," Jax said, laying a hand on his chest. "Great job."

He tried to grin. "That's why I get paid the big bucks. August is getting away, though."

Nick spoke up. "This time. Next time he won't be so lucky."

Suddenly he remembered August's terrible claims, his story of betrayal that ran all the way to the presidency. He wanted to ask if it was true, if Nick had known. But he was too exhausted to talk anymore. Then Daria came into his line of vision, and he'd never seen anything more beautiful.

"Ryon?" Her face was wet with tears.

No sound would move past his throat.

"Always gotta be a hero, huh?" she said, stroking his face. He tried again to reply, but she shushed him. "Rest. You're going to be all right now."

He wasn't so sure; everything hurt so bad. But he'd trust her. With a deep sigh, he let the darkness close in, and everything faded away.

*   *   *

Daria jumped from the helicopter the second the creature began to change back into Ben. As her former lover crumpled in the dirt, unmoving, she ran to her mate and dropped to her knees. Ryon lay on his back, staring up at the people around him. She could've sworn she'd seen him talk, but he didn't have the ability now.

"Ryon?" She put a shaking hand over her mouth. Hot tears slid down her cheeks. His lips moved, but he didn't speak.

"Always gotta be a hero, huh?" She stroked his face, cutting off his second effort to talk. "Rest. You're going to be all right now."

He closed his gorgeous blue eyes, heaved a deep breath, and lost consciousness. His body was bathed in blood, his hair matted with it. He must've gotten those injuries when the creature threw him to the ground. Her hand trembled as she smoothed back the strands of blond hair. Long lashes rested against his cheek. God, he was burning with fever.

"Christ Almighty," Jax murmured. "Somebody get a stretcher. We've got to get him home."

Micah took off.

Nick's hand landed on her arm and squeezed gently. His eyes were calm. "He's going to be okay. Trust me."

She searched the commander's face for any sign of deception. "Is that your word as a PreCog?"

"It is. He'll have a rough go of it, and it'll be a near thing, but he'll survive."

"I have a feeling that's more than you usually say to people about the future."

He gave her a faint smile. "You're right. But then, I think you've earned the truth, especially if it's good news."

She swiped at her tears. "Thank you."

"No, thank *you*." He winked. "And I have a feeling Ben will be full of gratitude, too."

Micah returned with the stretcher and, working together, they got Ryon situated. She was hardly aware of another group off to the side working on Ben. Her sole concern right now was for her mate. Inside, her wolf paced anxiously.

Ducking well clear of the whirling blades, Jax and Micah got Ryon into the helicopter. Then Micah gave her a hand up and a shy smile that pulled at his scarred face. As though realizing how he might appear to her, the man turned away and busied himself with Ryon. She was saddened that Micah was going through such a tough time, and she prayed he was getting better.

And not relying so much on the pills she'd seen him popping more often than maybe he should. But she couldn't dwell on that at the moment.

"Go, go!" Jax yelled to Aric, and then they were airborne.

She stayed by Ryon's side and prepared for the two-hour flight home. The compound, *home*. Such an odd concept. But it filled her with warmth to realize she was about to make her place with such awesome people.

Reaching down, she took one of Ryon's big hands in hers. His palms were as hot as the sands of the Sahara. His face was deathly pale, eyes closed. Although the helicopter's deafening noise prevented her from hearing, she could see the jerky rise and fall of his chest as he fought to breathe. Despite Nick's prediction, she couldn't help but be fearful. She tried their mind-link.

Come on baby, stay with me.

Tightening her grip on his fingers, she pressed a hand over his heart. Every sluggish beat pulsed as though mired in glue. As the sun rose higher, and the minutes ticked by, the deep, telltale rattle in his chest worsened. She remembered something he'd told her not long ago, when Micah had been hurt and she'd been so afraid.

I'll always move heaven and hell to come home.

Now her fears had come to pass.

Aric's anxious voice filtered through their headsets. "How's he doing?"

Jax shook his head. "Hurry, man."

Aric pushed the bird full throttle, eating the miles rapidly. But as the forest below rolled by, Daria could feel Ryon slipping away in spite of his fierce battle. In spite of the commander's words. His breathing had become shallow, his features slack. She couldn't stop touching him. His hair, his face. As if she might somehow keep his soul bound to this world.

"I love you, my mate. Please don't go," she whispered, even though he couldn't hear. The men were listening through their headsets, but she didn't care. She kept talking to him.

Her brave wolf gave it everything he had, right until

the compound came into view far below. Any minute, Ryon would be in good hands.

Daria gazed down at him, and froze. Underneath her palm, his chest had gone completely still. No rattle, no movement at all. He wasn't fighting any longer, wasn't breathing. Horror washed over her.

"Oh, baby, *no, no*! Jax, my God!"

"Come on, buddy, Nick's never wrong. Don't do this," Jax begged. He looked at Micah, his face white. "Get his head. I'll do the compressions."

They worked together, each passing minute an eternity, carrying a man they all loved beyond reach. Their frantic efforts met with failure, and by the time Aric put the chopper down, it seemed hopeless.

Ryon was gone.

As long as she lived, the sight of Mac and the others rushing away with his lifeless body would remain burned in her memory. Hardly aware of her actions, she stumbled after them, a zombie. A moan built in her chest, and escaped in a painful wheeze.

Halting in her tracks, she clapped her hands over her ears. "Nooo."

Suddenly, Nick was there. His strong arms were pulling her backward, enfolding her. She buried her face in his chest and let the black wave take her. How long they clung to each other, sharing their terror of the news that she was certain would come, and the stark anguish, she couldn't have said.

Finally, Nick stepped back and raked a hand through

his dark hair. "You love Ryon, and he's a good friend. One of my best men. Remember, I said he'd have a battle, but that battle is *not* lost. We'll face this together, okay?" He held out a hand.

The simple gesture touched her. "Absolutely," she whispered, and put her hand in his.

Together, they walked inside.

Under the watchful eye of Ryon's many friends, Daria paced the small waiting room. Prayed harder than she ever had in her life. She couldn't stop trembling.

The doctors had resuscitated him, but only after the promised battle. And they were saying damned little about his chances, despite what Nick had said.

Complications from the creature's bite and the gunshot wound in his leg were the ultimate concern. The bacterial infection had spread through his bloodstream, ravaging his internal organs. He'd developed pneumonia, and his fever had climbed to a frightening one hundred and eight degrees.

Anyone but a shifter would've been dead.

They were pumping him with massive doses of antibiotics, along with painkillers. After several hours with no change, Nick left to make a few phone calls. One of which included notifying General Jarrod Grant of August's claims. Daria had pulled Nick into a room and told him in private every single hateful word August had gleefully related to them. Nick's blue gaze had darkened with every word.

"I knew absolutely nothing about this," he had said

in a low, dangerous voice. "But I will get to the bottom of it, take out August and everyone invoved in this horror, if it takes the rest of my life."

And she believed him. She didn't envy Nick and the general the unpleasant task of starting that investigation. Nick returned shortly, taking a seat across from the group.

Jax eyed him. "What's up?"

"When Ryon's out of danger, I'm calling a meeting and I'll tell all of you at the same time." He exchanged a knowing look with Daria that the others didn't miss. But they didn't push.

Daria rubbed her arms and shivered as Mac appeared, her expression kind. Daria's stomach dropped to her toes.

"Ryon can have visitors now. One at a time, and keep it brief."

Daria lurched to her feet. "Please, how is he?"

"Hanging in there," she said with a gentle smile. "That man has the willpower of an ox."

Jax nodded at her. "You go first, honey. We'll wait."

"Thanks." She studied each of them, taking at least some comfort in the way they were rallying around her. In a short time, these wonderful men had become very important to her. She could see why Ryon was close to them.

Daria turned and made the walk down the corridor, the longest of her life.

And tried desperately to convince herself that, if the worst happened in spite of Nick's prediction, she would be strong enough to say good-bye.

*   *   *

He was suffocating. Drowning in an ocean of pain. He tried letting himself sink and fall forever into the darkness just to escape it. But each time, they tormented him, pulling him to hover just below the surface. To stare into the soothing peace of death on one side, the beautiful light of life on the other, allowing him to reach neither.

"I want my mate," he told them, repeatedly. Or dreamed he did. Perhaps they heard, because each time he whispered the word, something strange and pleasant swirled through him, chasing away the agony if only for a while.

He clung to that lifeline, the word and the warm feeling after. It was all he had to hold on to. All that mattered.

Until he heard her voice.

She told him to hang on, that she loved him. Would always love him. She said so many things, but all he grasped was *I love you*. Harder than ever, he fought to rise from the endless void. For her.

"Daria?"

"Hush, baby. You're very sick, but you're going to get better. Just rest and get stronger. I love you so much."

"Don't leave me."

"I won't," she whispered. "Nobody can make me, staying right here. Sleep."

Ryon drifted, relishing Daria's cool fingers raking his hair, messaging his scalp. Stroking his face and lips.

When the pain became almost too much and his soul was tempted to slip from its exhausted shell, he called to her. A soft touch, the quiet strength of her presence became his reason to cling to this earth.

Slowly, however, the fog began to part. His thoughts became more lucid, awareness of his surroundings sharper. His eyelids still refused to budge and his limbs were encased in cement, but he sensed that Daria did leave for short periods of time. He understood.

She never stayed away for long. She was steadfast, urging him to get well.

For his mate, anything.

"Hey, you."

For a full minute, Ryon didn't comprehend that he'd awakened and opened his eyes. The fog parted gradually as he rose to the surface. Gentle light filtered through the filmy haze covering his vision. By slow degrees, the haze dissipated, and he found himself staring into a pair of huge brown eyes.

"Baby," he rasped.

Eyes that immediately filled with tears. Happy ones, he guessed, from the way she beamed down at him. Her smile crinkled her nose, and she grasped one of his hands tightly.

"I thought I'd never hear you call me that again," she half-sobbed, choking on the last word. "You shaved a couple of decades off my life, mate."

"That close, huh?"

She leaned over and brought his hand to her face,

rubbing it against her cheek. "You weren't breathing when they brought you in. We thought you were gone." She gave a watery laugh. "Except for Nick, of course. He swore you'd make it. Guess we should learn to trust him."

"Guess so." Jesus, his head was muzzy and he hurt all over. Ryon attempted a smile, but his face wouldn't cooperate. "How long have I been out of it?"

"Four long days. Everyone's been visiting, and taking bets on who'd end up in here next. Meanwhile, Nick has been on the phone nonstop with General Grant."

"Really?" He tried to sit up, but vertigo and nausea swamped him. "What did Nick say about all that government conspiracy shit? Did he know about it?"

Daria eased him back. "Whoa, no sudden moves, big guy. To answer your questions, Nick didn't know a thing about it, and he was furious. He and the general aren't sure how much of what my uncle claimed is true, if any of it, but they're starting an investigation."

"A real quiet one, I'll bet."

"You bet right. Nick had a meeting and told the team about it, and they were shocked and upset, as you can imagine."

"The day we were turned was one of the worst of my life," he murmured. "All of our lives. Even if August was lying about some of it, a lot of what he said makes sense."

"Like how it happened that all of you ended up in Afghanistan, in the same unit?"

"And how those of us who survived each have a Psy gift. I know we won't rest until we have the truth of who was behind it all." He paused, and asked a question that was burning in his gut. "Have you seen Ben?"

Giving him a soft smile, she shook her head. "No, honey. He's been asking for me, but I wanted to wait until you woke up."

That surprised him. "Why?"

"Because you're my mate. If you don't want me to see my former fiancé, I won't out of respect for your wishes."

"But you'd be unhappy," he said, shaking his head. "I'd never do that to you, baby. My wolf might be possessive, but the man isn't that stupid or insecure. You both need closure after all you've been through, so go see him."

She smiled through her tears. "Thank you."

"How is he?"

"Noah tells me he's dealing. They haven't said much else since he wants to talk to me in person."

"Then you shouldn't wait."

The bed shifted slightly as she leaned over him, and pressed her lips to his. The soft, sweet kiss warmed his toes. And, in spite of his battered body, one very happy part of his anatomy.

She touched his cheek. "I love you, Ryon Hunter. More than I ever dreamed possible. You're a part of me and always will be, no matter what."

"I love you, baby. I can't imagine my life now without you."

"Simple. Don't."

"I turned out to be more trouble than you bargained for, and the challenge isn't over yet. Are you sure about having me around for keeps?"

"Gee, I don't know." She snorted, rolling her eyes. "Now that I've been through ten kinds of hell, living in terror that I'd lose you, I think I should give you the boot. What do you think?"

"That I should quit while I'm ahead?"

"Good idea."

He looked straight into her eyes. "You know, I have the woman I love hovering and fussing, nursing me back to health. Life is looking pretty terrific, except for one detail."

She frowned, little worry lines creasing her brow. "What's that?"

"I know we're already mated, but there's something else that would make me happy." He rushed on before his nerve fled. "My angel, will you marry me?"

Well, hell. Making her cry seemed to be all he was capable of doing. Her eyes rounded and filled, like two big brown marbles. He held his breath, heart hammering. The discomfort from his healing body he could take, as long as Daria was his.

"Yes." She laughed. Then she threw herself against his chest, hugged him tightly. "Yes, *yes!*"

His arms went around her, happiness flooding him. She took his face in her hands and covered him in kisses. His shout of joy came out as a pitiful wheeze, but he barely noticed. Daria was *his!*

"When?" Excitement laced her voice.

"Even if we have to marry in this hospital room, I couldn't care less."

"It's a date. But *after* you're out of bed and walking under your own power. Your team will want to be there, too."

"You're right. It's a plan."

With that, he pulled her down and kissed her, thoroughly. He tasted the salt of their mingled tears and knew life didn't get any better.

With this woman at his side, he could endure the weeks of recovery ahead. Then they would lay the past to rest and begin to build their future.

Together.

Daria walked toward Ben's hospital room, unable to squelch a tiny bit of dread.

True to what she'd told Ryon, she hadn't come by before now despite a couple of inquiries from the man that had reached her through Mac and Noah. She knew how frightened he must be, how anxious. That he was ready to talk, however, had to be a good sign for his recovery.

Ahead, Phoenix emerged from an exam room. The tall, lithe man with long, dark blond hair moved like a supermodel, graceful and sexy. Looking at him, smiling at Mac as he took his leave, it was hard to believe the man had been rescued from one of Bowman's hellholes just a few weeks ago.

He gave her a blinding smile. "Daria. It's good to see you looking recovered from your ordeal."

"Thanks. You're looking pretty good yourself." She was mated, but *damn*.

"I saw Ryon earlier. I've never seen him so happy."

"We both are. You coming to the wedding?"

"Wedding? Congratulations!" Laughing, he gave her a hug. "Wouldn't miss it. When's the big day?"

"As soon as my mate is on his feet. We'll have it here, I think."

"Then I have no excuse." Peering past her, his gaze took on a predatory quality. Then he returned his attention to Daria. "Well, I have to go. Talk soon?"

"You bet."

After giving her a kiss on the cheek, he strolled past. Curious about his behavior, she turned to see that Noah had just rounded the corner. He was carrying a stack of file folders, head down, and was totally not watching where he was going.

Which was why he had no idea that Phoenix smacked into him on purpose, then pretended it was an accident.

"Shit, I'm sorry!" he exclaimed. "Here, let me help you."

"Damn," Noah grouched. "I just spent the last three hours on these." Squatting, the cute nurse joined the other man and started to gather the files. Then he looked up to find himself the recipient of the blinding smile that had been bestowed on Daria moments before.

Only this smile was completely different—the heat could've melted the paint off the walls.

Noah blushed, visibly flustered. "I—I . . . thank you."

"Don't mention it." With a wink, Phoenix resumed assisting him.

Poor Noah looked as though he'd been hit in the head with a tire iron.

Well, now, wasn't *that* interesting? Chuckling, Daria pushed into Ben's room. Her amusement faded as she saw her former lover staring listlessly at the television mounted on the wall.

"Ben?"

His head whipped toward her, and he sat up a bit. "Daria! Please, come in."

Moving to his bedside, she sat in the chair and put a hand on his forearm. "You're looking well."

"Thank you." There was a sadness in his green eyes she'd never seen in the normally confident attorney. A vulnerability. "I'm glad you agreed to see me."

"Why wouldn't I have? We parted amicably, and I consider you a friend."

"Really? After all I've done since then?" he said, choking up.

Shaking her head, she used a no-nonsense tone. "The creature did those things, not you. The man was not in control. Do you even remember the things *he* did while in that form?"

"No, nothing except flashes of looking through his eyes, feeling the rage and confusion. Maybe I blocked out the rest. But I—he—killed people," he whispered. "I knew the beast had done something bad because I was covered in blood. I had an awful feeling."

"That wasn't you," she reiterated.

He was silent a moment. "I never knew it was your uncle behind my kidnapping, until it was all over and I ended up here. I defended him in a criminal case once, and that was the thanks I got. Nick told me the man apparently waited until our breakup and then had me taken to Bowman. I had caught their eye as a perfect test subject."

"And they weren't concerned that you're a prominent attorney with colleagues and a client base who would miss you?"

"I guess not. They were that arrogant."

"Or that stupid."

His lips curved. "It's really good to see you. Are you happy?"

"I am." He was still fragile and she didn't want to hurt him in any way, or rub in her bliss. But she told the truth. "He's my other half. We mated, and we're going to get married as soon as he's up and around. Living here will be perfect, too. That way I can continue my study of the wolves—the real ones."

"That's wonderful." His voice rang with sincerity.

"Would you be interested in attending? I'd love to have you if—"

"Thank you, but no," he said quietly. "It's best that I go home, get my life in order. But I do wish you all the best, and I'll be thinking of you."

"All right, I understand. And thank you."

"I can't thank you, Ryon, and the Pack enough for risking so much to save me. I'm forever in your debt. If any of you ever need a good criminal attorney, I'm a phone call away."

She laughed. "I'll be sure they know. And you're welcome. Like I said, you're my friend and there's no way I was going to leave you to your fate."

"You're a rare woman, Daria. I was a fool to let you go."

"Yes, you were."

They both laughed at that, knowing the real story. The decision to part was mutual, their lives too different, going in different directions. They would remain friends. Whether she'd ever see him again, she didn't know. But she hoped so. Some people, like Ben, were worth holding on to.

And no one more than her amazing mate, whom she loved to distraction. He was worth any risk.

Here, with Ryon, she'd found her home at last.

Sixteen

Ryon stood at the altar, which was really a simple white archway decorated with all sorts of flowers he couldn't name. He didn't care—he had eyes for only one beautiful flower in the entire vicinity.

Daria walked up the aisle, escorted by her father, Charles. They were both smiling, but it was her brilliantly happy one that caught his breath. Her face was radiant. Raven hair was piled on top of her head, spilling down on the sides of her face. Brown eyes devoured him, shining with love and promise.

As they reached him, Ryon was a little nervous about taking her from the older man, but the transfer took place without a hitch. Ryon liked Charles and hadn't really been worried since the feeling was mutual, but still. The man was "giving away" his daughter. But Charles seemed thrilled for his baby girl, and as long as she was smiling, Dad would, too.

The ceremony passed quickly, in part because they'd shortened it to the essentials. It was meaningful and not rushed, they just chose not to let it go on and on because Ryon was still healing. By the time it was over he was leaning on the handle of his cane a bit. A small ache, nothing he couldn't bear. He was anxious to make nice with their friends.

And then get on with claiming his new bride. His wolf growled in agreement.

Soon he was kissing the bride, and didn't release her until the audience starting hooting and catcalling, making a good-natured fuss.

"Come on, man," Aric shouted. "There's beer waiting!"

Everyone laughed. Ryon reluctantly stepped back from his mate. The local preacher, a friend of Sheriff Deveraux's, announced them as husband and wife. They turned to face the crowd, and everyone cheered.

Through all the usual wedding stuff, Ryon endured his friends' backslaps and raw jokes about the wedding night. They took loads of pictures, ate lots of food.

Zan walked over, holding a beer. The man had gotten back from his vacation to learn he'd missed a major op, and hadn't been thrilled. But he was still learning to compensate for the loss of his hearing. He could read lips pretty well, and his speech was okay, if a little odd. The biggest issue was how he'd do once placed back in the field. They just didn't know yet.

The Healer stopped and hugged Ryon. "Congrats!"

Ryon made sure his old friend could see his mouth. "Thanks. Having fun?"

"You bet." He waved his bottle at their resident Fae prince. "Good thing Blue can glamour his appearance, or that might give the preacher a shock."

"It would be entertaining, for sure."

"Yeah. But the last thing we need is more publicity. People might find out what we really do here."

That's what they were all secretly afraid of. If the world knew that paranormal creatures existed—not to mention that the government had allegedly experimented on humans and shifters—the fallout would be huge.

His friend grimaced. "Sorry. This is your party, so no heavy stuff. Right?"

"Right."

"I'm gonna go get another beer. Congrats again, man."

"Thanks."

Just as Zan ambled off, Ryon caught sight of Micah standing alone at the corner of the building. He was sure he glimpsed a prescription bottle in the man's hand as he tucked it into his coat pocket. Then the younger man definitely popped something into his mouth and washed it down with his wine.

"I'm worried about him, too," Daria whispered into his ear.

He kept his voice low. "He's addicted, isn't he?"

"I'm not sure, but I hope not. He's taking a lot of pills."

Ryon's heart sank. His mate, however, was having none of it.

"Hey." She stood in front of him. "This is our day. Tomorrow, we'll see about our friends. We'll go to Nick if you want."

"Okay. He might not know, and he'll be able to help us watch Micah. We should tell Rowan and Aric as well. His sister wouldn't appreciate being kept out of the loop."

"I agree." Slipping her fingers into the vee of his dress shirt, she toyed with his chest. He hadn't worn a tie, and now he was damned glad. "Let's do the cake, then go for the icing—in our quarters."

"Lady, I love how your dirty mind works."

They called everyone over, tossed the garter to the guys, the bride's bouquet to the girls. Then they cut the cake and shoved their pieces into each other's faces, giggling. They stayed just long enough to get all their guests served, and then ducked out. Jogging toward their room, Ryon grew more and more excited.

"I didn't tell my dad good-bye," she said suddenly.

"He'll still be here tomorrow. And do me a favor—do not say the word *dad* again once we get to our room, or you'll wilt a perfectly nice erection."

"I doubt anything short of nuclear war could do that."

"Why risk it?"

Inside, Ryon left a trail of clothing—shoes, jacket, pants, shirt. When they reached their bedroom, he stood only in his socks and underwear. His mate laughed and his eyes narrowed.

"What?" she asked innocently. "You look cute."

"I'll show you cute." He stripped off his briefs and his cock slapped his stomach.

Stalking her, he turned her around and went to work on the tiny zipper at the back of her dress. It was tasteful, a slim lovely column that accented her body like a glove. And he wanted it off, now.

Once she was naked, he led her to the bed, striving not to jump her like the starving wolf he was. He wanted to be gentle, but there was a greater fire tonight. A passion that wouldn't be denied. He wanted to take charge. The answering heat in her eyes said she wanted it, too.

Pulling her onto the bed, he grasped both wrists in one hand and pulled them over her head, pinning them to the covers. He loved that position, the way it made her look vulnerable to be taken by him. At his mercy. The way it exposed her breasts to him, ripe and waiting to be sucked.

"I'm going to suck and lick every inch of you," he asserted. "Then I'm going to slide my cock into you and fuck your sweet pussy until you scream."

"Talk is cheap."

Giving her a feral grin, he proceeded to do as he'd warned. Bending, he sucked her pretty nipples—one, then the other, nibbling them until they stood proud and tight. She squirmed, and he liked that.

"Don't move your hands."

Leaving her arms over her head, he moved lower. Licked a path down her flat tummy, to her thatch. Then lower, he mouthed the lips of her sex, chuckling when she spread her legs wider to give him better access.

"You like that, my pretty slut?"

"Yes," she whimpered. "I need you."

"What do you need me to do?"

"Eat me, please!"

With pleasure. He licked her mound, swirling his tongue until she was writhing. Twice he had to remind her to keep her hands still, and that seemed to excite her even more. Then he plunged his tongue between her folds, fucking her for a while, getting her nice and slick. He loved her taste, and pretty soon he'd relish her blood when he claimed her again.

He suckled her clit, not letting up until she was begging, hips bucking. He knew she wanted to reach down and pull at him, but he wouldn't let her. His control heightened the eroticism. Finally, he moved up and crouched between her legs.

Lifting her thighs, he draped her legs over his shoulders. Her ass was in the air, her sex spread and glistening. Waiting for him to master.

Mine!

Neither he nor his wolf could wait another second. Lining up his cock, he plunged into her moist, hot depths. She screamed, a sound of pure ecstasy. She loved this, craved more, and he gave it.

Cupping her ass in his hands, he pounded into her tight channel, spearing home again and again. Their joining was raw. Primal. Filled with lust and need, and the air around them reeked of pheromones and sex. It was real.

His climax built, and he felt the tingle at his spine. The tightening of his balls trying to climb into his body as it prepared for release. And then he exploded, shooting inside her again and again, the force and sheer pleasure of it almost turning him inside out. This surpassed every time before. He'd never come so hard in his life.

Lowering her to the bed, he fucked her toward release. His fangs descended and he nosed into the curve of her neck and shoulder. And struck, her blood like honey on his tongue.

Her orgasm shattered and she cried out, writhing on his rod and squeezing out more of his juices as he rode the aftershocks. At last they came down together, and he withdrew his fangs, licking the wounds closed. Then he wrapped her in his arms, her head on his chest.

"That was perfect," he murmured, kissing her head. "I love you, my wife. My mate."

"And I love you." She nuzzled his chest, snuggled close. "I'm so glad we found each other."

"Me, too. I think it was fate."

"Same here. I never dreamed I'd meet the love of my life while studying wolves. Not to mention that he would *be* a wolf." He heard the smile in her voice.

"Not long ago, you weren't so thrilled about that."

"I was scared," she said simply. "Now I'm nothing but happy and in love with my mate."

"I'm glad you feel that way, baby. Because you're stuck with me from now on."

"That's the best news I've ever heard."

Drowsy, they drifted off to the sounds of the party still in swing outside, blissed-out and at peace. Daria had completed him, had tamed his restless, lonely spirit—not to mention the real spirits that had once plagued him. He didn't have to run anymore. She loved him, and was home with him, with the Pack, for good.

A man couldn't ask for more.

Miles away, the white wolf sat on her haunches and howled out her grief. Her pain. She hadn't gotten what she'd come for, her plans delayed time and again.

But soon. The day was coming when she *would* find peace.

That would be the day Nick Westfall paid for his sins.

In his own blood.

Turn the page for an exciting glimpse into the world
of J. D. Tyler's alter ego Jo Davis,
with a preview of

Sworn to Protect

The first in the Sugarland Blue series.

1

"It's way too damned quiet around here."

Several other cops groaned and a couple of them shot Taylor Kane the death glare. Shane Ford just smirked, getting more comfortable with his booted feet propped on his desk and crossed at the ankles.

His cousin, Christian Ford, a recent transplant from the Dallas, Texas, PD, wadded up a sheet of paper and launched it at Taylor's face. "Thanks a lot for jinxin' us, dipshit," he drawled. "Even the dumbest rookie knows better than to let the *Q* word pass his lips."

Taylor slapped a file onto his desk with a grimace of disgust. "I'm just sayin' I'm sick of investigating vandalism and stolen bicycles, that's all. It's a waste of my rather large and brilliant brain. Shut up, Chris." At the other man's snort, he threw the paper wad back, missing his target.

"Hey, there's a lot of money to be had fencing bikes," Shane said, crossing his arms over his chest. "And a crime is a crime."

"I know, but it's *boring*. Since Jesse Rose and his bunch got shut down last year, nothing exciting has happened around here," their friend griped. "I'm about to lose my frickin' mind."

Shane suppressed a shudder. Jesse Rose was a homeland terrorist who had planned to blow up their fine city of Sugarland, Tennessee, and had damned near succeeded. A Sugarland Fire Department captain by the name of Sean Tanner, along with Shane and the entire police force, had been instrumental in stopping the bastard just in time. Tanner had since been promoted to battalion chief, and it was a well-deserved honor as far as Shane was concerned.

Another new hire, Tonio Salvatore, spoke up. "That case Shane and Daisy solved last month was pretty exciting. . . ." An uncomfortable silence fell over the room. "What? What'd I say?"

Shane's good mood did a belly flop and curdled in his stomach. It always did whenever someone mentioned Daisy Callahan's name and the case that had almost gotten them both killed. Or, worse, when he was forced to exchange polite, professional conversation with the stunning blond juvenile officer. Especially when all he wanted to do was bend her over the nearest flat surface and fuck her until she screamed his name.

Yeah, their passionate affair hadn't been such a great idea before, and that fact hadn't changed.

Easing his legs off the desk, he studied the other officers' faces. Most reflected curiosity, the barely disguised desire to pry. So they didn't *really* know, just likely suspected. Chris was the only one who knew, and it seemed he'd kept his promise not to say anything to the others. Their friends were merely attuned to the sudden tension that snapped like a rubber band whenever

Shane and Daisy were mentioned in the same sentence, or the two of them were in a room together.

Shane wasn't about to satisfy their avid curiosity.

"Our lack of excitement means nobody has been murdered," Shane said dryly, sidestepping the reference to him and Daisy. "Let's not borrow trouble."

"Too late for that." Their captain, Austin Rainey, swiped a trickle of sweat from his rugged face with one hand as he approached. "Goddamn, this heat is already bad enough to poach an egg, and it's not even spring yet."

Shane studied the man's grayish pallor. Austin wasn't just his supervisor; he was a good friend who'd been through a rough time in the last couple of years. The man's bitch of a wife was really putting him through the ringer lately. Shane feared for his health, as did the men and women who respected and loved him.

"You okay, Cap?" Shane asked him. "It's February and it's not that hot in here. You're not looking so good."

Austin waved off his concern as usual and addressed his detectives. "We've got a body in the gulley out on 49. White male, no ID, shot once in the back of the head, execution style." He gave Taylor a baleful glare. "Since you're so fucking bored, you can take this one with Shane. Oh, and you can do all the reports, too."

Taylor grimaced as a few others snickered. "Thanks a million, Cap."

"Don't mention it. Get the lead out. Eden and the FU are already on their way."

Shane had to smile a little at that—Eden and the FU, as though they were a rock group. But it was appropriate, since Nashville's taciturn medical examiner and the

Sugarland PD's forensic investigations unit sort of went together like a guitar and strings. Though they were employed by separate entities, they worked toward the common goal of finding and analyzing clues that would help the police locate and apprehend the bad guys.

And then there was the shortening of FIU to FU, which one of the uniformed officers had jokingly said stood for Fuck U, because the science geeks thought they were smarter than a bunch of cops.

"On it." Taylor grabbed a set of keys off his desk and jingled them, looking at Shane. "I'll drive."

As they headed out, Shane fell into step beside him. "Happy now? You got the murder you wanted, and a messy one, too."

The other man shrugged. "I'm not happy someone bought it, but it happens."

"You like solving the puzzle. A lot of us do." That might seem strange or morbid to some, but to them, the need to make the pieces fit, the satisfaction they felt when they were successful, was normal.

"For me, the seemingly random pieces are more like snippets of a story, and aren't usually random at all," Taylor said thoughtfully. "The body is the last chapter, and I have to read the story backward to find out what led up to it."

"Never thought of it like that before, like reading a book in reverse."

He pondered that as they pushed outside and the frigid air hit them, slapping them like dozens of tiny needles. But that wasn't the only reason he suddenly felt as though he were suffocating.

Daisy Callahan was striding purposefully up the steps

to the precinct house, and all the spit dried up in Shane's mouth at the sight of her. Like the other detectives, Shane included, she wore street clothes consisting of dark pants and a casual shirt, a holstered gun and badge at her hip. But there the similarities ended. Blond hair was pulled back into a ponytail, emphasizing an angular face adorned with little makeup, large blue eyes, and a wide mouth. The woman was a long, tall drink of water on a scorching day, five feet, ten inches of lean muscle and confident stride that should have made her seem mannish, except she was anything but.

Her breasts were full, and he knew from experience how they spilled over a man's hands, ripe and tasty. He knew how smooth her skin was, how small her waist was just above the slight flare and curve of womanly hips. How toned those long thighs were, just how fantastic they looked wrapped around his waist as he—

"Earth to Shane?"

He blinked, becoming aware that he and Taylor had stopped in front of Daisy. Taylor had greeted her and they'd exchanged a few words, and now they were both regarding him with two completely different expressions—Taylor with amusement and Daisy with a polite detachment he'd grown to hate.

Completely my fault. I'm a first-class jerk.

"I'm sorry. What?" He hoped his smile gave no indication of just how desolate he felt inside. Given the unnatural tightness of his face, he suspected he'd failed.

"You guys caught the body out on I-49?" Her look was cool, appraising.

"Word travels fast as always," he said, striving to keep his tone even. "Yeah, we're headed out there now."

She made a face. "You and half the county, no doubt. Good luck, once the news people decipher the dispatch that went out on the scanner. I figure you've got an hour, tops, before the real madness hits."

"Shit. We'd better make tracks." But he couldn't get his feet to move. Daisy turned to go, and on impulse, he called after her. "Wait!"

She blinked at him, surprise causing the mask to slip. "What is it?"

"Can I . . . have a word with you?" He sent a pointed look at Taylor, who nodded and walked toward the parking lot. Thankfully without comment.

Once Taylor was out of earshot, his former lover gazed at Shane coolly. "Is there something about the case that you couldn't say in front of Taylor?"

"Of course not." He ran a hand through his hair. Never had he felt more awkward around a woman, and it was his own fault. "Dammit, I hate this weird distance between us."

"Really?" She gave an incredulous laugh. "That's funny, considering distance is exactly what you wanted. And lots of it. Which I gave you." Her last words were clipped. Angry.

"We were friends before and I ruined that. You'll never know how sorry I am," he said quietly.

The blunt edge of growing hostility disappeared as quickly as it had begun to form, and her face softened. "Me, too. But I guess I can't blame our failure solely on you. I'm the dumb-ass who slept with a friend—a fellow cop—and I should've damned well known better. So, lesson learned."

A raw lump formed in his throat and he spoke with

difficulty. "I'd like to think we're *still* friends. Or can be again." He waited, but she didn't let him off the hook. "Want to grab a beer after work sometime? Or coffee? I'm free Sunday—"

"Stop." Looking away, she regained tight control of the abject misery that had flashed across her beautiful features. "Just stop, okay? I'm not there yet. Maybe I won't ever be, either. And if not, that's a loss we'll both have to own, and move on."

Oh, God. The stab to his gut was sharp. Powerful. Had he honestly thought she'd forgive him, and they'd simply go back to the place they had been? Somehow, he mastered the unexpected pain and managed a sad, lopsided smile.

"I suppose we will at that." He glanced toward where Taylor stood by the car, studying them with undisguised interest. "Better go."

"Let me know what you find," she said, all business again. "I doubt it'll overlap with any of my cases, but you never know."

"You bet."

Before Shane could say anything more, she turned and walked into the building without a backward glance. As though they'd never been anything to each other at all. Which was how he'd wanted it. Right?

Numbly, he went to meet Taylor at his friend's beat-up vintage Chevelle, a "project car" that in Shane's opinion should have been sold for scrap twenty years ago. In an effort to deflect the questions he knew were coming, he scowled at the wreck. "Why can't we drive a *cool* car, like Starsky and Hutch, or Steve and Danno?"

His friend grinned at him as they climbed in and

slammed the doors. "So buy yourself one and we'll drive it. You're the guy with all the money." He started the ignition, and the car sputtered before roaring to life. "Or, better yet, fix up this one."

Shane rolled his eyes. "First, stop saying I'm rich just because I own a nice house on the Cumberland. Second, I like my truck just fine, and even if I was into muscle cars, I'd buy my own beater instead of pouring a small fortune into yours."

Taylor rolled his eyes. "Oh, sure. Compared to the rest of us, you're shitting money. You're like fuckin' Batman—you don't need a job; you just like to play superhero," he shot back, pulling out of the parking lot.

"Nah, I don't have a really cool, snarky butler. That's a superhero requirement, in case you missed the memo."

"Good point." They rode for a couple of minutes in silence before Taylor glanced at him, his tone growing serious. "So, you and Daisy . . ."

Crap. The man wasn't going to be put off so easily. "Me and Daisy, nothing. Nada."

His friend wasn't buying. "I knew it! Christ, of all the good-lookin' ass in town, you had to tap hers?"

"Daisy is *not* just some piece of ass," Shane said in a low, dangerous voice. "So watch your mouth." Too late, he realized his friend's ploy.

The man laughed and slapped his steering wheel. "Oh, you've got it bad! You never get all protective and snarly over your random hookups. So what gives? How did you two happen?"

Shane sighed. His cousin had been bad enough, but Taylor was a pit bull. He wouldn't let this go until Shane gave him something. "We've been attracted to each other for years, but it's not such a great idea to get involved with a colleague. You know?" His friend arched a brow, waiting. "So, while we were working the case, we got a little too close to the subject we were researching . . ." He shrugged. "That's how."

Taylor whistled through his teeth. "Man, that's heavy. Something tells me it wasn't a one-time thing."

"No, but it should have been. I let the relationship go on too long, and that was wrong of me."

"Why?"

He stared at Taylor. "Why? What do you mean, *why*?"

"Why was it wrong? You're both consenting adults, and you guys clearly aren't over this thing between you."

"Um, other than the rule about not dating fellow cops, the one that could get one or both of us fired for breaking it?" he replied sarcastically. "Gee, let me think."

"Don't give me that bullshit. You wouldn't be the first couple to ever fall in love at work."

"Whoa, nobody said anything about *love*." Jesus, he should've called in sick.

"Well, then, just bang each other in secret. You wouldn't be the only ones in the department doing it, and it's not like you haven't done it before. Hellooo, remember Leslie, from patrol?"

Shane frowned. "The problem is, Daisy deserves better, you moron. Unlike Leslie, she's not a *bang-in-secret* kind of woman—which is why I had to end it." His friend just snickered, as if he knew something Shane didn't. "Taylor?"

"Hmm?" He appeared way too satisfied.

"Shut the fuck up, okay?"

headline
ETERNAL

FIND YOUR HEART'S DESIRE...